The Secret Life
of Deacon Henry

The Secret Life of Deacon Henry

A Novel

Curtis O. Sanders Jr.

Copyright © 2015 Curtis O. Sanders Jr.
All rights reserved.
ISBN: 0996847405
ISBN-13: 9780996847407
Library of Congress Control Number: 2016906055
New York, New York

Dedication

This book is dedicated to what I term "The Twelve Wonders of Faith."

1. *To everyone whose personal growth has been stymied by his or her religious upbringing.*
2. *To everyone who watched a loved one die, after his or her pastor proclaimed he or she was healed in the name of Jesus.*
3. *To the nine parishioners of Emanuel African Methodist Episcopal Church who were murdered during prayer service.*
4. *To those who died before the Holy Ghost manifested their earthly dreams.*
5. *To all children in hospice care.*
6. *To all children born with an egregious physical or mental disease. To children whose only experience in life is starving to death.*
7. *To my ancestors who died during the middle passage.*
8. *To my ancestors who survived the middle passage.*
9. *To those who died in the name of ethnic cleansing.*
10. *To those who died in natural disasters, commonly known as acts of God.*
11. *To victims of senseless murders, random acts of violence, and countless disease.*
12. *To those who cannot accept that human suffering is part of a divine plan administered by a sovereign, loving, merciful God.*

---◆---

Acknowledgments

A NOVEL WAS inside of me long before this book made it to print. Thus, I will start with the end product and work my way back. I want to thank Will Vaultz for the cover design and photography (WillVaultzPhotography.com), Calvin A. Ramsey for letting me hold on to his coattails, and my editor, Mellissa Scott, for a second eye. (Mellissa can be reached at needasecondeye.com)

While this story was in my head, my mentor, cousin, and friend relentlessly encouraged me to put my story on paper. What started as a short story was elevated to a series of e-mails. These e-mails became the basis for a never-performed comedy script, which was transformed into an unpublished magazine article. When I spliced them all together, I had my novel. My cousin did not view me as flippant. He viewed me as someone seeking to grow as a person and to define his own truth. For this I am truly grateful.

I take great pride in my family and my family history. My relationship with my mom and dad was complex. The more I experienced life, the more I learned to love them for who they are and for the trials and tribulations they have passed. I feel extremely fortunate to be 100 percent Wilber (my mom's side) and 100 percent Sanders (my father's side). Together, I was exposed to a number of aunts, uncles, and cousins who made it clear to me that life is a little more than a collection of untold, fascinating stories.

To my sister, brother-in-law, nephews, first cousins, and son, I am sure that at some point, reading this story will make you cringe. Hopefully, you will find refuge in the fact *Deacon Henry* is a story about ideals, not a personal attack against the solace that many people find in God.

A true friend has enough confidence in your friendship to practice tough love. A true friend will tell you when it's time to straighten up and fly right. When you talk to Jesus, his response is almost always dictated by some emotional response within, not a direct verbal response that facilitates a healthy exploration of ideals. With this I thank my closest friends and extended family. You know who you are because at some point I gave you a part of my book and asked for your feedback. If I did not love you and respect you, I would not have asked for your opinion regarding such a personal endeavor.

Contents

PROLOGUE

---※---

The Gospel according to Deacon Henry

JESUS WILL ALWAYS live in the hearts of the faithful. For many, religion is the essence of their being. They live for God. They are fully committed to living what they perceive as a godly life. Many of the members of my childhood church could not read and had no real concept of theological doctrine. They declared their love for Jesus based on what they felt in their heart. I have no incentive to discourage faith of this nature. My objective is not to persuade the faithful to relinquish their faith. If faith in God brings happiness and purpose to someone's life, I see no reason why anyone would find this objectionable. On several occasions my favorite bartender has declared that she thanks God every morning for her health, her family, and her job. She then pours me a gin and tonic, and I say amen. She epitomizes what I consider an earnest faith based on what God has done for her, not some religious doctrine. She is expressing how grateful she is for the life she is living.

Unfortunately, too many religious people feel obligated to infringe upon the rights of others as part of their religious convictions and doctrine. Evangelical Christians use the bromide that Christianity is not a religion but a personal relationship with Christ. This is deceitful and academically false. Christianity is a religion, with all the attributes of any other religion. These people use Christianity to achieve a political or financial agenda. Whenever Christians are warned that unless they vote for a candidate of a peculiar party because they represent Christian values, they are being used to achieve a political end. These same Christians assert that Sharia Law in Islamic countries is despicable. Yet, they are adamant that federal laws are passed that reflect their religious doctrine. A prominent eevangelical Christian pastor and scholar declared that America is under the wrath of God because President Obama was reelected. This preacher adroitly presented scriptures that justified his obligation as a Christian pastor to warn true believers. He presented scriptures to validate every conservative Republican position. To make his biblical arguments, he conveniently ignored the Constitution of the United States and our entire political process. He also presents Christianity as an issue of fact, not faith, and the Bible as absolute truth. I aggressively rebuke these types of claims. These claims transform faith from an issue of individual solace to issues that can be debated. Such debates demand that the Bible be supported by independent evidence. I contend that a critical reading of the Bible, scrutiny of religious testimonies, a review of biblical history, and the history of Christianly decimate any claim that Christianity is an absolute truth. Moreover, I contend that such beliefs are detrimental to the advancement of humanity.

On a very personal level, as an African American, I resent the first Black president being stigmatized as the president who brought forth God's wrath.

I live in Harlem, and on any given Sunday, Black churches are filled with tourists from all over the world. I have had meaningful conversations with some of these tourists regarding how much they enjoy the liveliness of the Black church. Overall, they view the Black church as a powerful spiritual experience. They love gospel music. They love the unique style of African American preachers. Some have commented that if church was this lively back at home, they would go to church more often. I share my experience of growing up in the Black church. The uniqueness of the Black church is a reflection of the uniqueness of the African American experience being rooted in slavery. The role of the "Church" in Black culture is different from the role of "Church" in the White community. An understanding of both experiences is enriching for all.

My desire to become a deacon started as a young Black male growing up in the sixties. I was a solider in the army of the Lord. Armed with the Bible and the bloodstained banner of Jesus, I committed to fighting for justice. While on the battlefield, my faith was attacked by reason, logic, and the role of Christianity during the slave trade. My only recourse against these attacks was to engage in critical thinking and examine every aspect of my Christian faith, the Black church, and theism in general. I was impelled to search for a truth I can live with. I share this truth with you using my Christian experience, essays, and theological arguments.

Deacon Christopher Henry II

PART 1

My Walk with Jesus

CHAPTER 1

— ✦ —

Come Sunday

THE ONLY MEMORIES I have of my grandmother is that she was always sick and refused to go to the hospital. She slept in a hospital bed and had an oxygen tank in her bedroom. My grandfather spent most of his time in the living room watching a console color TV, which was a real status symbol back then. One hot Sunday afternoon, Grandma's house was full of anticipation. Grandma hadn't slept all night. My mom and all my aunts were in Grandma's room. The grandkids were watching TV with Grandpa. Going to the bathroom, I peeked into my grandma's room. She looked miserable, and this frightened me. My aunt Louise would come into the living room every ten minutes or so. She would announce "They should be here soon" and go back into Grandma's room. I didn't know who "they" were, but I knew that everybody wanted them to hurry up and get here. My aunt came to the window again and shouted, "Here they come." Like all good-natured kids, I ran to the window to see who it was that everybody is waiting on. I saw two distinguished-looking Black men approaching the house. They were wearing black suits, with white shirts and black ties. They were also wearing white gloves. They were carrying Bibles, and one carried a small black box. My aunt greeted them from a distance "Here we are, Deacons." It seemed that it took them forever to enter the house. My aunt and my mom greeted them, and then they acknowledged my grandfather. They entered my grandmother's room truly like men on a mission. They had a confidence and a presence that while I did not know who they were or why they were here, I had a feeling that everything was going to be all right. I walked into the hallway and watched as they greeted my grandmother. My grandmother actually smiled, which was a rare occasion. Then one of the deacons read a scripture and said a few words. My grandmother nodded in agreement while my aunts and mom gave the amen. Then one of the deacons opened the black box and started to serve communion. At that time I had no clue what communion was, but I was able to tell that it was extremely important to my grandmother, my mom, and my aunts. Then one of the deacons started to pray. In African American culture, prayer is almost an art form. It is like listening to a symphony of words telling the story of life. When the deacon prayed, it was more than petition and praise. It was biographical and passionate. He challenged God to be merciful and challenged us to be worthy of God's mercy. There was a rhythm and cadence to his prayer reminiscent of a Miles Davis's solo. The deacon's prayer was a story of how he found joy in a world of misery by the mercy of God. After his prayer everyone sung a hymn:

> Precious Lord, take my hand
> Lead me on,
> let me stand
> I am tired, I am weak, I am worn
> Through the storm, through the night
> Lead me on through the light
> Take my hand precious Lord, lead me home

By the time the hymn was over, the room was full of tears. There was peace in the house. When the deacons left, my grandmother was at rest. I watched her sleep with a radiance that I had not witnessed before. That was the day I knew I wanted to be a deacon. That was the day I knew God called me to visit the sick, feed the hungry, and comfort the brokenhearted.

Like most African Americans in the sixties, I was brought up in church. My favorite Sunday school songs were "Jesus loves me this I know for the Bible tells me so" and "He's got the whole world in his hands." These songs gave me a real sense that there is a God above looking over me. At a very early age, I developed a belief in "divine justice." I can't explain why. I simply believed that if God has the whole world in his hands, he would see that justice is done. "What a friend we have in Jesus" is another song that gave me a sense of security and assurance that God is looking over me. I often wonder if the comfort I found in Jesus was to compensate for the comfort I never felt at home. My parents were good parents and good providers. But, like many African American families at that time, there was little interaction between parent and child. My father worked two jobs to make sure that I had the money for band trips and Pop Warner football. My parents owned a home in a White neighborhood, and we never missed a meal. My dad supported his family, which was his way of showing how much he loved us. Speaking such words was not acceptable. The idea of family interaction and activity was something my dad placed no value on. My mom believed that as a man I had to be tough and work out my own problems. Both of my parents would show up at band concerts and football games. I was not able to talk much with my parents. If my communication with my parents had been better, I probably would have spent less time "talking to Jesus and telling him all about my problems."

My mom made sure we made it to Sunday school and church on a regular basis. My dad never went to church. I have no clue what his religious beliefs were. I do know that whenever we had guests over for dinner, as the man of the house, he would say grace. My experience growing up in church was mostly positive. My world at that time consisted of home, school, and church. As in most Black churches, one of the main attractions was the music. As a child it was exciting watching the choir march down the aisle. The robes had a soothing flow as the choir members would take a step, a slide, and a stomp. In perfect harmony they would march down the aisle as the congregation would move to music. They would turn on a dime and then stride up to the choir pit. I never understood why people would pay to see a gospel concert. I have yet to hear better gospel music than what I heard as a child. The passion of the singing, along with the words of hope, could move mountains:

> Its a highway to heaven
> None can walk up there
> but the pure in heart.
> \ I am walking, up the Kings highway \
> \ Christ walks beside me, Angels to guide me \
> \ walking up the king's highway \

At that moment in time, the whole church was on the highway to heaven. Tears of joy and happiness were flowing, and shouts of "Glory! Hallelujah!" filled the church. I would envision walking into heaven with all the pure in heart. I never questioned if heaven existed. Heaven was as real as the music beating against my eardrum: "I heard of a city called heaven, and I started to make heaven my home." I can't remember a day that I did not believe in Jesus and heaven while I was growing up in church. I knew that one day my pain, heartache, and suffering would soon be over and I would shout hallelujah as I walked into glory.

My church family really was an extended family. I was known as "Esther's boy." I would always get a word of encouragement from the brothers and sisters in church. My church was what most would describe as very progressive. About half the congregation hated the pastor. It seems that in every Black church, about half the congregation hates the pastor. As a young Black man, I admired that church was about the only place I could see Black men in charge. The pastor was a Black man with power. The deacons and trustees were leaders in the community. Most owned their own home and were married to a deaconess. Some of them owned their own businesses. A few of them were financially well off. Most men who attended church had some leadership position.

The pews on any given Sunday would be packed with women. Most of the women who attended church would bring their kids. It was never clear how many of them were married. Overwhelmingly, Black men did not attend church other than those who were leaders. The same holds true today. It took me years to figure out why.

The men and women in church had a tremendous amount of pride in their church positions. Brother Johnson was the head usher. My church had several usher boards, and he kept a close eye on each of them. He made sure that ushers were well trained, polite, had proper uniforms, and made everyone feel welcomed. Brother Trent was the superintendent of Sunday school. He ran our Sunday school as if it was an Ivy League university. Brother Knowles was the head chef. His kitchen stayed spotless. He made sure every meal served was cooked to perfection.

One of the most memorable members of my church was Sister Smith. Sister Smith would get happy every Sunday. She was a sermon within the sermon. As the preacher preached, Sister Smith testified to everything coming forth from the pulpit. Sometimes she would get so happy that the ushers had to fan her down. As kids it was fun to imitate Sister Smith getting happy. At some point I wondered what was really going on with Sister Smith. I considered myself as loving Jesus, but I was never inclined to shout about it in church. I had assumed that because of her age and experience walking with the Lord, she must know God on a much higher level than me.

When I attended a church Bible study, I learned that Sister Smith could not read. Unfortunately, this was the norm for so many African Americans of her age, and this made me angry, but it was a reality of our history. This became an issue when I started listening to all these evangelical preachers who insisted you can't know Jesus without studying the word of God for yourself. They emphasized that unless you rightly divide the word of God, you cannot grow as a Christian. Where did this put all the Christians I knew who couldn't read? To be truthful, I think most of the older members of my church couldn't read. I am sure they had the intelligence to read and comprehend religious theology if given a chance. But the reality was educational opportunities for them were limited, if they existed at all. This was probably my first crack in determining what it takes to be a Christian. I grew up believing that being a good Christian was a matter of faith, only to find out that for some it's a matter of the correct doctrine.

I grew up in a church where Christianity was presented in terms of faith in God. Later I was presented a view of Christianity that if you interpreted one passage wrong, you're doomed to hell. The pastor of my church held a master's in divinity from Princeton University. This put him at odds with what some would call "That old-time religion." I didn't fully appreciate my pastor until I moved to the East Coast and learned how many Holy Roller churches were led by pastors with limited reading skills and absolutely no theological training. The success of their ministry was essentially based on their ability to convince their flock that they were "anointed by God to preach the Gospel." They were very charismatic and definitely able to get the church shouting and dancing in the spirit. They presented a very simple view of the Gospel. You were either saved or going to hell. If you were saved, you avoided the pleasures of this world. No drinking, women don't wear pants, no dancing outside of dancing in church. No secular music or concerts, no sex before marriage, limited sex within marriage. They don't play cards and essentially commit themselves to church. Fortunately, some church activity was available most days of the week and all day on Sunday. For men who married church women, this was a great deal. They were able to spend quality time with their girlfriends. I enjoyed watching women in Holy Roller churches dance. A booty shaking is a booty shaking.

Growing up in church, everything I know about God made sense. I had one point of view regarding everything about religion. I knew that Jesus loved me and died for my sins. I took communion once a month. I would confess my sins, drink the blood of Christ, and eat the body of Christ. I actually enjoyed the grape juice and loved the way the bread tasted. I believed that God could make a way out of no way. I believed that God would open doors I could not see. I was a proud soldier in the army of the Lord. I believed those less fortunate than me would be much better off if they would just trust in the Lord. I was never accused of not being saved. My religious beliefs were never challenged. I was commended for holding up the bloodstained banner. I believed the testimonies about what God has done for others, and expected

9

him to do the same for me. I read the new testament from cover to cover. After years of attending Sunday school, I knew most of the prominent Bible stories inside and out. I lived in a world where everything made sense and everything went unchallenged. I was determined to serve the Lord until I die. Sometimes I miss this world. But once you leave it, you can never return.

CHAPTER 2

Christopher Henry II, Junior Deacon

I MUST CONFESS that as a child I looked at my pastor with a sense of awe. I always wondered what it was like to be called by God. He radiated a sense of power and confidence that was second to none. His robe added to this presence, along with the way the deacons and church members would cater to him. My pastor could preach. I still remember some of his sermons forty-plus years later.

Among my favorite sermons was "That Drum Major Instinct." He preached about the inner desire to be a leader. I was in high school and was not comfortable with being a leader. This helped me put leadership in perspective. Another memorable sermon was "David, a lightweight fighting a heavyweight battle." It covered all the elements of how sometimes in life we are required to fight battles that apparently we cannot win but eventually do win. One sermon that I found to be very profound was "Do you have your rather right?" It was a thoughtful lesson regarding how to discern your choices in life. If you are dating Cain but would rather be dating Abel, you may need to dig deeper on why you're dating Cain. Sometimes what you rather be doing is what you should be doing.

Growing up, I was preoccupied with being both a good Christian and an exemplary Negro. Race was the subtext of almost every conversation. My uncle would talk about how far out in the woods my aunt would have to walk to take a piss while they were driving in Alabama. He would go to the gas station, get his tank filled, but was not allowed to use the toilet. He was trapped. He needed the gas to get the hell out of there. With pride he told stories about how he could be buried on the friendly plantation. It never occurred to me growing up that both my uncle and aunt were half white. I saw them as light-skin Blacks with straight hair. When I learned more about Black history, I realized that there is a good chance that they were the result of rape or a secret side-piece. Open interracial dating was virtually inconceivable when they were born.

There is a rumor my uncle killed a White man in Alabama and immediately left. It is easy to believe because he had all traits of a warrior. He always carried a knife and would tell stories about when and how he used it. I always wondered why my uncle was constantly smiling. It turned out he wasn't smiling. Half his face was paralyzed by getting hit in the face with a two-by-four. I can easily see my uncle standing up to some redneck and taking him out. He moved to California and joined the merchant marines to make a living. He would occasionally visit his family in Alabama. My uncle became like a second dad to me. He loved to laugh and loved to drink. He was an avid Dodger fan because the Dodgers signed Jackie Robinson. He played in the Negro leagues and had a true passion for the game. I remember him attending church once in about twenty years. My aunt and my mother attended church as much as possible.

I remember visiting my aunt and watched her lay hands on the TV as she prayed along with some White preacher. I found this to be funny on the verge of crazy. I never said anything because back then questioning grown folks was grounds for a whipping.

My mom would walk around talking to Jesus, which I also thought was strange. While I loved Jesus, I knew some things about Jesus didn't make much sense. My mom loved the Lord and always talked about how Jesus brought her out of sin; yet, she seemed miserable most of the time. The other thing that puzzled me was my dad and all of my uncles would have nothing to do with going to church. In the meantime, I pledged that I would be one of those few men who attend church with their wives.

I started to notice the White families I saw on TV were nothing like mine. I remember watching *Father Knows Best* and wishing our family was like theirs. I don't remember hearing anything about Jesus on *Father Knows Best*. I also noticed that on TV, married couples would get dressed up and go out for dinner at a fancy restaurant. I didn't know any married Black couples who got dressed up and went out for dinner at a restaurant. I do remember that for holiday dinners the men and women would dress to kill. Historically, the only occasion for Black people to get dressed up was church and holiday dinners. Some Black folks would get dressed up to go grocery shopping.

In high school I sang in the church choir and served on the Young Adult Usher Board. What I really enjoyed about being an usher was it gave me a chance to hang out with my friends. I still remember all the usher hand signals. Our usher board actually gave house parties. Dancing, food, and alleged spiked punch. A good slow dance would make me bust in my pants. Christine was the best. She was tall, slender, and was able to arch her back and hit the spot. Every summer my church would have vacation Bible school. I attended it as much as possible as a child. During my senior year of high school, I was very involved in vacation Bible school and began to have some intriguing conversations with my pastor. I eventually became a junior deacon. With great pride I held the title Christopher Henry II, Junior Deacon. My identity as a junior deacon became so prevalent that my nickname became Deacon Henry.

Every fifth Sunday I would lead the Youth Service. I would get to sit in the front of the church lookout and see the congregation. Looking out at the congregation, I felt a sense of prestige, and power mixed with humility, and intimidation. I would lead the church in prayer or read scriptures. Occasionally, I would give a mini sermon. My commitment to the Christian faith far surpassed my peers. Most of them attended church but did not have the type of commitment to walk in the light as I did. I was truly a Christ bearer as reflected in my first name, Christopher. I was metaphorically and in reality someone who carried Christ in his heart.

As a junior deacon, I would help bring senior citizens from the nursing home to church. We once raised money to buy Christmas gifts for church members who were convalescent. I truly enjoyed the spiritual satisfaction and accolades that came with being a junior deacon.

I was committed to spreading the Gospel. I wrote a Christmas play that highlighted how Jesus was God's gift to the world. He came to set us free from Adam and Eve's original sin. God became flesh so that we can have eternal life. My number-one wish for humanity was that all would accept God's gift. I wrote an Easter play that portrayed Christ rising from the dead. I firmly believed that the resurrection of Jesus Christ was logical proof that God is real and there is life after death. Instinctively, I believed the best way to confirm life after death is to know somebody who died and then came back to life to tell his story. The resurrection of Jesus satisfied my standard of proof that God is real and Christianity is the only true religion. The resurrection of Christ is celebrated every year worldwide. I believed that those who witnessed the resurrection started the Easter tradition, and this was indisputable evidence that Jesus lives. If the resurrection of Christ was a sham, the celebration of Easter would not have lasted for two thousand years.

A few family members and friends predicted I would be a preacher someday. It was a given I would be a full deacon someday. I believed I was a child of God and my sole purpose in life was to seek and follow God's will. I believed that the Bible was the word of God. I believed that God exists and rewards those who diligently seek him. I could not understand why others did not see Christianity is the only true religion and ask Jesus for the forgiveness of their sins.

During high school, I knew I wanted to pursue college and was often accused of trying to be White by my Black classmates. When I told my White evangelical counselor that I wanted to go to college, he told me that people with my background should not go to college. However, he assured me my high school had plenty of shop courses, and he enrolled me in several of them. I truly felt that the only friend I had was Jesus. I was discouraged from pursuing college by my Black classmates because I was perceived as trying to be White. Likewise, I was discouraged by my White evangelical counselor from pursuing college, because I was Black. Jesus saved me from my sins, but he did nothing to deliver me from racism.

My high school was integrated in theory, but there was very little interaction between Blacks and Whites. Virtually none. The Blacks hung out with the Blacks, and the Whites hung out with the Whites. Most classes were either full of Blacks or full of Whites. I believe that busing had good intentions. I also believe it was a major failure. I talked with a White girl from Pacific Palisades who believed that busing was great. Her school won their league championship due to the influx of Black running backs. I asked if she had any Blacks in her classes. She said no. She didn't know any of the Black students. She only watched them play football. I can personally testify that sending Blacks and Whites to the same school only to keep them separate on campus is absurd. My nephews were bused and received the benefit of integrated gym classes.

After my counselor told me I wasn't college material, I started to ask a lot of questions. My first question was I was getting A s on all my exams but never received a grade higher than C+. Then I talked to a Black friend of mine who was in the White classes. I hideously discovered the truth. All Blacks were put in the same classes by default. The highest grades attainable in these classes were a C+, because the courses were watered down for Black kids. If your parents didn't bitch, you stayed in the Black classes. My friend's father bitched. I decided to bitch on my own behalf. The next year I had a new counselor, and my bitching began. I told my new counselor I wanted to go to college and study in the White classes. This counselor was once my band director and knew me. He was receptive to my request but had to cover his ass. The solution was I had to make arrangements to do a special project in all my academic classes. I had to prove I was worthy to studying with White kids. I accepted this challenge and succeeded. This left a bitter taste in my mouth. I walked into every White class with a chip on my shoulder and subconsciously a feeling that I really don't belong here. I speculate about what academic achievements I might have attained if I had been encouraged by my peers and counselors to excel. I accept this experience as a bitter pill that I will never cleanse. A few years after me, a Black female was put in the default Black classes. Her mom bitched. She was put in the White classes and graduated as class valedictorian.

My parents fell into the trap that sending your kids to a White school is the solution to the education problem. This is a misnomer. The solution is to send your kids to a school where they are surrounded by other highly motivated students, counselors who see their potential, competent teachers who challenge them, and a curriculum that prepares them for college. There are Black schools that have all of the above. They were around prior to integration, and they are still around. I know, because I live two blocks from Thurgood Marshall Academy, which has all of the above. Most of all, parents must take a very active role in monitoring their kids' education. Regardless of the school they attend.

I think it's pathetic that in the Black community, being smart is not cool. It's frequently perceived as being White. I despised being called "White boy." It was the farthest thing from being cool. Black women loved dating the cool guys. I was always intimidated by the cool guys. They had access to any woman they wanted. Not only was I not cool but also I wanted a relationship without sex. I firmly believed that I was going to find true love and be a virgin on my wedding day. I was confident that the Lord had someone especially for me. I was willing to resist the short-term temptation of lust in exchange for everlasting love. What I didn't know is that women assumed that if I wasn't trying to get into their panties, I must be gay. I was interested in some of the women in my church, but I lacked the cool factor and was ignored. I started to believe that while I had a commitment to and desire for Black women, I did not feel a sense of reciprocity.

I made an appointment with my pastor to discuss him writing me a college recommendation. The conversation went to a place that would take years for me to appreciate. His first question was, am I familiar with the use of birth control? I think I was still a virgin. I wasn't sure how deep I had to be in before I lose my virginity.

I was struggling like hell to remain a virgin until marriage. Now, my pastor warned that I should expect having female company and that not all of them will be protected. Some women, he warned, will get pregnant to trap me. Then he realized that I was totally disconcerted about this conversation. To comfort me, he disclosed that he's sixty and still gets busy with his wife. Then the discussion broached the subject of the Bible. For the first time, I heard a preacher proclaim that the Bible is mythology. I was stunned. I believed the Bible was the word of God, and my pastor was telling me it's a myth. This did not compute. I'm thinking the half of the church that calls him a wolf in sheep's clothing is correct. The fact that he held a master's in theology made things more confusing. I could not accept his claim. How much of the Bible was a myth? My pastor was adamant that he believed in the teachings of Jesus. We as Christians should be dedicated to helping the poor, healing the sick, and feeding the hungry. He quoted as follows:

Then shall the King say unto them on his right hand, come, ye blessed of my Father, inherit the kingdom prepared for you from the foundation of the world:

For I was hungered, and ye gave me meat, I was thirsty, and ye gave me drink. I was a stranger, and ye took me in:

Naked, and ye clothed me: I was sick, and ye visited me. I was in prison, and ye came unto me.

Then shall the righteous answer him, saying Lord when saw we thee an hungered, and fed thee? Or thirsty and gave thee drink?

When saw we thee a stranger and took thee in? Or naked and clothed thee?

Or when saw we thee sick, or in prison, and came unto thee?

And the King shall answer and say unto them, Verily I say unto you, Inasmuch as ye have done it unto one of the least of these my brethren, ye have done it unto me.

Then shall he say also unto them on the left hand, Depart from me, ye cursed, into everlasting fire, prepared for the devil and his angels:

For I was hungered, an ye gave me no meat: I was thirsty, and ye gave me no drink:

I was a stranger, and you took me not in: naked, and ye clothed me not: sick and in prison, and ye visited me not.

Then shall they also answer him, saying Lord, when saw we thee an hungered, or athirst, or a stranger, or naked, or sick or in prison, and not minister unto thee?

Then shall he answer them, saying, Verily I say unto you, Inasmuch as ye did it not to one of the least of these, ye did it not to me.

And these shall go away into everlasting punishment: but the righteous into life eternal. (Matt. 25:34–46)

These verses reflect the essence of being a Christian to many in the Black church. Martin Luther King was the de-facto pope for many in the Black church. The Black church was initially the only platform for Blacks to fight for civil rights. It was the only place Blacks could gather to strategize about how to improve the condition of the Negroes. Many argue the Black church was too political in nature and neglected what they proclaim the true message of Christ. This claim may have some merit, but the alternative was not working. It should be clear to everyone that the Holy Spirit did not change the hearts of White people. Change came by action not prayer. Maybe prayer was the fuel for the action, but it took action. Martin Luther King was concerned about the betterment of humanity. I submit that Martin Luther King was the paradigm of a true Religious Humanist who used the church as his vehicle. I am not inferring that King was not a man of faith. I am inferring that his vision of God was beyond what most preachers bring forth today. I have never heard King preach about tithing and prosperity. I never heard him preach that we are sinners, doomed to hell if we don't repent. I have heard him preach about the brotherhood of humanity. King preached that we are all God's children, which mandated that we all have equal protection under the law.

CHAPTER 3

❖

The Promise

BOTH OF MY parents grew up under Jim Crow laws. The impact on them was totally different. My dad was extremely indifferent to White people. To him a life without White people would be great as long as he could make a living. My mom always looked for an opportunity to be in the presence of White people. She wanted to prove that she was just as good, if not better than they are. They both believed that education was the key to the future success of Black people.

My education was a lot like the three little bears. I attended a predominately Black school, a predominately White school, and a very integrated school. The first myth I want to dispel about integrated schools is that they provide equal opportunity to Black and White students. Within a presumed integrated school, segregation is alive and well.

While attending a Black elementary school, I was not aware that I was getting a poor education. I was simply going to school. At the time we lived in a Black neighborhood, my friends were Black, and my church was Black, so I had no reason to assume that Black was inferior. I quickly learned that Black was by default inferior, by my mom. She was adamant that we move to a White neighborhood, which soon became a Black neighborhood, in spite of my dad's objections. I remember we moved into a White neighborhood on a Saturday. I also remember that on Monday our neighbor had a for-sale sign up. Maybe this was a coincidence. Soon after the house across the street went up for sale. Then the house next to it. Then the house two houses away from us. In all instances, Blacks purchased the houses that were sold.

Being the only Black in my class, my best friend was Jesus. I found the best way to be around White people was to stay to myself. I was occasionally called a Black nigger. I honestly can't remember what prompted my classmates to call me nigger. I guess it was a form of entertainment. Over time I discovered the two other Blacks who attended my school, and we formed the first Black Student Union of Creston Heights Elementary School. Our first pledge was not to tolerate any more nigger jokes. We would be one for all and all for one.

Some of the White kids showed a true interest in diversity. I remembered a White guy asking me if my blood was green. I asked why. He explained that someone had told him that Negroes had green blood because they came from apes and apes have green blood. I guess he did not do well in science. But who knows? Maybe he is a doctor today. Another White guy politely asked if he could touch my nose. Again, I asked why. He wanted to confirm that I had a nose like a gorilla. I told him to go touch the nose of a gorilla and ask the gorilla if it's the same as a Negro's.

My dad was a graduate of Langton University. For a Black man, to hold a college degree back then was a significant achievement. He was an accounting major, which meant that he was able to get a good government clerk job. He worked along White guys with high-school diplomas. It was a steady job with good benefits. He earned enough to buy a home and keep food on the table. For my dad's generation, the government was the prime employer for Blacks with college degrees, especially the post office. The bad news is that in many ways little has changed.

I never remember having a conversation with my dad that started with if you go to college. It was always when you go to college. For me not going to college was never an option. I had plenty of role models when it came to college graduates. One of my uncles earned his master's from USC. I have two uncles who graduated from college and became Tuskegee airmen. One stayed in the air force and became a major. The other, who was a fighter pilot, flew fifty-three missions in Italy, with thirty-five of those missions being bomber-escort missions. The Tuskegee airmen received the Congressional Gold Medal in March 2007, presented by President George W. Bush. My uncle expressed how much he loved to fly. Flying was his life. He wanted to fly as a career but soon realized he was not wanted. With pride he took his experience as a fighter pilot and became the first Black man entrusted to drive a Kansas City bus.

My mom and my aunt both earned college degrees in their fifties. My dad's mantra was an education is one thing the White man can't steal from you.

My first year in college I completed an honors course in The Thought of Western Civilization. This course was a revelation regarding the evolution of thought. The first thing that came to mind is how unfortunate it is that more Blacks are not enticed to attend college. I studied Plato, Aristotle, Socrates, Voltaire, Pierre Bayle, Saint Augustine, and a host of other scholars. I found this course to be fascinating. I felt I was learning what White boys learn. I learned how to read critically and challenge what the authors presented as truth. I quickly learned that human thought has dramatically changed over time. Probably the most important thing I learned was everybody is not Baptist. I also learned that very smart people can hold very different positions and support their positions using reason and logic.

For the first time in my life, I heard cogent arguments about why some people do not believe in God. The thought of not believing in God was unfathomable to me at that time, but I was captivated by listening to different arguments. I learned the difference between being an atheist, an agnostic, and a deist. Then I learned that describing God, Jesus, and the Holy Ghost was much more complicated than I what I learned in Sunday school.

The first thing I learned about atheism is that most atheists concede that they can't prove that God does not exist. Likewise, they contend that the existence of a God cannot be proven. They reject the claim that God exists. People with these beliefs are often referred to as negative atheists. Those who insist that there absolutely is no God are referred to as positive atheists. Only about 5 percent of atheists are positive atheists. In most instances, the gist of the problem is how to define God.

Two primary definitions of agnosticism is that God is unknowing and there is not enough evidence to determine if there is a God. Agnostics presuppose that given more evidence they could be convinced that there is a God. Atheists believe that there is enough evidence to support the claim that there is no God but will concede that the nonexistence of God cannot be proven.

Deists are natural theists. They accept the creation of the universe as an act of God, but they insist that God has no interaction with man beyond the natural laws of nature. Deists refute any claims of divine intervention, especially claims that the Bible, Koran, and the Torah are inspired by God. They believe in God only to the extent that claims can be supported by logic, reason, and science.

Not all atheists, agnostics and deists are created equal. You will readily find variances among these beliefs. One common element of all three is that they believe that humankind is responsible for making the experience of life on earth better for all. They all reject that man is subject to the wrath of God or that God intervenes on the behalf of man. Collectively, members within these groups often refer to themselves as Secular Humanists.

I also took courses in comparative religions, which exposed me to Eastern religions. To my surprise, Eastern religions made more sense to me. They had a totally different perception of God and spirituality. In retrospect, I should have given them serious consideration as an alternative to Christianity, instead of an academic exercise.

When I studied astronomy, the big-bang theory started to make sense. The earth being made in six days did not seem plausible. The big-bang theory coincided with many of the principles I learned in chemistry. When I studied biology, the evolution of man from a common ancestor of monkeys did not seem farfetched.

My education escalated my intellectual curiosity to a level that was inconceivable a few years prior. However, I was determined not to be an educated fool. This was my way of not letting what I found to be intellectually correct impact my Christian faith. I held on to the biblical version of creation. There was a group on campus whose sole objective was to mitigate everything I was learning and keep me grounded in the word of God. College became more than a curriculum, it became a battleground for my morals, character, and Christian convictions.

My mom was involved in community politics. She went to a community meeting and was able to get me a job interview with the department of recreation and parks. I interviewed for a position as locker-room attendant. I got the job and was the only Black on staff. Once again, I was put in the position of striving to be an exemplary Black. I was the Black face for the staff and the public at large. I was exposed to White people on a whole new level.

At work I had to interact with White people. It was part of my job. Learning how to be a locker-room attendant was easy. Learning to work and be around White people was an arduous task. I found it almost impossible to ignore White people when I was working with them. I slowly learned how to be around them without becoming emotionally drained.

I expressed my interest in becoming a lifeguard, and to my surprise, I found the manager was open to my request. I had taken swimming lessons as a kid but did not really get that far. I truly enjoyed swimming and was willing to work. My attitude toward White people started to improve when I realized how many of the lifeguards took me under their wings and helped to significantly increase my swimming skills. I devised a workout schedule to improve my swimming technique, endurance, and speed. When management gave me the go-ahead, I took the required training courses in Water Safety Instruction and Lifeguard Training. Soon, I had mastered all the skills required to pass the city's required lifeguard swimming test.

Soon I began to see my coworkers as coworkers and not just a bunch of White people I have to put up with. I realized some of them are really good people. I once went backpacking with some White guys I worked with, which was unthinkable a few years ago. I also went to some White house parties. Black people and White people, back then, just did not party the same way. Black people would drink and smoke just enough to get a good grove on. White people would just drink and smoke all night. For the first time, I was exposed to White women. There was an old saying back in the day that every nigger wants a Cadillac and a White woman. My thought was why a White woman when there are so many Black women available.

I thoroughly enjoyed my first year of college. I was meeting new people and being exposed to new ideas. I appreciated the college environment. Especially, campus speakers. I heard lectures from Dick Gregory, Stokely Carmichael, a gay activist, and a transvestite. I had professors from India, China, and every other walk of life. I had mature White women accounting professors who candidly explained that their careers were limited because of their gender. They were CPAs, held at least a master's degree, but had limited career opportunities. I felt they identified with me and were in my corner. There was one Black professor who helped connect me with NABA, the National Association of Black Accountants.

I was eating lunch when two White guys approached me and asked if I knew Jesus Christ as my personal Lord and Savior. I said no. Not because I was not a Christian and didn't believe in Jesus, but because I have never heard the term "personal Savior" before. They proceeded to share with me what they referred to as the four spiritual laws. It was a very simplistic explanation of the Gospel. It presented an idyllic view of Christianity. A life with Jesus as Lord, who divinely guides you through life via the Holy Spirit. All you have to do is say a simple prayer and commit your life to Christ. They also adhered to what they termed discipleship, which was a concerted effort to ensure that your view of Christianity is congruent with their view of Christianity.

They invited me to a harambee conference. This was a special ministry of Campus Crusade for Christ to minister to the African American community, which in essence was a strategy to bring Black Christians back under the Master's control. I attended this conference and was surprised that two of my close friends also attended. I also knew one of the conference leaders. He happened to have a White wife, which bothered me a little. I read *Soul on Ice* and accepted it as a political statement.

I must admit that it was refreshing to meet so many Black people who seem to have the same dedication to Jesus that I had. We were determined to go back to our respective churches and enlighten our fellow church members in the manner Campus Crusade had enlightened us. For a brief moment, I had a feeling that the Black church had everything all wrong. Shamefully, I momentarily became a victim of White superiority in the name of Jesus. I reasoned that White folks are on top, so they must know something about Jesus that Black folks don't. I wanted to learn what it was. I was confident that if I pray like White folks, go to their Bible studies, and accept the Gospel like White folks, then I would get the same results in life that White folks get. If Black folks and White folks are worshipping the same God and getting such different results, Black folks must be worshipping God wrong. This had to be the case, otherwise Jesus is a racist.

Upon returning from the harambee conference, my friends and I decided to start a home Bible study at my house. We met with our pastor who was reluctant but rendered his support. He let us borrow the church's projector so that we can show a film produced by Campus Crusade for their harambee ministry. Our pastor wanted us to hold our Bible study at the church. We felt that holding it at my house would make people more comfortable about attending. In the back of my mind, I am still wondering how a preacher could believe that the Bible is methodology.

Our home Bible study was a success. I truly felt that I was doing the work of the Lord, and it was only a matter of time before I was ordained a full deacon at my church. What I was taught at Campus Crusade for Christ had assuaged my intellectual appetite to learn more about the history and background of Christianity. I also was discouraged from exploring Eastern religions further. I was only concerned with finding which Christian religion was the true Christian religion.

While my pastor at church was concerned with me using proper birth control and assuring me that the Bible is a myth, Campus Crusade had bombarded me with several seminars on how important it was to adhere to God's word and abstain from fornication. In the midst of this, I was surrounded by women willing to sleep with me. To complicate things, I had one friend who never talked about sex, which I must admit I found to be anomalous. I had a friend who had no intention to fornicate but did, and the rest of my friends tried to have as much sex as possible. My original intent was to be a virgin on my wedding night. I soon realized that this desire was unrealistic and imprudent. I eventually ended up engaging in sexual activity. I have never regretted becoming sexually active. I do regret being persuaded that sex out of marriage is a sin. This belief only hindered my ability to fully enjoy all aspects of making love without an undercurrent of guilt. I firmly believe that sex outside of marriage is part of developing healthy relationships. From my experience, the people who have abstained from sex until marriage have no better results than people who get busy on their third date.

By my junior year of college, I became an evangelical Black Baptist who had a reputation at work as being a born-again Christian. I would regularly go to house parties and secular music concerts. I was committed to dating only Black women, in spite of being surrounded by White women. I would vacillate between no sex before marriage and fornication.

My career as a lifeguard and swimming instructor was progressing. To everybody's surprise I became the second most-requested swimming instructor. This brought me attention from the managers and White women. How did this Black guy who could barely swim a few years ago become the second most-requested swimming instructor? By far, most of the kids I was teaching were White. Kelly a coworker told me that parents appreciated how patient I was with their kids. She felt that my level of patience was beyond what she had noticed in the other instructors. She admired my patience with the kids. She also encouraged me to pursue becoming a chief guard, which I did not take seriously. After all, teaching me how to swim was a staff project. Plus, I could not see a nigger like me managing a bunch of White guys. To my surprise, my manager also encouraged me to seek the position of chief guard. I never did, and this is something I've always regretted.

Kelly also recognized I was a Christian. She was a Catholic who went to a charismatic church. I found this to be extremely strange. I had never been to a charismatic church, which I thought was a Black thing. Kelly was Irish. She invited me to her church, and we started a dialogue.

I attended a prominent Black prosperity church, when prosperity preaching was in its infancy. I discovered another unique perspective regarding what it means to be a Christian. This church was very organized and had plenty of study material. They had a handout that must have had every scripture in the Bible with the word prosper in it. The same with healing, praising God, anointing with oil, speaking in tongues, and the power of the Holy Ghost. I never met so many people who claim everything in the name of Jesus. I always wondered what Jesus did when two people from the same church claim the same job. The pastor was arrogant and often bragged that he drove a Bentley while the local pimps drove Cadillac's. I found this church to be very entertaining but nothing to be taken seriously. The fact that this church was in the center of one of the more prosperous Black communities didn't help its credibility. Maybe if it was located in the middle of Compton and the members were becoming rich, I would have given it more respect.

Meanwhile, a classmate at school invited me to her church. This turned out to be my first encounter with a Black Holy Roller church. I saw the whole thing as part foolishness, part entertainment, and a little bit scary. I found the people to be sincere regarding their beliefs. I also found the claims made by the preacher to be incredulous.

My commitment to Christianity was not detoured by all of these conflicted positions regarding who is a Christian. I felt Pentecostals made the best arguments. If you are going to dedicate your life to Jesus, there should be some benefits, such as getting healed, compliments of the Holy Ghost. The problem was these claims blatantly are not true. My home church had the most practical approach to being a Christian. The evangelicals might have been technically correct. However, I found them to have no compassion and to be extremely callous toward humanity. I explored other Christian religions and came to the conclusion that the differences were a matter of preference not substance. Later, I discovered discrepancies within the Christian faith infringe upon the existence and credibility of the Holy Spirit. In retrospective, I did not realize that my desire to be a Christian was based on an emotional need. Intellectually, I had become a deist. I had developed a latent struggle between my intellect and my emotions. It would be a while before I realized this and resolved this conflict.

Kelly and I ultimately became lovers. My life became very fragmented at that point and remained that way for years to come. Somehow I became lovers with an Irish Catholic while being committed to marrying a Black woman. I attended an all-Black Baptist church but would attend evangelical Bible studies. I never took Kelly to my church. I believed that if God was real, he should be healing everybody and delivering everybody as proclaimed in the Pentecostal church. It was clear that these claims had no merit. I had an attitude with White people, but I was happily dating a White woman. I was working with a group of White people who were extremely supportive of all my endeavors. Definitely more supportive than my Black classmates in high school.

My family life was challenging. My mom had absolutely no respect for my dad, and this made me resent both my mom and my dad. My dad was trying to reach out to me, but I was already pissed, because it was too late in the game. I brought Kelly over to meet my family, and to say the least, we received mixed reactions. My dad laughed. My mom took it as a badge of honor. She saw it as an affirmation that she had raised her children according to the dominant culture. I never understood what she meant by this, but it sounded good. I think she was implying that if we were good enough to attract White folks, she must have raised us well. My sister saw this as poetic justice since I criticized her for dating a White guy. Through all of this, I trusted in Jesus. I had made a commitment to finish the race. I talked to enough deacons to know that life is a struggle. Several deacons admonished me to stay with the Lord. He will deliver me. There was something about suffering for Jesus that was ingrained in my Christian experience. Life was too tough to live without God. Troubles don't last always. Take your troubles to the Lord, and leave them there. My faith was being tested. I was in the wilderness, but God was getting ready to lead me into the promised land. I knew that by the time I start my career and get married, I would be ready to join the Deacon Board.

Beyond my faith I found refuge in the arts. Since fifth grade I was in the school band. To this day I love classical music. I joined the drama club in high school. I also joined the forensics club and won several competitions in the category of original oratory. I would rather go to an August Wilson play than any sporting event.

I find theater to be a great place to study human behavior. I appreciate how theater can transport me to life at a different place, at a different time. I believe a good play can be inspirational as well as a source of wisdom and knowledge. I refute the claim that everything you need to learn about the human condition is in the Bible.

I started to take acting courses on campus and off campus. I joined an African American Christian theater group and a secular theater group. The secular group was more fun. The leader of the Christian group had a grandiose vision of how God was going to bless his ministry. Faithful members of his ministry were preordained to be movie stars. During prayer sessions, evil spirits were being cast out, and miracle after miracle was being claimed, all in the name of Jesus. I found all this to be intriguing. I believed that all things are possible with God. The practical side reminded me that somebody always beats the odds, but most don't. I had no basis to believe a claim based on one man's vision. I also had no basis to deny what the future might hold. Members from both groups had some visible success in the film industry and TV industry. I still get a rush when I see someone I studied with in a movie or TV show.

I seemed to have more of an appeal to women in theater. For some reason, my lack of the cool factor was not an issue with them. I found this to be very refreshing. Maybe it was due to our common passion for theater. Maybe it was because I was a straight man interested in theater. Whatever the reasons, I connected with several of them.

Soon the racial divide between Kelly and I led to our split. The truth is the racial divide within myself caused us to split. Kelly had absolutely no problem with our racial differences. The race issue was solely mine. I know that I hurt her solely based on her race. I wonder if she felt like a Black woman not getting a job based on her race. Issues of race and justice are always complicated. I have lost all contact with Kelly. I trust life has been good to her. If I could speak with her today, I would profusely apologize for my racist behavior. Since dating Kelly I have been in other situations where there was a strong mutual attraction between myself and a White woman. I learned from my experience with Kelly to eschew these situations urgently. I do not want to cope with any interracial relationships again.

Camp Jesus

The summer before my senior year of college I decided to work as a lifeguard at a conservative evangelical Christian camp. This camp was desperately trying to integrate its staff. I had to live in a dorm with conservative evangelical White Christians. Akeem, a Black friend of mine, had broken the color line last year, and this year there would be a 300 percent increase in the minority workforce. Working at Camp Jesus was the first time I met anybody who did not adore John F. Kennedy. When one of my coworkers said the guy who shot JFK should receive a medal, I knew I was no longer working with liberal White hippie types. This was truly a new world for me. This will sound strange to anyone who lives in a major city, but for some of my coworkers, I was their first colored contact. They had seen Blacks on TV. Now they could actually talk to one. Camp Jesus apparently recruited from every White conservative city throughout the country. Working there took being an exemplary Negro to a whole new level. For a while I felt like Sidney Poitier in *The Heat of the Night.*

Occasionally, I had to listen to White folks complain about being victims of reverse racial discrimination. I had a conversation with a White guy who apparently felt that I had taken his job. I don't know why he didn't consider that someone White had taken his job. He apparently felt that I was hired only because I was Black and looked good in a red bathing suit. He was shocked when I told him about my previous work experience and that I actually had more experience than anyone hired this year. I am confident that management made sure not to hire someone with marginal qualifications, to avoid being accused of tokenism.

I truly resented the assumption that I was not qualified for my position. It is degrading that someone would assume that because I'm Black, I am by default less qualified than he or she is. This attitude followed me throughout my career. At what point does the playing field become equal in the world of perceptions?

I enjoyed working at summer camp. The environment was beautiful. There was a lake, horseback riding, good food, plenty of walking trails, two swimming pools, and just about every activity for kids you can imagine. Socially, I spent most of my time reading, writing, and working out.

For the most part, I was able to avoid controversial conversations. Most of my coworkers came from affluent families. They had no clue how different my life was from theirs and I was not going to tell them. All was well until Akeem decided to talk about how lost the Black church is in front of a bunch of White evangelical Christians. I went off. I'm sure some of the Whites came close to pissing in their pants. This was before Clarence Thomas and I could not believe that a Black man could hold such idiotic views. His whole argument was along that of Billy Graham's. Just bring people to Jesus, and ask the Lord to change people's hearts. If a nigger receives Christ and gets lynched on the way home, Graham did his job. The fact that a nigger got lynched was a government problem. Akeem criticized the Black church for being involved in the civil rights movement. He argued that for a church to advocate for anything other than Jesus was totally inappropriate. He believed that God called his born-again ignorant ass to get the Black church to merge with White evangelicals. He ended up working for Campus Crusade for Christ and soon became an intellectual zombie. Before Akeem got saved, we were running buddies, which means we smoked weed together, drank together, chased women together, and talked about White people on a regular basis. After he got saved, his life was Jesus. Jesus was the solution to every problem facing humanity. I was able to deal with him for a season. That season ended when he shared how proud he was to support George Bush for both terms. His sole basis for supporting Bush was Bush's claim to be a born-again Christian. Bush's incompetency was irrelevant, and he took pride in the fact that Bush would stick to a bad decision regardless of new evidence.

Akeem married a nice Christian Black woman. I emphasize Black because most of the women he pursued were Whites. They abstained from premarital sex as proscribed by their religious convictions. If you do things God's way, your marriage will last. Shortly, after they got married, Akeem had a serious stroke and never fully recovered. Everyone is susceptible to a stroke. However, everyone does not go around preaching Jesus wants you to live an abundant life. I see nothing about having a serious stroke that contributes to living an abundant life. Akeem spent his entire career being a role model of the abundant life that Jesus promises believers. I believe he got shortchanged. His stroke added stress to, what in my opinion, was already a piss-poor marriage. I suspect that Akeem became overconfident about his marriage vows. Apparently, he assumed that he can treat his wife like shit and she would not leave him. Fortunately, his wife woke up and divorced him. This did not help Akeem's living the abundant-life testimony at all. During the course of his marriage, I never saw the benefit he received from abstaining from sex until marriage. Today, I can be cordial if need be, but I have no respect for him as a Black man or as a Christian. I will assume the feeling is mutual.

Upon returning from the camp, I renewed my commitment to the Black church. I was excited about my last year of college. I had not been in a relationship for a while and decided I would date a committed Black Christian woman. We both agreed to no sex before marriage. That was a great decision. Not because we got married. Not because it improved the quality of our relationship. The only benefit is she married someone else and remained a close family friend. It is very heartening when I'm talking with her husband to know that we never crossed any sexual boundaries. This was my only serious relationship without sex. I plan to keep it that way.

I finally graduated from college. I never went to my graduation ceremony. I decided to pass the CPA exam before I started my career. I also wanted to give writing and acting a shot before I pursued a real job. I completed a screenplay that took place in New York City. I took full advantage of being young and naive. I took my life savings of $600 and moved to Jersey City.

CHAPTER 4

⚜

Life in Jersey City

A FRIEND OF mine had some cousins living in Jersey City. He told them I was moving to NYC and asked if I can stay with them if I share in paying rent. I did not know they were Holy Rollers. I also did not know that Holy Roller Land on the East Coast is like a trip to ridiculous. I was living with saved college students. I quickly learned that being saved in Holy Roller Land was not the same as being saved in the rest of the world. I was having Sunday dinner with a mixed crowd. I asked, "What clubs do you go to?" There was dead silence. Everyone looked at me to see if there were horns growing out of my head. I was totally clueless of why all of them reacted like they did. Then I was verbally assaulted by one of the Church sisters, "I thought you said you were saved." I responded, "I am saved. I just want to know if there are any good clubs to go dancing." Then the big question came. Do you speak in tongues? I said no. Her reply was intense on the border of furious, "How're you going to fight the devil if you don't speak in tongues?" I looked at her like that was the stupidest question I ever heard. To me fighting the devil was a cartoon theme. I could not imagine college students who did not like to party. This explained why they dance so much in church, which I always thought should be reserved for prayer and worship. I found Holly Roller churches a good place for senior citizens to party. One of my roommates intervened and stated that once I get saved, the Lord will deliver me from the world. I actually like the world. I have no intention of being delivered from it.

I was in a real bind. I had to attend church with them at least in the short term, since I could not afford to be asked to leave. My next challenge was learning to tolerate everything as being a blessing from God. Praise the Lord or praise him was a salutation, benediction, and everything in between. I found church service to be a sideshow. During church everybody got delivered from something. One sister got delivered from smoking. We went to the park during church break, and she admitted that she just got delivered from smoking, but she wanted a cigarette and had one. One brother was delivered from his lust. He later got busted for attempted rape. I asked him about what happened. He blamed his pastor for claiming that he was delivered. When I talked to him, he was out on bail. I never found out if he served time. Another brother who warned me that I better get saved ended up a crackhead and left his wife. What I found really funny were the number of sensual women who were constantly being delivered from lust. The plain Janes talked about these women like they were whores at the navy yard. The plain Janes were also the first ones to get pregnant.

I would always sit in the back of the church. One evening service the pastor got in my face and said, "God told me to pray for you." I did not want to make a scene and tell the truth, "Hell no, I can pray for myself." So I lied in church and said OK I stood there, and his deputy pimps got ready to catch me just in case the Holy Ghost hits me. I had no reaction at all, and the pastor left me alone henceforth. This confirmed to me that Holy Roller Land is nothing but a sideshow that fools a lot of people. Everything in his prayer was bullshit. It had nothing to do with my life. It was clear that he made assumptions about me and prayed accordingly. I can assure you that nothing he said came from God. To the believers, this was the power of the Holy Ghost at work. God spoke through their pastor, and I was delivered.

I did some temporary accounting work as I pursued my acting career. I am convinced that Denzel Washington should send me a thank-you card. I am sure that we both auditioned for the role of Malcolm X at a NYC theater. The only reason he got the part was that my phone was disconnected when they made the callback. No problem, Denzel. I think you should have won an Oscar for your portrayal of Malcolm X. If you find some time, I would love to do a scene with you. Maybe in the context of a TV reality show. I will try not to upstage you.

Some close friends of mine were working on Broadway. I was able to hold on to their coattails and pretend that I was in the business. I might not have been a performer, but that did not prevent me from attending after parties. Many Black singers got their start in church. I was invited to a Bible study that was geared toward Black artists. I loved it. I met some great people. Mostly women. I knew that guys in the chorus are likely to be gay. I am not gay. I am not antigay. I like women and figured that women in theater are probably freaks. I met two women whom I had a keen interest in. I knew they were close friends, but that did not keep me from talking to both of them. Over time, I developed a closeness to both of them. Over time, I became amorous with both of them. Over time, I found out they were once lovers. This was my first encounter in my quest for love on the East Coast.

For the most part, I was able to keep a flow of women in my life. Initially, I had a problem getting stuck on friends, which I hate. There is nothing worse than being with a woman and she's talking to you like you're one of her girlfriends. I was with one woman, and all she talked about was how much she missed screwing her ex-boyfriend. One woman I dated wouldn't give me none because she had already introduced me to her mom. She had a house rule. She does not screw anybody she brings home. I was like, Bitch, why didn't you tell me this before you asked me over for dinner? I would have gone to McDonalds and taken the pussy. I once dated a divorcee. She was going out with me but screwing her ex-husband and her new boyfriend. Again, no pussy for me, and I got stuck in the good-friend zone. She got pregnant and invited me to her wedding.

I had to seriously check myself. My first reaction was that these women must be thinking I'm gay. Once I addressed this issue, I still wasn't getting laid. I soon discovered that all those relationship seminars I attended at Campus Crusade for Christ were destroying my game. I was indoctrinated with too much "let's be friends, and wait until marriage" propaganda. This had to be corrected. There is a small window to get laid. Once I get laid, I can work on the friendship. Once I was designated as a good friend, I never got laid. This went against everything I had been taught, but it was true for most people in the real world. My new approach worked. I would seek sex first, and all else came second. I was attracted to the women I approached beyond sex. However, from the beginning I let them know that I was not interested in a platonic relationship. As a result of this new approach, I developed a friendship that lasted a lifetime.

I met Nicki on a Circle Line cruise. I was lit up, and we connected right away. A couple of dates later, we were lovers. This was my first relationship with a woman who had a child. This was a major adjustment for me. She was also in college. Her son spent the summer with her parents in the Caribbean. This provided us an opportunity to have a summer romance second to none. Once her son returned and she started school, we agreed that it would be best to chill. That lasted until the holidays. We became more than friends and lovers, but we never got married. Again, I put that on me. I am not sure why I never married Nicki, but I am sure that we proved that being close friends before having sex is a misnomer. The outcome of our relationship would not have been any different if we had abstained from sex. In fact, Nicki was a virgin when she got married. She complied with her religious upbringing and refrained from sexual intercourse until her wedding night. She got pregnant early in her marriage. She was living according to the word. Her marriage was off to a great start until she found her husband in bed with another woman. Again, destroying the notion that abstaining from sex until marriage will ensure a successful marriage. Our friendship has survived me having a son, me getting married and divorced, and quite frankly, me treating her in ways that I am totally ashamed of. Over twenty-five years later, I call her just to let her know that I am alive and healthy. The same with her. What started off with a few drinks and talking crap on a cruise down the Hudson has ended in a lifelong friendship. I know too many Christians who have played by the book and have never come close to the relationship that Nicki and I shared, in spite of us never getting married.

A female friend of mine put it this way. Men will play all kinds of games to get the pussy. She decided to give up the pussy early and see what she has to work with afterward. She is happily married today. I went to her wedding. It was the most elaborate wedding I ever attended. It was clear that after the pussy, she and her husband had plenty to work with. It seemed that every year I was learning that what I was taught at Campus Crusade did not hold true as my life unfolded. It seemed that life happened with or without Jesus.

CHAPTER 5

---------- ⚜ ----------

It's Good Work If
You Can Get It

ONCE I REALIZED it was too late to catch up with Denzel, I decided to get a real job. I was fortunate enough to get a job at a major commercial bank. Working in banking gave me access to a new class of White people. It was also a work environment that matched my personality. I believe in working hard and playing hard. The bank gave me an opportunity to do both.

My first observation working at the bank was that most of the Blacks being hired with college degrees were replacing Whites without college degrees who were retiring. The term given was upgrading the department. The second thing that I noticed was that the area I worked in was mostly minorities with White management. The third thing I noticed was that White managers could have any background. The fourth thing I noticed was that there was a lot of nepotism among managers. The fifth thing I noticed was that my boss did not have a college degree.

I did not like any of the above, but I was in the door. I started at the lowest level possible. I had recently passed the CPA examination and was keying in general ledger tickets. My break came when the bank decided to put in a new general ledger system, and I was part of the design and implementation team. Miriam, a Jewish coworker of mine, gave me a lesson that changed the course of my career. I was testing the system and had logged several system problems. I shared them with a coworker who presented them as her own work. As soon as the coast was clear, Miriam went off on me. She told me to never let anyone take credit for your work again. Then she really made me feel stupid. Everything she told me was 100 percent correct. I thanked her and realized she was a Jewish woman who had my back. She had some grudges of her own with management, but she was a fighter. She taught me that in corporate America a little fight and arrogance goes a long way. Many will argue that I might have overcompensated on the arrogance part, but I got results. When it came time to appoint a project manager, I was skipped over for my coworker who presented my work. Miriam was pissed at me, my coworker, and management but mostly at me for letting it happen. I had put a lot of time into this project and knew the project inside and out. When my coworker started to embarrass management by distributing bad information, she was reassigned, and I took over the project. If her performance had been anywhere close to par, I would have never been considered. This was a reality of the world I was now working in. I did not like the way my opportunity came. I resented not being considered for the starting lineup. My only consolation of becoming project manager under these circumstances was that I redeemed myself in the eyes of Miriam, and everyone figured out that my coworker was incompetent. The project was a success. I was selected to demonstrate the new general system to the controller of the entire bank and played a key role in rolling out the new system. I even traveled upstate to assist with implementation. I soon was promoted to accounting officer.

With my new title came a staff, office, and new attitude. A good friend of mine hooked me up with his tailor and showed me where to buy custom-made shirts. Life was good. I moved from

Jersey City to Park Wood Village. I was exposed to good wine and good cigars. Two things I still enjoy. Going out for dinner and drinks after work became a norm. There were plenty of women to go out with. I was a having a great time. I could only imagine what the view from the top must be like.

I was still recovering from living with Holy Rollers, and my goal of being a deacon was put on hold. I still had faith and prayed daily, but for a season regular attendance to church was not happening. I would watch some TV services and listen to Christian tapes. Sundays became my day of rest in very real terms.

Most of the Blacks I worked with were raised in church. About half of them were backsliders. I did not encounter any White evangelical Christians at work. For the Whites I worked with, religion appeared to be a formality. It seemed strange that according to prosperity preachers, the key to prosperity was Jesus and becoming a financial partner with a prosperous ministry. Overwhelmingly, Whites and Jews had the best jobs in the company. I never heard any of them talk about tithing, speaking in tongues, being members of a mega church, or praising the name of Jesus. Most of them were very generous when it came to supporting charities. It had to do with accountability. My favorite was the March of Dimes. Helping babies is tangible. Their financial statements are audited, and I can see how progress is being made and how babies are being helped. This seems to be a better way to donate money. I don't understand why a prosperity preacher needs to live in a mansion and fly on a private jet, at the expense of his congregation. It's not like being a CEO where profits are being distributed to shareholders. If a company does well, the shareholders have a clear benefit. What is the benefit to a tithing member of a prosperity mega church beyond bragging privileges of how well their pastor lives? There is no evidence to support that members of prosperity churches do better financially. A lot of testimonies from a select few, but no evidence other than claims made by the preachers. There is a correlation between prosperity and race. A statistically strong correlation.

I enjoyed working at the bank and all the perks that came with it. To give back to my community, I would tutor in East Harlem. My bank had an annual global day of service where employees would volunteer working on community projects. I always looked forward to participating in this event. I also liked being in a position to give to charities and causes I believed in. Since I was not attending church, I would give away about 10 percent of what I earned to charity or to the benefit of someone other than myself. I did give to church when I attended. I understand that churches have to keep the lights on. I concede that some churches are very involved in their local community and provide essential services to those in need. I think that Christians who only donate to church are very shortsighted. The United Negro College Fund, Jerry's Kids, cancer research, and other charities have objectives that benefit humanity.

JB Syndrome

I had an uncle who married two women twice. That's four divorces alone. Plus, he had several other marriages, divorces and, numerous girlfriends in between marriages, and sometimes during marriages. My family members affectionately called this JB Syndrome. On my mom's side and my father's side of the family, solid marriages were few and far between. I was determined that as a good Christian man, I was going to break this trend. I fell short on the no-sex-before-marriage goal, but I still considered myself to be a good man, with a good heart, who knows how to treat a woman. I soon discovered that JB Syndrome might be a genetic defect. I admired my uncle JB and apparently picked up JB Syndrome.

I was entertaining quite a few women on different levels. Because of JB Syndrome, I gravitated toward women who surrounded their emotions with the Great Wall of China. I had a coworker who declared to the whole department that men are no God damn good. She was not falling in love with nobody. All she wanted was a man to get her pregnant and leave her the hell alone. My ignorant ass fell in love with her and got her pregnant. As a supreme idiot, I was expecting her to repent regarding her talk about raising a child by herself. This is when I learned to listen to what people say. It does not matter how ridiculous the words are coming from their mouths, listen to what they say. She told me point-blank to go on with my life that she was going to take care of everything. This was her baby! I was much cheaper than going to a sperm bank. She assured me that she had enough love for both a mother and a father. She thanked me for getting her pregnant. She expected her child to be smart and tall, which he turned out to be. I took her advice and left both of them alone. I never mentioned to my family that I had a son because I truly believed that I didn't. I was merely a sperm donor.

My career at the bank continued to progress. I was mysteriously recommended for a job as divisional assistant controller. The interview was arranged before I knew about the opportunity. My first thought was that my boss wanted to replace me with one of his preferred managers, which he did. I never confirmed how this interview was arranged. I know that according to corporate policy, to transfer to another department, you had to sign up for mobility. I had been pitched to join other areas from managers I had previously worked with. I never heard of a prearranged interview.

None of my colleagues, Black and White, had heard of a prearranged interview. I went to the interview and got the job. I took the opportunity but again did not appreciate how the opportunity materialized.

My new position was located in the bank's corporate headquarters. I got more perks, including an onsite gym. I worked mostly with credit officers who were highly paid, came from Ivy League schools, and of course were virtually all White. They received crazy annual bonuses. Because I was not directly a part of the Controllers group, I was able to receive an annual bonus also. I learned two things by working in this area. I discovered what I call the racial default. I also witnessed White folks living on a whole new level.

There is a story about JFK that illustrates the racial default. Reportedly, Kennedy was walking off Air Force One, and he asked why he didn't see any Negro honor guards. The next time he walked off Air Force One he did see Negro honor guards. Kennedy did two things that I feel most Whites neglect. First, he asked the question why. Second, he used his power to implement a solution. Unfortunately, my experience is that most Whites lack the type of awareness that JFK had. The default for most Whites is honor guards are White. There is no issue to address.

I had some interesting conversations with some senior managers at the bank. One senior manager told me about how much he learned from mentoring in the inner city. Yet, he made no effort to bring diversity to his own staff. This pattern was prevalent among the senior managers I interacted with. These were people with tremendous power and hiring authority.

Thanks to e-mail, I experienced the next level of racial default. It was not intentional, there was no malice, but it's simply a way of thinking. I had written a memo regarding how to handle some issues with foreign debt. My memo eventually made it up to executive management. I was invited to attend a meeting with the chief credit officer, the bank's controller, and a host of other senior managers. I walked in with a White manager. The bank's controller congratulated the White manager on writing such a comprehensive memo. My colleague politely let it be known that I wrote the memo. The default was that my memo had to be the work of a White guy. This happened on several occasions. I would attend a meeting, and my colleagues assumed I was White. One of their favorite questions was if I have ever eaten at Sylvia's. This frustrated me sometimes, but it was something I could not control. I would talk to other Black managers, and they experienced the same phenomenon.

I have a theory on why Blacks excel in sports more than in corporate America. It is due to the selection process. In sports, the evaluation of a player is more objective. No one can take a subordinate's work, dress it up, and present it as his or her own. Often in business, a manager can hide behind the work of a subordinate. It is very difficult to evaluate how two different candidates will perform in any given position. Unfortunately, it is rare, if at all, that one candidate gets a shot for a few months and then another candidate gets a shot for a few months and their performance gets reviewed. I have found that few Blacks get a chance to be in the starting lineup. They are often called from the bench. I read the biographies of several Black CEOs, and their stories confirm my suspicions. Whites seem to interpret affirmative action as replacing qualified Whites with unqualified Blacks. Blacks see affirmative action as acknowledging that qualified Blacks are often ignored by default and should be given an opportunity.

I overheard a White manager declare that he would not hire any Blacks or women if it was not for human resources.

He had absolutely no track record of promoting any people of color. Based on my experience in the corporate world, getting rid of affirmative action is like getting rid of internal affairs at the NYC Police Department. Everybody wants to think that all cops are good, but you need someone to look over their shoulders just in case.

The Holy Ghost Strikes Back

I continued to struggle with JB Syndrome. A colleague of mine hired the most beautiful woman I had ever met. Lena had a gorgeous face and a dynamite body. She dressed extremely sexy. She was a woman who I proclaimed would look good under my arms. Then I talked to her. Immediately, big Christopher and little Christopher had a major conflict. I could not believe that such an incorrigible mind could be trapped in such a great body. This beautiful sexy woman was a genuine Holy Roller. She wore dresses with high splits and low-cut backs but did not dance or drink. She went to church at least four days a week.

Lena dated a local drug dealer and womanizer. I guess she felt that the Holy Ghost would save him. She loved him dearly, and they got married within weeks of her getting pregnant. Lena had no intention of sex before marriage. She had the Holy Ghost, and in her mind, going to a man's apartment at two in the morning did not mean that having sex was imminent. She was saved, and she expected the Holy Ghost to deliver her from lust. They had a daughter together, and her marriage worked until she caught him in their bed with another woman. She divorced her husband and essentially raised her daughter by herself. Her ex-husband spent most of his time incarcerated.

The most bizarre thing about Lena was she never dated men in church. This was another case of my ignorant ass getting involved in a hopeless situation, aka JB Syndrome. Lena invited me to her church for a concert. That should have been our last encounter, but it wasn't. I was intrigued with how her Holy Roller mind worked. Lena would dress like a first-class call girl, but dancing was against her spiritual principles. I later learned that living a double life is the norm in Holy Roller Land. I must admit that dating Lena did restore some of my dormant Christian values. She reminded me that I was once committed to no sex before marriage. When I started to see Lena, I was having sex with a married woman. I was thinking a woman like Lena might be what I needed to get back on the path to becoming a deacon. I joined a prominent Baptist church and renewed my commitment to the Christian faith. My relationship with Lena was a real dilemma. I liked to party, she didn't. Her priority in life was church. Mine was work hard, play hard. She liked gospel music, I liked jazz. Our biggest difference was I went to church and went home. She let church dominate her life.

My solution to some of these problems was simple but naive. She would go to church on Friday nights, I would go to a club on Friday nights. I had a variety of women to go to clubs with. I was not sleeping with them; thus adultery was not an issue. I would go to church with her but often waited in the car when things got crazy. When she attended church with me, she would catch the evening service at her church. Sex was a serious issue with us. I revert back to what I learned earlier but neglected to follow. If getting the pussy is a problem, you are in the wrong relationship. This is a rule that should be taught to every man in America. Lena and I eventually had sex before marriage. What a disaster! I never imagined making love to a woman and in the morning she is hysterically crying about what happened. This was coming from a woman in her mid-thirties, her sexual peak. Her guilt was beyond belief. I agreed to attend church with her to show emotional support. I was astonished when she burst into tears again as she confessed to Sister Williams that she made love with her boyfriend. This is why I am sure that JB Syndrome is a genetic mental defect. I should have gotten the hell out of this situation and hired someone to beat the shit out of me on general principle. My ignorant ass stayed with her. Now, I was in a relationship that is focused on not having sex more than anything else. This was a terrible foundation for building a relationship. Sister Williams would call Lena at work to make sure she was not sleeping with me. She should have been calling her own daughter who got pregnant at eighteen. Lena and I eventually got married, but that did not resolve our sex issues. First, Lena had a limited sex menu. The items on the menu were great, but the menu was limited. Suffice it to say, I found a solution to this problem. The second issue was that her pastor would put the church on a fast, which meant no sex. WTF! If I say hell no, then I would not be supporting her spiritual life. If I say yes, I would not be getting laid. Either way I was screwed. In addition, Lena believed you have to suffer for Jesus. This was when she would either voluntarily refrain from sex or have a church shut-in. A shut-in is when she would lock herself up in church for a week and pray. From what I understand, this warrants prestige and praise from other church members. A female friend would always warn, "Deacon how long can you live like this?" The answer was less than two years. There was nothing about my marriage that was normal, including the equitable distribution of assets upon our divorce. My attorney advised me that I was making payments that legally she was not entitled to. Since I wanted the divorce and she didn't, my attitude was give her what she wants so I can get the hell out. Years later Lena left her church. She apologized to me for in essence letting her church pimp her. I was happy that she saw the light, but at a tremendous cost.

After a reasonable cooling-off period, I was able to establish an amicable relationship with my ex-wife. Her daughter, Briana, ended up getting pregnant in high school. This was not a surprise considering that the only guidance she received from her mom regarding healthy adolescent sexual development was how to choose the correct-size sanitation napkin.

When Briana was facing challenges with her son, she would occasionally seek my counsel. As a result, we maintained a step-father-stepdaughter relationship, often to the dismay of Lena. Lena confronted me when she found out Briana bypassed her and called me for advice. Briana was facing serious issues regarding her son. I gave her my advice and supported her in what was by any standard a tough decision. Fortunately, she made the correct decision. They both received counseling to address several issues. They became closer and were able to use this experience as a step in personal growth. Her son will be graduating from college this year. I rebuked Lena and advised her to have a conversation with Briana regarding why she reached out to me. Maybe Briana did not believe that prayer was the solution to her problem. I was asked for advice and support, and I provided both. I would do it again.

Regrettably, Lena had a stroke and heart attack, as a side effect of removing a tumor that would have eventually killed her. I had a serious conversation with Lena the day before her surgery. I had done some research on her condition and knew that her operation entailed serious risk, including death. I attempted to delicately discuss what preparations she had made just in case something goes wrong. The possibility of something going wrong was never a consideration to her. She insisted that God had already told her that he was going to deliver her. She had earned a master's degree in sociology from Howard University. She recently had earned a master's in theology from Princeton University. She had secured a position as a hospital chaplain to start in about six weeks. According to Lena, this was God's way of preparing her to be a faithful chaplain. She would be a better witness to those she ministers to once God delivers her. This conversation made me angry. My first issue was that she neglected to provide her daughter with basic information needed to cover healthcare-cost and other financial issues. I was also piqued that no medical directives were given. I also found that her arrogance about what God had told her to be troubling at best. I immediately signed a do-not-resuscitate directive and gave it to my family.

Soon I realized that Lena's comments and preparation for her surgery were very consistent with her beliefs and faith. Her entire life she had been taught that God was watching over her. She believed that God will heal his faithful servants. She had no reason to doubt that God would heal her. To her facing the reality that something can go wrong was not a matter of dealing with reality, it was a concession to doubt, which was the work of the devil.

In my sinister moments of weakness, I want to ask Lena, "How come God did not deliver you like he said he would?" If your surgery was successful, I'm sure you would be giving a testimony in every church that has a pulpit, about how you trusted in God and he delivered you. Why don't you go testify that God did not deliver you in the manner you expected? Praising God that you are still alive is not the same as praising God for a full recovery. Either you heard God wrong, he lied to you, or what you've been taught in church for years is a bunch of bullshit. Which is it? What is the point of praising a God who is so unreliable? You dedicated your whole life to trying to please a God who by his goodness and mercy blessed you with two master's degrees and then deprived you of the opportunity to use them for his glory. To any rational person, this does not sound like a God who is worthy to be praised, as you would exuberantly encourage your church members' week after week. If you had known that this was your fate, would you have spent less time in church and more time enjoying the things of this world?

Lena's misfortune prompted me to examine my own professions of faith. I have been a victim of the same religious enigma. I started to correlate my success with being a blessing from God. However, I always justified my failures to be a result of my own shortcomings. By associating my success to the intervention of God (supernatural), I developed a dependence on the supernatural more than my ability to use logic and reason to make sound decisions. Emotionally, I became dependent on the supernatural. Regardless of what reason and logic dictated, I had programed myself to walk by faith and not by sight. This is a formula for eventual self-destruction. I now accept my failures are a result of making bad choices and not taking advantage of opportunities presented. My success is the result of making good decisions and taking advantage of opportunities presented.

I divorced Lena over twenty years ago. Yet, to support her and Briana, I caught a train to visit her in the hospital and several times since. My first reaction was that all of her dreams are dead and she has no clue. She took a "before picture" with everyone who visited, as evidence of how she was before God manifested his healing. Lena will never be able to take care of herself for the rest of her life. Briana now takes care of her. What I find incredible about Briana is her mom would take her to church and ask her pastor to cast out evil spirits. I am not that forgiving. I would have a hard time taking care of my mom if she put her church before me. Her lifelong pastor who took great pride in letting me know that he has known Lena since she was a child, has not visited her. I guess once Lena left his church, Jesus's teachings regarding visiting the sick became void. I guess that showing love and concern for someone who helped you start your own church stops once he or she stops tithing. I am sure that Lena's former pastor uses her misfortune to warn his flock of the perils of leaving his ministry. Sister Lena left the anointing of my ministry, and God let the devil have his way.

My bank went through several mergers. This hindered my career progression. I ultimately left the bank and accepted a controller position at a nonprofit community-development company. The company was an auxiliary to my church. This was the first time I worked for a Black company. It was an experience that I found to be invigorating. My technical skills, management skills, and leadership skills all faced their ultimate challenge. I also realized that political skills also become important in senior positions. Since we were a community group, going to and hosting fund-raisers was part of the job. This part of my job was somewhat fun, but at times it was very annoying.

The most disturbing issue regarding working in community development was the lack of resources. I went from being a phone call away from having just about any problem resolved to how this can be addressed. A vice president described the challenges faced by community-based nonprofits as deeply comingled. I agreed with her assessment. I also learned that the nepotism I complained about at the bank was present here, only the benefactors were Black. The company was technically bankrupt and was going through its first change in senior management. I felt privileged to be a part of that change, and the company was back in the black when I left. It is very frustrating working in community development knowing that in every deal everyone is making a profit except you. There is a huge difference in a company making a profit and a nonprofit making a decent return. Profit is distributed to its principals. In nonprofit there are no principals. While my experience in nonprofit brought me a tremendous amount of personal satisfaction, that did not translate into career growth. I wrote an article that was published in the *Journal of Accountancy*, based on my experience working in community development. Beyond that I was not able to capitalize on the experience I gained working in community development.

CHAPTER 6

———— ✦ ————

A Walk in the Wilderness

As I APPROACHED my fiftieth birthday, I reassessed my life. Now might be the time to join the Deacon Board. I entered into a spiritual wilderness and confronted the darkest side of my inner being. I discovered the magnitude of the schism between who I am and who I wanted to be. In the wilderness I saw my clouds of disappointment and my rivers of success. I found new meaning in that old Negro spiritual:

Nobody knows the trouble I've seen
Nobody knows, but Jesus
Glory, Hallelujah

My worldly friends can't understand my spiritual conflicts, and my Christian friends trivialize them. I learned that life is complex. I learned that temptation only has an appeal when it promises to assuage some disappointment or heal some wound. I have yielded to temptations and have paid the consequences right here on earth. I found light in the wilderness when I looked deep down inside and realized that the wilderness is part of my journey called life. My life has not been all that I wanted it to be, but it is better than most. I may not enter the land of milk and honey, but I have a good view. For now my prospects for being a deacon are nil. My church requires that deacons are to be married to a deaconess.

Love and marriage have to be the most perplexing dream to fulfill. If the mandate of marriage is "until death do us part," then one is hard-pressed to define what constitutes a successful marriage. My parents stayed together until death, but they were miserable together. I know couples who are total atheists, have never considered marriage, and have been happily living together for over thirty years. I know women who got married as virgins, only to catch their new husbands in bed with another woman. I know men who were completely dedicated to their wives until death but also kept a girlfriend on the side. I know couples who used the Christian play book and it worked. I dare say there are no rules when it comes to love and marriage. Perhaps the only question is, how long do you search if you have not found it?

Julia

Several times in my life, I've experienced what I consider love at first sight. I have no rational explanation for this phenomenal. I only know that occasionally, I meet a woman and connect with her on all levels. The fact that I know nothing about her does not mitigate my initial connection with her. For me this is a rare but enthralling experience. It is an aspect of the human experience that I unwittingly, embrace, relish, and succumb to.

My position required me to interact with personnel from several departments. I called Julia to resolve some reporting issues. When I heard her voice I was smitten. I knew that behind her voice was the woman of my dreams. When we eventually met, I was captivated with her beauty and charm. Julia was a natural composite of the positive elements of my previous lovers. She was physically attractive, had a sense of humor, enjoyed a good glass of wine, and was a good dancer. She loved theater and classical music. She was a vice president and made good money. I fell in love with Julia effortlessly. In my mind Julia was my soul mate. I would be at a jazz club thinking she should be here with me. Not only did I think she was my soul mate but also our mutual friends expressed the same sentiments. We had a mature female friend who was a mentor to both of us. She gratuitously warned me that my emotions toward Julia are beyond that of a friend. She accused Julia and I of having a love thing that was inappropriate for a married woman. Of course, I denied that I was in love with Julia. But my charade didn't work. I knew Julia loved her husband and was fully committed to her two children. Initially, I was not looking for a wife. I was looking for someone to love. I did not see myself competing with her husband. I saw myself as completing Julia. This was not about sex. To equate an affair with sex is a naive way of addressing the complexity of human emotions. Extramarital sex is not an affair. Affairs have captured the minds of great playwrights and novelists over the centuries. An affair is when two people create a place for themselves that only they can touch. They become each other's refuge. They find within each other what they need to live a more fulfilling life apart from each other. I did not have an issue with Julia being married. I had been with married women. My problem with Julia was that my emotions drifted into the forbidden territory. I wanted Julia to be more than my lover, I wanted her to be my wife. That was not going to happen. Julia was faithful to her husband. I once again attributed this experience to JB Syndrome and moved on.

For my fiftieth birthday, I had an opportunity to visit Mali and Senegal with a good friend. She was a featured speaker at a celebration on Goree Island. I had invested in a Juice Bar on

Goree Island via a connection of a friend who was a Peace Corp volunteer. The grand opening was during our visit. The Juice bar had running water and electricity. The homes of the owner had neither.

The image of my motherland was shattered. I loved the people but nothing else. I would describe both countries as enclaves of Europe in the midst of African people. Both countries are primarily Muslim. Our guides were not religious. They came from polygamous families, and both were looking for their second wife. They had a totally different concept of love and marriage. For them a wife is a role. They were adamant that each wife was treated equal. There was a proper protocol to introducing a potential new wife to the current wife or wives. I could tell that they did not appreciate our Western prejudices regarding this topic. They also were very defensive about the role that Africans played in the slave trade. They seemed to have a guilt trip. The gist of their argument was that Africans were forced to sell Blacks into slavery, and they believed that slavery in America was not brutal.

On my way home, I appreciated that I live in America. I would not want to live in the countries I visited. In the slave castle, there is an exhibit that clearly explains the role that Christianity played in the slave trade. There was a conflict between missionaries, slave traders, and slave owners regarding if slaves should be converted to Christians. Based on the assurance that Christianity would make Africans better slaves, the slave traders and slaveholders granted missionaries the permission to convert Africans to Christianity. The missionaries were correct. Christianity did make Africans better slaves. To this day there are Christians who see nothing inherently wrong with slavery since it is sanctioned by scripture. To many the abolitionist movement was considered anti-Christian. The only problem with slavery was a few bad slave masters, who did not treat their slaves in accordance with biblical teaching. This gave slavery a bad reputation.

When I turned fifty, the reality of having more days behind me than ahead of me changed my perspectives on life, death, and Christianity. Heaven lost its appeal. I felt good about my fifty years of life and determined that whatever happens henceforth will not take away from this. After visiting two African countries, the disparity in life became disconcerting. I realized that my satisfaction with life can be attributed to what Warren Buffet refers to as "The Vagina Lottery" more than me being a Christian. I was born into favorable circumstances. I was afforded certain opportunities in life that resulted in me living a lifestyle I truly love. This does not define who I am, but it does define my experience on earth. Emotionally, my faith in God was embedded and subconsciously impaired my ability to make sound decisions. Once I realized that Christianity had such an emotional influence on me, I had to make a very conscious effort to purge the emotional influence that Christianity had on my life. Thus, I embarked on a mission to scrutinize every aspect of my Christian faith. My search for the truth about God, the Holy Spirit, heaven, hell, and life after death was resurrected. This time my search for truth was rooted in fifty years of life experience, intellectual curiosity, a dedication to use critical-thinking skills, and the Internet.

PART 2

Scripture according to Reason

CHAPTER 7

❧

Heaven

A Place Where the Righteous Call Home

PRESUMABLY, HEAVEN IS the hope of every Christian. It is the hope of heaven and the fear of hell that prompts most folks to walk down the aisle and give their hand to the preacher and their heart to God. In the Black church, a good choir can convince a staunch atheist that he is walking up the King's highway. Preachers warn, "You don't want to live in hell on earth and then end up going to hell when you die. Only the blood of Jesus can wash away your sins. No man knows the time or place of his death. Come now before it's too late." The Bible says that "whoever was not written in the book of life was cast into the lake of fire" (Rev. 20:15).

As a child, I certainly did not want to go to hell and was thoroughly convinced that there is a heaven. My vision of heaven was mostly based on what I heard through songs and preachings. There would be no dying there, there would be no crying there, there would be many mansions there, and I would dwell in the house of the Lord forever. For most of my life, I was not certain of my future but was certain of my place in heaven. My belief in heaven was planted deep within me before I developed critical-thinking skills. The same goes for my belief in God and sin.

Nigger Heaven

In my opinion, too many people in Black churches are obsessed with going to heaven. I submit this obsession can be traced to the African American religious experience during slavery. Christianity served a dual purpose during slavery in America. First, it made Blacks better slaves. Second, it justified slavery to the slaveholders.

African Americans' acceptance of Christianity was more the work of the whip than it was of the Holy Ghost. Slavery in America entailed more than being chattel property, it meant complete subjugation of the masters' wishes. It was in the best interest of a slave to accept Christianity. Slaveholders convinced slaves that the Bible was the word of God and it should not be questioned or challenged. Here are a few of the scriptures that slaveholders used to keep their slaves submissive:

Let Slaves regard their master as worthy of all honor. (I Tim. 6:12)

Slaves, obey your earthly masters with fear and trembling, with a sincere heart, as you would Christ. (Eph. 6:5)

[Exhort] Servants to be obedient unto their own masters, [and] to please [them] well in all [things]; answering again; not purloining, but shewing all good fidelity; that they may adorn the doctrine of God our Savior in all things. (Titus 2: 9–11)

Servants, be subject to your masters with all respect, not only to the good and gentle but also to the unjust. (1 Pet. 2:18)

And that servant who knew his master's will but did not get ready or act according to his will, will receive a severe beating. (Luke 12:47)

Christian slaveholders successfully convinced uneducated slaves, under the threat of punishment, that they are nothing but sinners who by the blood of Jesus have been delivered from eternal damnation. They used the word of God to keep slaves submissive and obedient to their master. God had delivered them from Islam or some other pagan religion and blessed them with good Christian masters. According to scripture slave and slaveholders are one in Christ. Unfortunately, being one in Christ is worthless on earth. The slave was forbidden to learn how to read and develop any critical-thinking skills at all. When a slave accepted Christianity, the slaveholder owned his or her body and soul. For slaveholders introducing slaves to Christianity was a superior method of giving hope to a hopeless people. Keeping niggers focused on heaven was good for niggers and good for the masters.

Regrettably, even today a vast majority of Black Christians accept Christianity without any intellectual challenges to their faith. They believe the Bible is the infallible word of God based on a few scriptures within the Bible that claim that the Bible is the word of God. This is not evidence that the Bible is true or reliable. Few Blacks make any effort to research how the books of the Bible were chosen, by whom, and when. They don't study the history of Christianity, the history of religion, the psychology of religion, or the basic views of other religions. They only study well-defined scriptures to reinforce what their church advocates.

Black preachers have enormous influence over their congregations. Again, this can be traced to the influence that preachers had during slavery and during the civil rights movement.

Most Black Christians are quick to celebrate how far we have come by faith, leaning on the Lord. They have no clue that it was our dedication to the Lord that made us such good slaves.

I'm Going to Walk All Over God's Heaven

When I was a child, I was presented the choice of either going to heaven or burning in hell. I chose going to heaven. For me going to heaven was something that was instilled at such an early age that I could not conceive of not believing in heaven. When people die they go to heaven to be with Jesus. This made perfect sense to me as a child. It was the reward for being a faithful soldier in the army of the Lord.

I first questioned heaven when I learned about slavery. There seemed to be something inherently unfair about slaveholders and slaves going to the same heaven. If we are all God's children, then why were Blacks relegated to being slaves? It made no sense that slaveholders would have the privilege of owning slaves in this world and then be equal to slaves in the next world. I would imagine a slave making it to heaven only to be greeted by his former master. "Welcome buckwheat, you were one of my best niggers on earth. I've been waiting for you. Go fetch me some water, boy." I also wondered if there is a nigger-only section in heaven. Maybe the slave masters used angels for slaves, and niggers spend all their time in heaven singing and dancing. I find it very difficult to imagine how being a nigger on earth is compensated once you get to heaven. It seems to me equality in heaven is useless. We have one life on earth. Why should the people who give you hell on earth make it into heaven? It seems to me that if God truly loves niggers as much as he loved the masters, there wouldn't be any niggers. It seems to me that God totally ignored niggers who prayed for their freedom. However, God did answer the prayers of slave masters who prayed for good obedient slaves. God has a funny way of answering prayers. For niggers, to get their prayers answered, it took a civil war, and freeing niggers was a side issue. It's not like niggers prayed for freedom and the Lord changed the heart of a country to end slavery. It was a matter of the economic devastation of a new country, and niggers were the gist of the problem.

Maybe Heaven Is Not What It's Cracked Up to Be

A friend once asked me, "Can I have as many women as I want in heaven?" As an evangelical Christian at the time, I said no and thought that was a ridiculous question. I let my friend know that heaven is not a place of rampant sin. It is a place of sanctity. We are brothers and sisters in Christ. We are no longer free nor bound. We are washed in the blood of Jesus. Praising God for all eternity. Then a sobering thought crossed my mind. I don't like most Christians. The thought of having Jerry Falwell as my neighbor is horrific. What if I get placed in the middle of a bunch of right-wing conservative Republican Christians? This would be pure hell. Maybe heaven and hell is the same place depending on your perspective.

What really discouraged me from wanting to go to heaven was when I went to a Pentecostal church and the church was on fire, everybody was shouting and praising the Lord. Women were having spiritual orgasms and passing out on the floor. Men were crying like a bunch of bitches. Everybody, except me, was dancing like a bunch of lunatics and running up and down the aisles. Then the pastor quoted some scripture about heaven is a place of constant praise. He then warned me that if I don't praise God in church, how am I going to praise him in heaven? He did not call me by name, but it was evident he was talking to me. I declared to myself, if heaven is anything like this, I would rather go to hell and have a couple of drinks. Again, it occurred to me that heaven and hell could be the same place depending on perspective. If upon my death I am surrounded by drums, tambourines, and Holy Rollers, then I will know I was sent to hell.

Many Are Called But Few Are Chosen

I have attended more funerals than most. I recently attended a funeral that caused me to look at heaven, funerals, and the Christian faith from a whole new perspective. I realized that Christian theology and songs about the highway to heaven have some major defects.

Mr. Baker was the husband of the late Evangelist Baker. Evangelist Baker had two sets of bastard kids, three kids with a married man, and three marriages before she got saved. Once Evangelist Baker got saved, she became totally dedicated to church and the work of the Lord. Of course once she saw the light, she made sure that all of her kids were brought up in church and instilled in them the fear of the Lord. Mr. Baker was her last husband, and they had two kids together.

Over the years Evangelist Baker built a reputation as being an outstanding Christian woman. She was known throughout the Holy Roller community. When she died church delegates throughout the community came to pay tribute to a woman whose life was a testimony to the power of salvation. They danced, shouted, and proclaimed that Evangelist Baker was now in heaven and they would see her again someday. Well almost everybody.

At Mr. Baker's funeral, the preacher made it clear that Mr. Baker never went to church, never got saved, and that he can't preach Mr. Baker into heaven. He said the only thing he knew about Mr. Baker was he married Evangelist Baker. He assured those in attendance that Evangelist Baker was saved, and he will see her again someday in heaven. He did not expect to see Mr. Baker. He went on, "I am a man of God called to preach the truth. I am tired of preachers who stand before grieving families and lie to them. Mr. Baker never talked about Jesus, never attended a prayer service, never pretended to be saved, and I'm not going to pretend that he was saved now." I will be one angry saint if I see Mr. Baker in heaven.

To my surprise, everyone, except Mr. Baker's biological kids, thought this was a great eulogy. They admired a preacher who stood up for Jesus and told the truth. Mr. Baker's kids were pissed and felt that this eulogy was disrespectful to their father. They felt that the preacher should have focused on Mr. Baker being a good father and a good husband and left everything else alone.

My first reaction to Mr. Baker's eulogy was that telling the deceased family that their loved one has gone to hell lacks human compassion. It seems to me that the preacher should have focused on Mr. Baker's life without any mention of an afterlife. I have been to plenty of funerals where a preacher is hired by a funeral home. He or she meets the family fifteen minutes before the service starts. They give words of encouragement to the family, a few words about the deceased, and leave everything else alone. I find it quite amusing when you go to a funeral of someone who never went to church and the funeral becomes a church service. This prompts the question, how many people literally believe in heaven in contrast to adhering to traditional burial rituals? For many people the notion of their loved ones going to a better place is comforting. This comfort is not necessarily connected to a religious belief but is more of a way of coping with grief.

Assuming there is a heaven and you make it in, how much of your life on earth do you remember? Mrs. Baker had over forty grandkids, all of whom she loved dearly. Is she watching them grown up from heaven? Is she mourning over those who walked away from God? Did she see Mr. Baker get cast into the lake of fire? I hear that when you're in heaven, you are in the presence of the Lord, and all of these things are irrelevant. This makes sense. Otherwise, watching your loved ones go to hell might be a damper on heavenly joy.

Jesus Is the Only Way to Heaven

To be an evangelical born-again Christian, one thing that you have to embrace is that most people are going to hell. Devout evangelicals are adamant that there is one absolute truth about salvation and they know what it is. They are unapologetic that billions of faithful Muslims are going to hell. A Muslim man who diligently studies the Quran, prays five times a day, attends mosque regularly, keeps Ramadan, and adheres to other tenets of Islam is wasting his time and energy if he hopes to get into heaven. Even if he is brought up in a Muslim country and that is all he has been exposed to, he is doomed to hell. It does not matter how faithful he has been to his beliefs, how good he has been to humanity, or how much he prayed to and trusted God. He is not a Christian, and therefore cannot enter into heaven. However,

Muslims should not feel bad. Devoted Jews are going to hell also. In fact, regardless of your religion, you are going to hell if you don't accept Jesus Christ as your personal Lord and Savior. If you are a Christian, you still might be going to hell. When I was a Christian, I was told that I was going to hell because I did not speak in tongues. Fortunately, I learned that people who speak in tongues are being deceived by the devil and they're the ones really going to hell. I also learned that the Catholics are going to hell along with the Jehovah's Witnesses. What I decided to do was read a variety of books on all sides of the argument. I learned that they are all equally flawed.

Rafael and I have been friends for over thirty years. We started our careers together and have supported each other during life's ups and downs. Rafael has a very deep faith in God. He prays daily, studies scripture, and worships on a regular basis. I listened to his admonishments that God requires a pure heart to get into heaven. He deeply believes in heaven and hell, with hell being reserved for the vile among men. One day I broke the news to one of my closest friends that he is going to hell. It was my duty as a former believer to inform him that according to the teaching of evangelical Christians, he is going to hell because he has not accepted Jesus Christ as his personal Lord and Savior. Rafael reminded me that he attended Catholic school and had always questioned the divinity of Jesus. He decided to worship Allah, the one true God, and converted to Islam. He also advised me that within Islam, there are those who declare that all Christians are going to hell. We agreed that extremes on both sides give religion a bad name. Maybe if God zapped all the people who are worshipping him faithfully but through the wrong religion, the rest of us could make a better decision. We would know that whatever religion or religions that are left can be trusted.

To me Christianity has perplexing rules regarding who gets into heaven. Jesus was crucified between two criminals. One criminal asked Jesus to forgive him for his sins. Jesus assured this criminal he will join him in paradise. Now this may be good for the criminal, but I suspect it pissed off a lot of people. This story is meant to show the extent of God's grace and mercy toward the criminal. What it doesn't show is how the victims of the crimes felt. The story of David Berkowiz, aka the Son of Sam, is a good example of how the rules for getting into heaven has too many loopholes. In the summer of 1977, women in NYC were in fear of the Son of Sam. Berkowiz shot thirteen people killing six. While serving his 365-year sentence, with the help of some evangelical prison ministry, Berkowiz found the Lord and got saved. Glory be to God, another sinner has repented and will have everlasting life with Jesus. Then I thought about his victims. Maybe some of his victims were not saved. Then I thought about the family of his victims who are not saved. Then I came to the conclusion that this salvation thing is inherently amiss. The victim spends eternity in hell, the family of the victim spends eternity in hell, but the murderer spends eternity in heaven since he repented and accepted Jesus Christ as his Savior. Maybe if there were some special provision in the salvation clause that allowed victims of people killed by converted Christians to enter heaven, I would see some justice. I find no justice in a system of salvation that condemns good people to hell for not being a Christian, while a multi-murderer can get into heaven by repenting.

Death in My Family

The first funeral I ever attended was my grandmother's. I was about seven years old and for a long time wished I had skipped the funeral and stayed with my cousins. I remember my grandfather giving my grandmother a final good-bye kiss. When I walked by for my final viewing, I was told my grandmother is sleeping and I will see her again in heaven. I knew she was dead. She was dressed in a night-gown and looked very peaceful. I didn't understand why everyone was crying. This was the first time in my life I saw my mother cry, and I found this very disturbing. After the funeral, we went to the repast. Sorrow turned into food and drink. A lot of food and drink.

My father's death had a profound impact on me and challenged my views on heaven. My relationship with my dad was volatile. But he was my dad. He had a serious stroke that took him out in about three weeks. I went to visit him in the hospital to make peace before he died. He could not speak but was able to blink to communicate that he knew what I was saying. I assured my dad that he did a great job raising me. I told him I am successful and I will take care of mom. I made sure that he understood that I loved him before I left. I knew he was going to die, and this was my last time seeing him alive. This did not bother me. What did bother me was not being able to end his life myself. He was not religious at all. I had absolutely no inclination that he was in God's hands. The thought of my father going to a better place never crossed my mind. That God had the final say on taking him home seemed like a ridiculous notion. All I saw was my dad suffering, and if there was a Dr. Kevorkian bottom to take him out, I would have pushed the bottom and ended what was left of his life right then and there in a very respectful manner. I felt as his son I should have the legal right to end my dad's suffering. I do not see any role for God when it comes to ending human suffering. I knew my dad well enough that he would have been proud of me taking him out. He would have received my actions with a sense of pride and honor.

After my dad died, we took him to Arkansas to bury him in his home state. His funeral was held in the church he attended as a child. From what I understand, his mother was very religious, and his father was a heathen. Besides saying a prayer at special holiday dinners, I have no clue what my dad's religious beliefs were. I gave him some Christian tracks once, but he did not take them too seriously. I am certain that my dad was not a devout Christian.

My dad's death prompted me to take an intense look at my beliefs regarding life and death. After my dad died, I had no concern, whatsoever, regarding if he went to heaven or hell. I had no inclination to see him again either way. I soon came to the conclusion that the existence of an afterlife is irrelevant to me. I have no need for it. I realized that my dad instilled in me certain values that I have carried throughout my life. That's good enough for me. Accepting that my dad had died was relatively easy. What I found difficult to accept about my dad's death was that I had no clue about how he felt about the life he had lived. I only know a small portion of my dad's life. Unfortunately, I found the portions that I knew about to be very unappealing. This changed my approach to life and to death. Living a good life started to make a lot more sense than living to get into heaven. I made sure to get my fifteen minutes of living the good life. My dad died in 1987. To this day every time I put on my tool belt, I hear my dad saying to me, "Christopher Henry, I told you that you needed to learn how to do some of these things for yourself." I respond "OK, you were right. Now leave me alone, I have to fix this toilet." At times like this, I realize how big of an impact my dad has had on who I am. This is far more important than being able to see him in heaven. Besides the chances are my dad is not in heaven anyway

My dad died not knowing he had a grandson. While I felt like a sperm bank, it did not negate that I biologically had a son I never met, and never disclosed to my family. Several years after my dad's death, I met my biological offspring. His mom made it clear that Anton was her child and that I was merely a necessary evil. I would like to say that meeting him was a moral awakening, but it wasn't. Meeting Anton was like meeting the child of any ex-lover, and little more. I was emotionally neutered from him. It was a price I had to pay for indiscreet screwing. When Anton turned eighteen we had an adult to adult conversation. Before we talked I braced myself for a good cursing out. I had no remorse about not raising him. My only preoccupation was how do we move forward. I was raised by my dad and resented how little I knew about him. I declared to myself that if Anton is going to be a part of my life, he is going to know who I am. I never had an aversion to being in his life under what I considered acceptable circumstances. I knew that eventually Anton would have to decide if he wants to be a part of my life or write me off.

To my surprise, Anton never showed any animosity toward me. If he does have animosity toward me he hides it adroitly. I am grateful that Anton accepted my unfounded terms of engagement. I consciously share with Anton my experiences in life, our family history, and what I think about damn near everything. I am proud of his reciprocity to my endeavors. I don't tell him how to live his life. I respectfully tell him what I think about how he's living his life. He returns the favorite. I do what's in my province to succor Anton getting his fifteen minutes of fame.

I surmise that Anton knows more about me than he bargained for. I often get questioned about what is it like to develop a relationship with a son I did not raise. I always give the same answer. It would be nice to see more family traits (he would say vices). Moreover, he supports me in my endeavors and buys me good cigars. Beyond this, I hope my imprint on him surpasses the imprint my dad had on me.

My oldest sister died of cancer. I was devastated when I found out that she had six months to live at best. Our family came together better than anyone could have hoped for. My sister's church family was also there for my sister and for us. I flew from New York to California to give as much support that I could. I took time off under the family-leave program so that I could be with her as she went through chemotherapy. My sister lived in Northern California, and the rest of the family lived in Southern California. Our original plan was to take her back to Southern California and give her treatment there. Then 9/ 11 hit, and we had a major change of plans. I would stay in Mountain View until her treatment was complete. Then we would fly her back to Venice Beach. This was probably the most emotional period of my life. Also the most fulfilling. I paid for a good portion of the cost related to her transition from Mountain View to Venice beach, including moving her furniture. I only mention this because being able to do this provides a personal satisfaction that is second to none. I really learned to appreciate being in a position to make things happen.

I vividly remember my sister's last day on earth. Her oldest grandson made it to her bedside to say good-bye. He was her heart, and we all sensed that this was what she was waiting for.

My sister was a devout Christian and a dedicated member of her church, in her later years of life. I remember all the family holding hands and singing gospel songs to her delight. She lifted up her hands and said hallelujah. This was the last word I heard my sister speak. To me this was her signal to Jesus saying, "Come and take me home." Indeed, that night my sister died.

To my family members who are strong believers, my sister's faith was a witness to the power of the Holy Spirit. Her pain and suffering was over, and she went home to be with Jesus. I was fixated with her suffering. In my mind the going-home-to-Jesus theme was meaningless. I only saw the end of suffering. I started to realize how much I hate human suffering.

Similar to my reaction of my father's death, my focus went from my sister's death to how much did my sister enjoy her life? While my sister did become a devout Christian, from my point of view, most of her life was troubled.

She was the child my mother wanted to abort and probably would have aborted if abortions were safe and legal in 1948. This is not speculation on my part. This was a lucid confession made by my mom to my sister who shared the same with me. Being an unwanted child, born to a single, ambitious mother fermented into behavior that justified the resentment my mom had toward my sister. This led to a cycle of self-destructive behavior. Thus, what you have is an innocent child born into unfortunate circumstances. I submit that my sister's life was so troubled that Christianity truly did become her refuge. I have heard hundreds of testimonies about "God has brought me from a mighty long way." I never heard a testimony about why God made my journey so hard in the first place.

Watching my sister rot away from cancer caused my natural views of the world and my Christian views of the world to clash. My natural view of the world accepted my sister was a heavy smoker for most of her life. Smoking causes lung cancer. She developed lung cancer. It metastasized and spread to her brain, and she died. From a natural view of the world, her life and death were simple to accept. However, if you believe that once you become saved, you become a new creature in Christ, then the question becomes, what are the benefits of becoming this new creature? God may have forgiven her sins, but he did not spare her from cancer. Since most of her life was troubled, why did she have to suffer so much at the end? Since she gave her life to Christ and turned her life around, why didn't God show some mercy toward her while she was on earth? The standard response to these questions is don't question God. That is a great answer for someone with the mind of an infant. These questions are the core of what giving your life to Christ entails. These questions must be asked and answered if one is to believe that at some point, based on faith, God intervenes in the affairs of humankind. There is a schism between the comfort a believer can find by giving his life to Jesus and the reality of what that means. For some the only purpose of accepting Christ is to avoid hell and go to heaven. This is a good reason only if you believe in heaven and hell. It totally negates the need for prayer. If God is not going to intervene to help his faithful, then what is the purpose of prayer and worship? Just accept Jesus, and wait until you die.

My mom's death was somewhere between my father's death and my sister's death. Mom slowly deteriorated from natural causes. She suffered from dementia, and we eventually put her in a nursing home. I have always known my mom to be a very religious woman. My mom, like my sister, declared that she lived in the world before she got saved. My mom attributed the deterioration of her marriage to her coming out of the world, while my dad stayed in the world. I view my mom as a woman submerged in guilt. So much guilt that even Jesus could not deliver her. It seemed that it was almost impossible for my mom to chill out. I later found out that my mom's past probably included prostitution. My uncle proudly disclosed this information to my cousin who was busted for prostitution as a teenager. His intent was not to degrade my mom but to encourage my cousin. He was using my mom as an example of how you can turn your life around if you choose to. Truly, my mom became an exemplary community leader, church member, mother, college-educated career woman, entrepreneur, and a good Christian woman. She had the vision to provide for her children long after she left earth. I am proud that my uncle offered my mom's experience as a lifeline to his daughter. My cousin never overcame her circumstances in life, but my mom did. I wish my mom had been able to relinquish her embedded guilt and fully embrace her humanity. My mom is physically dead. This does not preclude me from telling her she has nothing to be ashamed of. It only makes what she accomplished in life that more amazing. When I measure success, I look at the starting point. Using this standard, both of my parents reached a level of success I can only hope for.

I mention my mom's past because it is typical of the stories behind many of the women you see shouting in church on Sunday morning. The problem is that instead of discreetly sharing their experiences to encourage others, there is a tendency to keep their past buried and condemn those "still living in sin." My personal experience with women who are extremely religious is that they have extreme personalities outside of religion. I have been with church women whose behavior is more outrageous than anything I experienced with non-saved women. They seem to have a problem with moderation. Some have confessed these sentiments to me. Part of the attraction of giving your life to Jesus is that you can expunge your past transgressions. For many people being washed in the blood of Jesus gives them new hope. They truly do become a new creature in Christ Jesus. I do not belittle the sinner-to-saint phenomenon found in church. I do submit that this type of change is not exclusive to Jesus, Christianity, or religion in general. People can change their course in life regardless of their religious belief or nonbelief. I endorse anything that genuinely contributes to someone's quality of life, happiness, and personal growth. My only qualm is when religion is manipulated for financial, political, and personal gain. Too many people are unwittingly seduced and suppressed by pulpit pimps. To these I offer an alternative.

When I saw my mom on her deathbed, I did not see a woman looking forward to seeing the Lord. I saw a woman who was tired of suffering and was ready to check out. She told me to shut the door, which I did. She then looked me straight in the eyes and said, "Get me out of here." I knew exactly what she wanted me to do. We both knew that she did not want to continue living in the condition that she was in. My mom was always a very independent, energetic woman. She was the type of woman who would never accept being totally dependent upon caretakers as a life worth living. Again, I wished there was a Dr. Kevorkian bottom to push. I would have pushed that bottom with pride and dignity. It would have been a privilege to grant my mom her last wish. To leave earth at the hands of her only son. But instead, I did the only thing I could think of as an escape. I told her there is nothing I can do and asked her to pray. I left, knowing this was the last time I would see my mom alive.

After the death of my mom, my expectation of going to heaven seemed like a foolish childhood wish. I realized my belief in heaven was ingrained in me before I had the critical-thinking skills needed to determine if my belief in heaven was valid. Like with my dad, I have no inclination to see my mom again in some afterlife. Whenever I get in a situation that requires aggressive behavior, I hear one voice and one voice only. It's the voice of my mom telling me to fight back. Again, this is a true testament to the influence my mom had on my life. I now see heaven as a comforting thought at a funeral, but little more.

I hope that when I die, I leave the type of impression on others that my mom, my dad, and my sister left on me. There is some truth to "Those you love never die." But it is not the result of some supernatural spirit living in the afterlife coming to visit. It is because of how that person lived and influenced you while he or she was alive. As a very practical matter, I can't imagine anyone paying a medium to talk to a deceased loved one. I know exactly what my parents would say about damn near everything that has happened since they died.

Heaven Deacon Henry Style

If there is life after death, I have my own vision of what it would be like. First, I would go watch a live Duke Ellington show, swing dance, and drink all night. In my heaven all the great musicians would have their own club. Then I would look for Bank Henry. He is the oldest member of my family whom I can trace back to. I would talk to him about his experience of life on earth. I want to hear firsthand his experience as a slave. Then I would visit each of my ancestors through the middle passage, back to Ghana. According to my DNA test, my Y chromosome (NRY), I am a descendent of the Ashanti tribe in Ghana.

Next, I would check in on earth to make sure the core values that I held while I was alive on earth are still going strong. I would want to make sure that there are still men and women on earth who believe in and are working for peace on earth and the betterment of humanity. I would be encouraging them from heaven. Then, and this is why I believe there is no heaven, I would want to visit the nigger section of heaven. But the nigger section of heaven would be totally equivalent to the White section of heaven with no exceptions. It would be like having a Black nation that is the equivalent of Sweden. In fact, the nigger section should be better than the White section. This is to compensate having to live life as a nigger. Finally, I would want to join the *USS Enterprise of Heaven* and visit other galaxies, other solar systems, and other planets.

CHAPTER 8

———— ✦ ————

I Am Not a Sinner

All men have sinned and have fall short of the
glory of God.

—ROMANS 3:23

I WAS TAUGHT I am a sinner saved by grace. I believed that if
it was not for Jesus dying for me on the cross, I would die and
go to hell. I prayed nightly that God would forgive me for my
sins. I was persuaded that I could do nothing without God and
vigorously pleaded for God to bless me. I wanted God to order
my steps in the world. I believed that God had a plan for my
life, and I diligently pursued God's will. If I avoided sin and
praised God for his goodness and mercy, I was convinced that
God's plan for my life would be revealed to me. Everything in
my life was by the grace of God, who showed mercy on a sinner
like me.

In retrospect, I can see how my faith in God supplemented
my lack of self-confidence. My dependence on God eroded my
confidence in my own abilities. This created a dilemma that took
years to resolve. How much of my success was a result of my hard
and good decisions, and how much of it was a blessing from God?
Likewise, how many of my failures were a result of my lack of
preparation, poor decisions, or bad luck, and how many were

simply a matter of not being God's will? Believing I was a sinner killed my self-image. When something bad happed, I believed I was a sinner who deserved it.

I noticed that self-confidence, self-discipline, and the expectation of success can mitigate this notion of being a sinner. This explains why the impact of being a sinner is often a nuisance for some while devastating for others, especially African Americans. Again, slavery is a prime example of how the fundamental tenets of Christianity have a completely different impact on the Black community. To privileged White Americans, being a sinner during slavery was merely an intellectual concept, not a reflection of their life. The concept of being a sinner to people who are powerless, is almost a justification for their status in life. It is a bridge to accepting that you deserve to be a slave. Your life resembles the life of someone God has condemned. If White folks are sinners and God has blessed them with freedom and wealth, niggers must really be sinners. God has already showed some of his judgment against niggers on earth. The only hope niggers had was that Jesus would show them some mercy in heaven. This mentality is ingrained within many Black Christians today. Fortunately, I started to read the Bible critically and learned that my concern about being a sinner was unwarranted.

For anyone struggling with the problem of original sin, I suggest you listen to fundamental evangelical Christian preachers. They will provide you with the arguments needed to determine if you need to be concerned with original sin. The foundation of Christianity is that all men are born into sin. This is the result of the original fall of Adam and Eve. If the book of Genesis is not literally true regarding the creation of the earth, and Adam and Eve being the first two humans, created directly by God, then the Bible and Christianity is just another religious myth. Without Genesis being literally true, Christians cannot biblically explain where and when the fall of Adam and Eve took place. Thus, Christianity would be on par to any other religion, something that is abhorrent to any fundamental evangelical Christian. If you believe that the universe was created in seven days, then you truly should be concerned about your sins.

When you scrutinize the content of the Adam and Eve story, you get a better understanding of God's role in the origin of sin. God got bored and made Adam. Then Adam got lonely and asked for some companionship, so God gave him Eve. Now we have two people in the Garden of Eden. They are living in paradise, and God talks to them directly. At this point, there was no need for heaven since there was no sin on earth. Then God decides that Adam and Eve have life too easy. God decides that he will put in the midst of the Garden of Eden the fruit of the knowledge of good and evil. Since God made Adam and Eve, it is reasonable to believe that he knew they would be curious about the fruit from the tree of good and evil. To compound this problem, God made Satan perfect but then allowed Satan to figured out a way to become evil, to tempt Adam and Eve. More about Satan later. Adam and Eve fell into the temptation of Satan. God kicks them out of the Garden of Eden, and sin enters into the world. Thus, we have humankind being born into the fallen state of sin.

The germane question is, why did a loving God, who just created man and woman, put the fruit of the knowledge of good and evil in the garden in the first place? Why did God allow Adam and Eve to be tempted by the devil, if he loves them? If God hates sin, why create sin in the first place? Adam and Eve had no clue what sin was. Adam did not yell up to God and say, "Hey God, we're bored, will you tempt us with sin?" The temptation of sin was initiated by God when he placed the fruit of the knowledge of good and evil in the garden. It seems that a loving God would have destroyed the devil as soon as he realized he made a mistake and protected the people he presumably loves from sin. For reasons that God never explains, he prefers to have men and women live in the fallen state of sin, send most of the people he claims to loves to hell, and let a few chosen ones into heaven. For those few who are chosen, they fervently believe that all those people who are sent to hell deserve to be sent to hell. This is why sin to me is an irrelevant issue. I prefer to see myself as a human being who has made a tremendous amount of mistakes in life. Like most humans, I am going to hell according to the divine plan of a loving God, who sends people to hell for being human.

I see God placing the fruit of good and evil in the Garden of Eden equivalent to a loving parent placing a red candy bar laced with poison in a basket of delicious candy and then placing the basket in a playpen with a three-year-old toddler. This parent then says don't eat the red candy bar because it's poison. A toddler does not know what the consequences of eating a poisoned candy bar is. It is unreasonable to believe that a toddler after eating the other candy is not going to eat the red candy. No responsible loving parent would even consider putting his or her child in such a perilous situation. When God put the fruit of good and evil in the Garden of Eden, he should have known the two people he just created were flawed and would fall into the temptation of the devil. Like a child who has no clue what poison is, Adam and Eve had no clue of the consequences of their actions. Adam and Eve did not create sin! They fell into a trap set by God. When they fell into God's trap, he kicked them out of the Garden, and the rest is history.

Genesis Is a Good Place to Start

The authority of the Bible starts in Genesis. According to the teachings of fundamental Christians, the writers of the Bible were inspired by God. Genesis is an accurate account of creation as dictated by God. The Genesis's account of creation should be accepted as completely literal and accurate. This provides a clear benchmark to determine the validity of the entire Bible.

The first issue that challenges the biblical view of creation is the order of creation. According to the Bible, the world was created in six days, and on the seventh day, God rested. I am not sure why an all-powerful God needs to rest, but he does. When the earth was created, there was darkness, and God said, "Let there be light." God made light the first day but did not create stars until the seventh day. Planets circle around stars and get their light from stars. The sun was created before earth. Earth would not have been dark and could not have been created before the sun. This sequence is contradictory to all the principles of astrophysics. These principles have credibility since man has landed on the moon, landed a vehicle on Mars, has created a spacecraft that has left our solar system, created a spacecraft that orbited Pluto within about eight miles, created a space station, and the Hubble Telescope has given us photos of space that are beyond what I've seen on *Star Trek*.

Genesis teaches that God created Adam and Eve, which means that there had to be incest. At best Cain and Abel had to sleep with their sisters. This assumes that Adam and Eve had a bunch of children not mentioned in Genesis. In Genesis God created Adam and spoke with him directly. No need for prayer. All of humanity should be linked to Adam's DNA. The problem is that DNA worldwide can be traced to the continent of Africa. This corroborates scientific claims that the evolution of man started in Africa.

However, there are multiple strings of Y chromosome (NRY). This dispels the claim that all men are the descendants of one man, Adam.

Next is the age-of-the-earth problem, which should be traced to the lineage of Adam and Eve. If Adam and Eve are the first two humans, there cannot be any humans before Adam and Eve. Bishop James Usher traced the lineage of biblical life to about six thousand years. The biblical account has several positive things going for it. It explains in very simple terms how man was created, why there is evil in the world, why women scream during child-birth, and the need for a Savior to save us from sin. Without Adam and Eve, there is no reasonable explanation of how sin entered into the world. Thus, no need for Jesus. Furthermore, the lineage to Jesus is based on the story of Adam and Eve.

Evolution teaches that man evolved as a species over billions of years. I applaud Christians who are reasonable enough to concede to evolution. However, their concession to evolution negates the entire Adam and Eve story. At best you would have to believe that God created everything but man over billions of years, and then God stuck Adam and Eve in the Garden of Eden about six thousand years ago as *Homo sapiens*. The fossil records of *Homo erectus*, Neanderthals, and other fossil records studied by anthropologists were planted by the devil to keep people from getting saved.

According to Genesis there was no death until the fall of Adam. Consequently, fossil fuel is not the result of dinosaurs that died sixty-five million years ago. It's from dinosaurs that died upon the fall of Adam about six thousand years ago. Death is an integral element of evolution.

The explanation of creation given by science spans about fourteen billion years and entails some understanding of physical anthropology, primatology, archaeology, ethology, linguistics, evolutionary psychology, embryology, genetics, and other sciences. It is much easier to comprehend that a supreme being took some dust and blew life into it, then it is to understand that earth and man evolved from stardust.

Some creationist comedians are quick to pronounce that they are not descendants of monkeys. This is a correct statement, but evolution does not teach that man is a descendant from monkeys. It teaches that man is a descendant of a common ancestor of monkeys. This is a critical difference when explaining the evolution of man. A difference that most creationists don't care to investigate. This explains why we still have monkeys and why monkeys are not evolving into humans. Thus, creationists often argue against something they don't understand.

I can understand why creationists look at evolutionary science and say this sounds like something from a *Star Trek* movie. Equally, I can understand how scientists look at the Bible and say it sounds like methodology. That being said there are some basic scientific evidence that creationists have to address to validate that we are all descendants of Adam and Eve.

Ninety-seven percent of scientists accept fossil records as proof that the earth is significantly older than six thousand years. Most scientists believe that the earth is about 4.5 billion years old and that *Homo sapiens* have been on earth for between 150,000 and 200,000 years. Oil companies spend millions of dollars searching for oil deposits, which geologists have determined are from dinosaurs that lived about sixty-five million years ago. Most scientists accept that it took at about five million years for the water in the Grand Canyon to rescind. Most scientists who refute evolution assert that their conclusions are based on their belief in the Bible, not their professional training.

The wages of sin is death. Without sin there is no death. The question is, should death be accepted as the consequence of sin or as the natural process of life? I can accept that some people do evil things and deserve to be punished. I have committed what the Bible describes as sin on numerous occasions. I consider my sin little more than experiencing life. I have paid for the consequences of my "sin" right here on earth. To me there is absolutely no justification for eternal damnation for any of the sins I have committed. Living with my sins, what I call my mistakes, for my entire life is sufficient punishment. I find the notion of sending humans to hell for all eternity for being born into sin and living a sinful life makes less sense than convicting an eight-year-old to a life sentence for stealing a Snickers bar. For the record, I have never committed a "sin" because I hate God. The notion that people commit sin because they are rebelling against God is foolish. There are enough scandals across all religions to substantiate that there are plenty "men of God" who commit sin.

CHAPTER 9

⚜

The Holy Ghost

THE HOLY GHOST is one of my favorite topics when it comes to Christianity, especially when it comes to Holy Rollers. I have never attended a church that did not claim what they teach is based on the word of God as interpreted by the Holy Spirit, more commonly known as the Holy Ghost among Black Holy Rollers. The best way to get a full understanding of the implausibility of the Holy Ghost being real is to read Christian books written by those who have different perspectives.

Read a book written by a charismatic preacher like Kenneth Copeland who teaches a full gospel approach to the power of the Holy Spirit. He will present every scripture that supports that God wants you to prosper. Using scriptures, he will teach you about the power of speaking in tongues. You will learn the biblical precepts of why when praises go up, blessings come down. Of course you will learn why dancing unto the Lord pisses off the devil and being slang in the spirit is evidence that the power of the Holy Ghost is upon you. Most of all he will teach you that if you withhold your tithes, which is a mandatory 10 percent, and your offerings, which is what you give above your tithes, according to how you have been blessed, you're robbing God. If you are robbing God, it follows that God has no recourse but to withhold his blessings from you. Needless to say, this makes Kenneth Copeland

and other prosperity preachers very rich, as their followers wait for their wealth to be manifested.

After you become fully engulfed in the full power of the Holy Ghost, according to Holy Roller Land, read a book by a fundamental evangelical Christian like John MacArthur. He uses the Bible to completely condemn almost everything taught by charismatic preachers. In fact, his position is that charismatics are false teachers who blaspheme the Holy Spirit. He sponsored a three-day seminar entitled "Strange Fire" to help true believers deliver charismatics from the deception of the devil to the true Gospel of Jesus Christ.

This is a critical impasse for anyone seeking to be a true Christian. How can "men of God," all whom claim to love the Lord, claim to be led by the Holy Spirit, and claim to base their teaching on the word of God as led by the Holy Spirit as they rightly divide the word of God, agree on nothing except that Jesus died for the remission of sin. The fact that this conflict exists is proof to many rational people that the Holy Spirit as prescribed by the Bible can't be valid. I find the arguments on both sides to be valid. I have examined both, and from my perspective they both have merit based on the hermetic they use. I find that charismatics present a cogent, biblical argument as to why someone would want to be a charismatic Christian. However, I find absolutely no observable evidence to support any of their claims. Likewise, I find that fundamental Christians have views that make no sense at some point.

My argument is that this division alone is evidence, by both standards, that the Holy Ghost does not exist. If there is one supreme Holy Spirit, it should be able to manifest itself in a manner that would resolve this vital conflict. What is the point of trusting in a Holy Spirit that does not have the power to send one unequivocal message to those who, on both sides, are sincerely seeking the proper way to worship God? Exactly what role is God playing to bring men to the truth of his kingdom? Why is a loving God allowing multitudes of sincere people who are diligently seeking him to be deceived unto eternal damnation? This is within the Christian faith. Not to mention the myriad false religions outside of the Christian faith. This reinforces my belief that there is little evidence of a loving God who is concerned with how many souls enter into heaven.

My disbelief in the Holy Spirit means that I have committed the unforgivable sin and am damned to hell. I have already explained why this is of no concern to me. However, it does not mean that I do not believe that there is a spiritual aspect to humanity. I contend that there is a human spirit that resides in every human being. It is a part of the essence of life. This is where love, hate, determination, wisdom, anger, and all other human emotions reside. Like the physical body, I believe that the human spirit is something that can be developed. I do not believe that there is another supernatural spirit that enters man upon request and only this spirit can get you into heaven.

What I really find amazing about the Holy Ghost is all the claims that have been made about its power. I was once healed from rheumatism by the Holy Ghost. I didn't know that I had rheumatism, and it only cost me a dollar. I have seen preachers deliver messages from God via the power of the Holy Ghost. God told one bishop that he was going to bless everyone in his church with a new car. A member of his church mortgaged her house to buy a new car. My friend's wife went to church and heard her bishop preach about the sin of alcohol. He told his members to get those evil spirits out of their home. She decided to heed to the warning of her bishop without consulting with her husband first. Her husband was livid when he found out she poured over $700 of premiere alcohol down the drain. First, he was pissed because his wife disrespected him as the man of their house. It was his booze paid for by his labor, in the house that he paid the mortgage on. Then he was pissed that he was not given notice. He could have least given his booze to his brother. He declared that if he had known his wife was going to get saved, he would have never married her. She truly changed horses in the middle of the stream. He was too far in to leave her. He was in a dilemma faced by too many African American men. What do you do when your wife falls victim to Holy Roller pimps? The first instinct is to go kick some bishop's ass. But this does not solve the problem since women eagerly attend Holy Roller services and await the God-given instructions of their anointed bishops.

You Are Healed in the Name of Jesus

It should be clear to any rational person who attends a Holy Roller healing service that these are people full of hope and emotion, with little understanding of basic science. I had a friend who was healed from asthma Sunday after Sunday. It never occurred to him that if he was truly healed last Sunday that he should not have to be healed the following Sunday. It is really astonishing that no one questions why the same people are healed each Sunday. Their favorite response is, I'm healed, but it has not been manifested yet. This is clever pulpit-pimp double-talk. According to every healing in the Bible, the afflicted persons were healed by the time they got home. No one who was healed by Jesus had to go back for a second dose of healing.

Elder Brown specialized in anointing believers with oil and delivering their healing in the name of Jesus. "The devil is a liar, you are healed by the blood of Jesus!" He would proclaim. Then he would give the believer a good rubdown in oil and speak in tongues. The church would praise God for delivering the same afflicted week after week.

If anyone understood the healing power of the Holy Ghost and the blood of Jesus, it was Elder Brown. That's why when he died from diabetes at the age of fifty, I got a little confused. I could not understand why a man with so much Holy Ghost power could not pour a little oil on himself and get healed.

Some of the testimonies about being healed are mindless claims totally devoid of any understanding of the human body and modern medicine. Let's start with some basics. The human body always tries to heal itself. When the Bible was written, laying on hands to get healed was as good as option of any. Some people would get healed and give God the glory while others would die because it was God's will. The laying on hands was comforting for the afflicted while the body tried to heal itself. Sometimes the body would win, and sometimes it wouldn't. Science has not solved every health issue out there, but science has come from a mighty long way. Today Holy Rollers who incur enormous medical bills for drugs and treatment, go to church and praise Jesus for healing them by the power of the Holy Ghost.

My favorite testimony is, "When the doctor told me I had six months to live, I said the devil is a liar and went to Dr. Jesus! Six years later I am standing here as a testimony to my God." For someone who has a limited understanding of science and the body's ability to heal itself, this seems like a valid testimony. The problem is this happens to people who are atheist. The best example is Stephen Hawking, who was diagnosed with amyotrophic lateral sclerosis (Lou Gehrig's disease) at the age of twenty-one. He was expected to live no longer than his twenty-fifth birthday. He is over seventy years old and is a self-proclaimed atheist. The human body is complicated, and most prognosis are based on probability. Doctors look at similar cases and, based on the outcomes of these cases, project what they expect going forward. Sometimes they are wrong. Moreover, sometimes they are wrong for very positive reasons. As treatment for a given disease improves, it is expected that a patient would live longer than a prognosis based on less effective treatment. In fact, I would argue that this type of testimony is a testament to the improvements of modern science.

Spontaneous remission is a recognition by scientists that the body is capable of healing itself, without any immediate scientific explanation. The key is spontaneous remissions are not a miracle reserved exclusively to those who believe in Jesus. There is a crucial difference between how the science community and religious community approach what appears to be miracles. The religious community accepts the explanation of being healed by God as a definitive answer. The science community sees the miracle as a question to be researched. The science community accepts that while they don't know the answer today, once they find the answer, yesterday's miracle will become tomorrow's science.

Unfortunately, there are cases where the truly faithful refuse medical treatment and die. This should be convincing evidence that faith alone does not heal. These are people who had the faith and expectation of being healed by God, but they die. This is a real legal problem when parents withhold medical treatment from their children based on their religious belief that God will heal them. The courts are now convicting these parents on various charges.

The argument that God uses modern science to heal is incongruous. Scientists spend decades searching for the cure of diseases. This research is necessary for those who lack the faith to receive their healing from God. To claim that God now refers the faithful to modern science for healing is an insult to both man and God. If God has the power to heal, he surely does not need man to take care of his faithful. The notion that God gives scientists the knowledge to cure sickness and disease is nonsense. Modern medicine has evolved over thousands of years at the cost of unmeasurable human suffering and loss of human lives.

Why should God get credit for what man has discovered at the cost of human suffering and life? If God gives scientists the cure for diseases, why does it take years of research? The germane question is, why does God allow sickness in the first place? According to scripture, sickness is the result of original sin. If God does not want man to suffer from sickness and disease, he presumably has the power to stop it. A true Christian fully accepts that sickness and disease is a part of God's divine plan and to question God is inappropriate. Well, maybe you can question God, but don't expect a reasonable answer.

❖

CHAPTER 10

Sweet Hour of Prayer

Sweet hour of prayer! sweet hour of prayer!
That calls me from a world of care,
And bids me at my Father's throne
Make all my wants and wishes known.

In seasons of distress and grief,
my soul has often found relief,
And oft escaped the tempter's snare,
By thy return sweet hour of prayer!

THIS IS ONE of my favorite gospel songs, and I still embrace much of its essence. There are parts of my Christian upbringing that I still adhere to in some fashion. My best example is the Communion Service. This is a monthly ritual where I would go before God and reflect upon my shortcomings and triumphs during the past month. I would drink the blood of Christ and eat the Body of Christ. During the service, the pastor would ask pertinent questions that would help me assess where my life was at that moment in time. I still find the concept of communion relevant, minus the drinking of the blood and eating of the bread. I feel the same way about prayer.

My assessment of prayer is perhaps the most challenging endeavor when examining the Christian faith. Mainly because at some point people who have prayed feel that God has answered their prayer in the affirmative. Likewise, at some point people feel that their prayers were not answered or they did not receive the answer they were seeking. At what point is the answer to prayer God's intervention or beating the odds? I find it amusing when someone who has not stepped foot in a church since Sunday school, wins the lotto and the first thing he or she does is thank God for giving him or her the winning numbers. This makes me think that beating the odds is not necessarily the work of divine intervention. I have been to prayer groups and have heard testimonies about how God has answered their prayer. The problem is that virtually all of the testimonies pertained to very predictable outcomes. This is especially true when I attended predominately White prayer groups. I was not impressed when a White guy gave his testimony about getting into medical school. He came from a prestigious rich family and had top grades. I really don't see Jesus having much to do with his admission to medical school. Distinguishing between good luck and the answer to prayer is insurmountable. The result of prayer is usually contingent upon who's doing the praying and what he or she is praying for. When it comes to praying for a job, God will answer the prayers of White people over Black people by a 2:1 ratio.

I will concede that there are situations in life when prayer is the last recourse and it brings comfort to those who embrace it. A prime example of this is a loved one on his or her deathbed. I have seen prayer bring comfort to all. It did not change the expected outcome, but it did help all gathered accept the inevitable. I submit this comfort is the result of people who love each other coming together to share a common experience. I do not believe that it is the intervention of the supernatural.

Another reason I am hesitant to discount the practice of prayer is on some level it is not a matter of supernatural intervention but an internal conviction that motivates individuals to achieve their desired results. I have witnessed people who used their faith in prayer to drive them to success. If the goal is to be successful, the means to get there should not be diminished.

My criticism of prayer is that it distorts cognitive mechanisms. This leads to the impairment of making sound decisions, especially when someone is under duress. Prayer generally evokes supernatural intervention. Since the effectiveness of this divine intervention cannot be verified, it is easy to attribute ones achievements to prayer, in contrast to one's own efforts. A reliance on prayer can give someone a false sense of security. Indeed, some preachers advocate that complete dependence on Jesus is the key to a closer walk with God. A believer is to submit him- or herself entirely to the will of God. Prayer is a key component to discovering God's will in one's life. The problem I have with depending on prayer for direction from God in life, is that everyone I know has been wrong at least once. This includes Pat Roberson who after praying and fasting announced that God had revealed to him that Obama would lose his second-term election. He had the integrity to apologize, explaining that he simply got it wrong. If the top guns in Christianity can get it wrong, what does that say for the flock? How can anyone be assured that he or she is correctly discerning God's will? I have witnessed a multitude of Christian conflicts. I don't care what the issue is, both sides invoke they have prayed for the Holy Spirit to lead them and have scripture to support their position. If everybody is praying over the same issue and God is giving everyone conflicting information, then either God is confused or, at any given time, fifty percent of those praying receive the wrong answer. Either way the credibility of prayer is jeopardized. The belief that God will intervene in the affairs of man based on prayer, is trying to negotiate with the supernatural, regardless of the religious affiliation or number of candles and incense used. The thought that a God who created the universe actually cares if you get into medical school is comforting and definitely will make you feel special. However, for every prayer answered, there are numerous prayers that go unanswered. Maybe those who fail to get into medical school won't feel so special. They just have to accept that it wasn't God's will for them to achieve their goal.

My experience is dependence on the supernatural can permeate one's subconscious over time. At that point the influence of believing in the supernatural is latent and can be very destructive. Inadvertently, decisions can be made factoring in expected assistance from the supernatural. This is different than making a decision based on identified risk factors. A dependence on God can be so ingrained that one must make a concerted effort to eradicate this type of thinking. Prayer and belief in God is a deeply rooted emotion. A person with a deep religious convention will strap a bomb on and blow himself up in a mall. A strong belief in prayer and faith in God can override reason and logic. What I find ironic is that most religions incorporate some type of relationship with the supernatural. A relationship with God is inherently a conversation with an entity you cannot see, hear, or touch. It is easy for any believer to look at a believer from a different faith and say he or she is just crazy. He or she is talking to the wrong God. At what point, is talking to invisible beings categorically crazy?

I have a daily routine of prayer and meditation. However, I don't pray to an external supernatural being and ask him to open doors I cannot see. I meditate to clear my mind so that I can make the best decision possible in any given situation. Meditation helps me focus and restore my energy. When I pray, I focus on what opportunities I want to pursue and look within myself to determine how to achieve them. I also focus on the people within my circle of influence. I have no clue if this benefits them, but thinking about them in this manner makes me feel good.

CHAPTER 11

⚜

I Am Hell Bound

I HAVE LITTLE to say about hell. Being a Black man in America, I am sure I can handle it. Dante's *Inferno* is the best depiction of hell that I have read. I can't vouch for hell in an afterlife. I declare that for too many innocent people, hell is right here on earth. I believe it is possible that some type of life after death exists. I say this because it is impossible to prove otherwise. If there is life after death, I believe it is a natural phenomenon that everyone experiences. If life is an energy force separate from the brain, that force may simply change form. I find it unreasonable to believe that there is some type of judgment after death where some go to heaven and some go to hell. However, if there is a hell, I know plenty of people who I think deserve to go there. Most of them are Republicans. This raises the question of Pascal's wager. What if I am wrong? I fully accept I could be wrong. If I had died when I was a believer, I would have been wrong based on my current beliefs. I have come to the conclusion that me being wrong is irrelevant. I call it Deacon Henry's wager:

1. If there is a hell, it's overbooked. There are Catholics who believe that Protestants are going to hell. There are Muslims who believe that Christians are going to hell and of course Christians who believe other Christians are going to hell because they have the wrong Christian beliefs.

Thus, if I picked the wrong religion, I would end up in hell anyway. I would consider myself the true winner of this bet because I did not waste my life adhering to a religion that leads me to hell anyway. Therefore, I conclude I am better off accepting that if there is a hell, that's where I'm going.

2. If believers go to heaven based on their faith and I simply die, which some religions consider going to hell, this is what I am expecting, so I have no downside.

3. If upon death, I am cast into a lake of fire, I would have a view of God that would justify it. Again, I win.

4. If hell is being expelled from heaven, which is what many believe, I again win, since I really have no desire to be around most of the religious people I know for eternity. I truly don't want to spend eternity worshipping a God who I think did a mediocre job of governing the world.

5. Finally, most of the people I know are going to hell if you believe the Holy Rollers. I would rather dance in hell with my friends than beat a tambourine with Holy Rollers in heaven.

I often wonder how a Christian would face his judgment day if God did not create man as sinners and Jesus did not die for man's sins. I envision God telling a Christian, that "I did not make all men sinners or evil. In fact, I think I did a pretty good job of making most men good, and some went astray, usually based on negative circumstances. I gave humanity everything they need to make life better on earth over time. I gave humanity the ability to love, intelligence, a human spirit, a conscience, humor, reason, logic, curiosity, and a host of other attributes needed to promote humanity. I am not a God who is going to pick a select few for heaven and send everybody else to hell for eternity. I am not that petty. Why would I want to send anyone to hell for eternity? That sounds like something you would do. I am much greater than your trifling desire for retribution against those who refused to believe like you. Finally, why did you put your faith in a book written over a period of 1,500 years, by people you don't know, over the experience of history, science, and the observation of nature? Especially, a book that depicts me as a cantankerous, capricious God who created the evil he hates but did not have the wisdom or power to destroy evil and spare humanity of suffering. Yet, I divided myself into three parts so I can get crucified to redeem those from the sin that I hate, but created.

"How come it never occurred to you that if I was a loving, all-powerful, merciful God who governed the world, the world would be a much better place? I left plenty of evidence that I created the universe about fourteen billion years ago. I am still creating. I am forming new galaxies and creating new stars. My universe is still expanding. I have plenty of work to keep me busy. Likewise, humanity has plenty of work left to make the human experience better for everybody."

I have listened to interviews and read letters form atheists and Christians who were terminally ill. What I find amazing is that they have more in common about dying than conflicts. Both say that the hardest part about dying is saying good-bye to their families. Especially those, who have younger children. The only significant difference that I noticed was that atheists focus more on the life they have lived without any expectation of an afterlife. They appear to have more gratitude for the life that they have lived. They simply accepted that death is a part of life.

Christians have an expectation that there is something much better on the other side of death based on their religious beliefs. Many Christians express a sentiment that there is always some-thing missing in this life. They often describe it as not being in the full presence of the Lord. I once had these same beliefs. Once I revised my views on God, the need to be in the presence of the Lord was eliminated. I started to see myself as a divine being living for a season on earth. The more I accepted that my life on earth is probably all I will have, each day became more precious and fulfilling. I accepted that for too many people life is hell on earth, yet I carved out a place in my life that is full of peace in spite of the world around me. I discovered my inherent purpose in life is to reach my full potential in all that I pursue, to enrich the lives of those around me when possible, and to serve humanity.

I am offended by Christians who have the best of what this world has to offer, yet complain about their life because they hate living in a world which is full of sinners. In my opinion these people are not worthy of hell. If there was a just God, they would be born in North Korea and have to find their freedom and Jesus on their own.

Religion is on the decline worldwide. Disturbingly, Christianity is increasing in the most underprivileged countries, which are vulnerable to religious influences. African Americans remain the most religious people in America and are still on the bottom of everything. Within the African American community, the fastest-growing group is the Pentecostal, charismatic, and Holy Roller-type churches, especially those who associate tithing with prosperity.

The profound question is, what should those who have broken the last shackle of Christianity due about those who are still in bondage? I am not suggesting that Black churches be abandoned. I realize that the Black church is a genuine place of refuge for many. For many, Jesus is all they got, and no one wants to take Jesus away from them. I am not against an individual having faith and praying to any God he or she chooses.

I am vehemently against what many do in the name of their God. The pride I once held as a Black Christian has been totally dissipated.

Most Blacks and Whites attribute the success of the civil rights movement to the work of the Black church and its allies from all races and religious backgrounds. Martin Luther King and other Black leaders cultivated a sense of if you serve God as a Jew, you are still my brother. If you are a Catholic, you're still my brother; if you are a protestant, you are still my brother; and if you are not any of the above, you are still my brother. The foundation of the civil rights movement was a fundamental belief that we are all brothers and sisters within the humanity of man. King never advocated that Jews need to convert to Christianity or that Protestants need to convert to Catholicism. He advocated that we can all sit together at the table of righteousness. The civil rights movement was successful because it promoted a common humanity. I was proud to be a part of a movement that advanced the cause of humanity, howbeit, through the leadership of the Black church. Now you have Black Christians who have joined the ranks of White Conservative Christians who have no interest in the cause of humanity. They are only concerned with the proliferation of Christianity and converting all non-Christians to a version of Christianity that they consider the absolute truth. Some Blacks rejoice that Christianity was forced upon us during slavery.

Every Sunday during Holy Roller hours, men and women who claim to be anointed by God give themselves a fancy title and appear to have enough Holy Ghost power to solve everybody's problems for about four hours. They have the power to deliver gay men from homosexuality, a thirty-five-year-old woman from her sexual desires, and an eighteen-year-old from his lust. They can heal the sick and give their members messages straight from God. They have the power to prophesize and cast out demons. When these same men and women fall, it's because they are human. This is an inherent contradiction. If at the end of the day you are merely a human, where did all this anointed power of the Holy Ghost go? The germane point of Humanism is that we are all humans who are basically good but flawed. We all make mistakes. Why is it that when a humanist errs, it is attributed to him not being saved and having the Holy Ghost? However, let a Holy Roller err; it will be attributed to an attack from the devil, and he will be delivered by the power of the Holy Ghost. The inconsistencies of behavior in Holy Roller churches is quite amusing. It's not what they do that is humorous, it's how they rationalize their behavior.

I submit that within the Black church, there is an unbalanced dependence on the supernatural. This dependence on the supernatural impairs critical-thinking skills and distorts cognitive mechanisms. When one's success in life is attributed as a blessing from God and failures as either not God's will or being robbed by the devil, the underlining cause of success and failure may be distorted.

I grew up listing to Gospel music. Some of the songs that gave me strength and encouragement, I find repulsive today. The song below is the epitome of giving praises to the Lord, at the cost of not recognizing the suffering and sacrifices of our ancestors. Racial progress was not the result of leaning on the Lord. It was the result of people of all races and religions working together during the civil rights movement.

We've come thus far by faith
Leaning on the Lord
Trusting in his holy word

He never failed me yet
Oh, oh, oh, oh, oh, oh
No turning around
We've come this far by faith

White folks sang "Praise the Lord and pass the ammunition." They never lose sight that freedom comes by the gun, not by faith. On the fourth of July or Veterans Day, rightfully so, America pays tribute to the brave men and women who fought for our freedom. America honors those who died on the battlefield for a better America. Many Black churches fail miserably to honor the death of Blacks, and liked-minded Whites, who fought and died for equal rights, and an America for freedom and justice for all. I have talked to Holy Rollers who claim that civil rights was all the work of the Lord. They have no concern about the three little girls who were killed at Sixteenth Avenue Baptist Church. To them, the death of Chaney, Goodman, and Schwerner made no contribution to making America a better country. They totally dismiss the fire hoses on kids, burning of churches, random lynching's, and the unity of various races and faiths marching for freedom and justice for all. It was the work of the Lord, and their only concern is spreading the Gospel. They have absolutely no identification with those who have died to make things better. I have been to two predominately White churches in NYC that displayed a better appreciation for the struggles of the civil rights movement than a host of Holy Roller Black churches. There is a movement among White churches that have adopted many of the tenets of the traditional Black church. They are often referred to as the emergent church. I find these churches more appealing than mega Black churches that in my opinion are run by pulpit pimps.

On an individual level, a dependence on the supernatural level can impair personal growth. In a competitive society, it is important to correlate actions that lead to success and actions that lead to failure. Claiming a job or groceries in the name of Jesus is not an effective correlation; there is definitely no correlation between being saved and prosperity. Yet, emotionally a belief that God will intercede on one's behalf, is entrenched in the psyche of many African Americans. I have personally been subconsciously influenced by religious beliefs instilled in me from childhood. I had to make a conscious effort to eradicate these beliefs from my way of thinking. I, like most African Americans who have denounced Christianity, have to navigate between rejecting Christian theology and not being offensive to most of my family and friends who are still Christians.

CHAPTER 12

Let's Go to the Word

I FIND NOTHING more amusing in Christianity than claims about the power of the word. Jehovah's witnesses, Pentecostals, evangelicals, Baptists, Presbyterians, atheists, yes atheists, and a host of others all point to the Bible to justify their beliefs.

Every religious group I have encountered have some form of Bible study. I was shocked when I found out how committed atheists are to studying the Bible. The problem is most Bible studies are extremely biased. Pentecostals are going to present all the scriptures that support dancing unto the Lord. They are quick to let you know that praise in the Old Testament was standard operating procedure. They know all the scriptures related to healing and prosperity. They study the word from the perspective of what they hear preached on Sunday morning. All other faiths do the same thing. There is no such thing as an unbiased interpretation of the Bible. Everyone who reads the Bible is going to bring forth a perspective of the word based on his or her personal experiences. Let's be honest that we are all biased and move forward.

The next issue that permeates the Christian religion is that the Bible is the word of God. This is an issue where Blacks are overwhelmingly complacent. I have found few Blacks will take a Bible as Literature Course, History of the Bible Course, or a History of Christianity Course. The biblical background of too many

Blacks is what they learn from a preacher who was called by God to preach but has little or no professional theological training. In fact, I have been to some Holy Roller churches that ridiculed seminaries because what they teach is relying on the teaching of man instead of the teaching of the Bible and the Holy Ghost. Two favorite scriptures to support that all you need is the Bible and the Holy Ghost are as follows:

> All scripture is given by inspiration of God, and is profitable for doctrine, for reproof, for correction, for instruction in righteousness: That the man of God may be perfect, thoroughly furnished unto all good works. (1 Tim. 3: 16–17)

> But the Comforter, which is the Holy Ghost, whom the Father will send in my name, he shall will teach you all things, and bring all things to your remembrance, whatsoever I have said unto you. (John 14:26)

A major problem with the Bible being the infallible word of God, is that the Bible itself often makes no sense. It is almost impossible to read the Bible using critical-thinking skills and accept it as the absolute truth from God. To believe that the writers of the Bible were not influenced by the society they lived in is somewhat naive. Then there is the problem of how do you substantiate that the men who wrote the Bible actually were divinely chosen by God? Go to your Christian book store, and you will find hundreds of books written by men who claim that they were led by the Holy Spirit to write their book. Try to pick out the fakes. Fortunately, there is a Master's College website that keeps a list of Christian books that are false teachings. Of course, this list is predicated on the notion that those at Master's College have discovered the absolute truth and that any teaching that goes against their truth must be false. This highlights the amount of arrogance needed to be a fundamental evangelical Christian. The fact that there are so many books based on the Bible, written by men all claiming to be led by the Holy Spirit, is sound evidence that either the claims of the Holy Spirit and the authority of the Bible are unreliable or there is one absolute truth and you must find it. I have come to the conclusion that either way most people lose.

For those who consider the Bible as absolute truth, I present to you excerpts from *A Letter to a Friend Regarding The Age of Reason*, by Thomas Paine, Paris, May 12, 1797. In this letter Paine responds to a Christian friend who was trying to convert him to Christianity. I must confess that I have an affinity for Thomas Paine since he was the only founding father who openly opposed slavery. His opposition to slavery was based on this simple proposition, since he would not want slavery imposed on him, he felt it is wrong to impose slavery on others. This is a very humanist approach to a practice that is sanctioned by the Bible.

But by what authority do you call the Bible the Word of God? For this is the first point to be settled. It is not your calling it so, that makes it so, any more than the Mahometans calling the Koran the Word of God makes it the Koran to be so.

You may have an opinion that a man is inspired, but you cannot prove it, nor can you have any proof of it yourself, because you cannot see into his mind in order to know how he comes by his thoughts; and the same is the case with the word revelation. There can be no evidence of such a thing, for you can no more prove revelation than you can prove what another man dreams of, neither can he prove it himself.

You believe in the Bible from the accident of birth, and the Turks believe in the Koran from the same accident, and each calls the other infidel. But leaving the prejudice of education out of the case, the unprejudiced truth is, that all are infidels who believe falsely of God, whether they draw their creed from the Bible, or from the Koran, from the Old Testament or from the New.

The above poses some serious issues for anyone who is going to dedicate his or her life to live according to the claims of one book. There are more mundane issues that those who profess to live according to the word should address. The basic question of how the sixty-six books of the Bible came into existence is paramount in determining how much credence to give the Bible.

Many Christians are under the false impression that what they believe about the Holy Bible was established immediately after the death and resurrection of Christ. They view the Bible as a sacred book that was directly communicated by God and carefully, without blemish, passed down for generations. The truth is the sixty-six books that today constitute the Holy Bible or the word of God were voted on. Constantine the Great was the first Roman emperor to convert to Christianity. Christianity was still an inchoate religion with different churches teaching from different books, which they considered Holy Scriptures. There were also differences regarding the status of Jesus. Some believed that Jesus was a good teacher but merely a man. Others believed that Jesus was God. This belief was consistent with many pagan beliefs at that time, which held it was not uncommon for God to come to earth in the form of a man. Others believed that Jesus was both God and man, a new concept that seemed to keep the masses happy.

In 325 Constantine held the Council of Nicaea and hired Christian Bishops to come up with one book that would be used throughout the Roman Empire, and this book would be called the "word of God." Emperor Constantine wanted to control what was being taught within the Roman Empire regarding Christianity. This was a way to control behavior and to instill a sense of unity and loyalty to the Roman Empire. The Council of Nicaea presented a recommended version of the Bible. At the Council of Trent, the Catholic Church rendered the final editing of the Bible and presented it to Constantine for his final approval. There is some dispute regarding what final decisions Constantine made regarding what the Bible would contain. There is no dispute that Constantine gave the final approval. Among the issues that many claim Constantine decided was the concept of the Trinity. They argue that Constantine decided that the Father, Son, and Holy Ghost would be taught as three components of God. Constantine ordered and financed fifty parchment copies of the new "Holy Scriptures" laying the foundation for future biblical translations. Most of the books that did not make it into the Bible were destroyed. Some are contained in the Holy Koran. Others are part of the gnostic church and are followed today.

Most biblical scholars do not believe that the Bible is literally true. Research in biblical archaeology has concluded that there is no archaeological evidence to support many of the major biblical stories. For example, there is no evidence that Jews were enslaved in Egypt, which would make the story of the parting of the Red Sea a myth as well as the forty years of wandering in the wilderness. At the alleged time of the Jews being slaves in Egypt and building the pyramids, Egypt was among the more civilized nations at that time and maintained superior records of its history, financial and otherwise. Egyptian history does not corroborate the Exodus story. First, craftsmen who worked on the pyramids were well paid and not slaves. Second, there is no record of a large Jewish population in Egypt. Third, a migration of the magnitude as described in Exodus should have been recorded in Egyptian history since it would have had a significant social and economic impact. The parting of the Red Sea would have been a major violation of the laws of nature. A miracle of this magnitude should have been documented by the Egyptians who witnessed it. The critics argue that Egypt was too embarrassed about the escape and hid the truth. My response is an event of this magnitude could not be suppressed. If the Egyptian army witnessed such a convincing miracle from God, it would be recorded in Egyptian history. It seems to me that a miracle from God, especially in a nation that believed in the divine, would have precedence over any embarrassment of having your alleged slaves escape.

My Favorite Bible Stories

I argued that most people who read the Bible are biased. I also suggest that if you read the Bible critically, you are more likely to accept it as myth. Those who accept the Bible as literally true do so because they are resigned to accept any action by God as good and just. I submit, in some instances, that if men behaved like God, they would not be considered good nor just men. The following are Bible stories from an admittedly humanist point of view.

Abraham Offers His Son to God

This is a basic childhood biblical story to show how faithful Abraham was to God and God's mercy toward Abraham. God told Abraham to sacrifice his firstborn child to prove that he was a faithful servant of God. Abraham takes his son up to the mountaintop, lifts up his knife, and is ready to kill his son. Then an angel of God steps in and stops him.

To thoroughly understand this story, you must realize that when Abraham took his son to the mountaintop, he did not know that God was going to change his mind and, tell Abraham this was a joke to see if you would do it. Imagine the fear in Abraham's son as he watched his dad raise his knife ready to kill him. Then ask yourself, would anyone other than a gangster ask someone to kill his or her son to show his or her loyalty? Why would a loving God, who has as one of his ten commandments "thou shalt not kill," ask one of his servants to kill his son? To reasonable people this makes absolutely no sense. Today if God tried this same stunt to test one of his servants, his servant would be locked up, and his son would be taken away and placed in therapy. I heard all the allegories about this is some precursor to God sacrificing his son for the benefit of man. That being said you still have a cruel irrational God. By the way there is no archaeological evidence that Abraham existed.

Elijah

Elijah was a prophet of God who was teased by some unruly youth over his being bald. Elijah being a prophet of God did not ignore the youth as being typical youth, and he did not take matters into his own hands. He called upon God to handle this situation, and God obliged. God sent two female bears to maul forty-two youths. To most rational people, this seems to be a little harsh punishment for teasing an old man about being bald. I was raised that sticks and stones will break my bones but words will never hurt me. I guess the lesson here is if you tease a prophet of God, God is justi-fied to go gangster on you, even if you're a youth. Apparently, the turn-the-other-cheek principle does not apply to youth teasing a bald-headed prophet.

Passover

Jesus celebrated the Passover with his disciples. The Passover story is a very encouraging story of God's grace as long as you're not Egyptian. God got pissed at Pharaoh for holding the Israelites captive. So he decided that he was going to kill the firstborn male and animal of every Egyptian. However, God did not want to kill any Israelites by accident, so he had the Israelites kill an unblem-ished lamb and place some of the blood on their doorposts. Thus, when God sends down his death angels, they will see the blood on the doorpost, pass over the Israelites, and only kill the Egyptians as described below:

And it came to pass, that at midnight the Lord smote all the firstborn in the land of Egypt, from the firstborn of Pharaoh, that sat on his throne, unto the firstborn of the captive that [was] in the dungeon; and the firstborn of cattle. And Pharaoh rose up in the night, he, and all his servants, and all the Egyptians; and there was a great cry in Egypt; for [there] was not a house where [there was] not one dead. (Exod. 12:29–30)

When I think about the outpouring from the Christian right over a woman's right to choose within three months of pregnancy and compare that with killing every firstborn child, I consider the right to choose as the moral high ground. Imagine if one day everyone in America experienced a death in the family, from a single event. 9/11 was an atrocity. Close to three thousand families lost a loved one from this single event. The country came together to grieve. Religious terrorists had attacked our nation, and we declared a war against terrorism. When you consider the type of violence God used to make his point, it's easy to understand why religious fanatics have no reservation against using violence to make their point.

Granted; Pharaoh was an asshole. So why not take out Pharaoh and, to prove you're a tough God, his family and friends and then say to Pharaoh's successors, do you want to be next. I think they would have gotten the message and let the Israelites go. This story takes a gangster mindset to a whole new level. Where is the justice to the Egyptian families that were only guilty of being Egyptians? Maybe some Egyptians wanted the Israelites to go free, just like some Whites wanted Blacks to be free during American slavery. Why would a loving, merciful God kill the firstborn of an entire nation because the leader of the nation is an asshole? God appoints those in leadership according to the New Testament. When George Bush took out Saddam Hussein, he had the decency to try to keep civilian deaths at a minimum.

Noah's Flood
As a child I loved the story of Noah's Ark. I never questioned why a loving, merciful God would destroy most of life because of sin. After all, couldn't God change the hearts of man to his satisfaction? He is God, the one who created man. On the sixth day of creation, God was pleased with what he created.

God saw all that he made and it was good. (Gen. 1:31)

Six chapters later God has creators' remorse as described below:

> And God saw that the wickedness [was] great in the earth, and [that] every imagination of the thoughts of his heart [was] only evil all continually. And it repented the Lord that he had made man on the earth, and it grieved him at his heart. And the Lord said, I will destroy man whom I have created from the face of the earth; both man, and beast, and the creeping thing, and the fowls of the air; for it repenteth me that I have made them. (Gen. 6:5–7)

This scripture shows that God takes full responsibility for his creation of man and that clearly God regrets his creation. The question still remains, how did a perfect, holy, loving God create men who are so inclined to wickedness that he regrets making them? This alone challenges the claim that God is perfect. At what point does God assume responsibility for creating wicked men? What role did God have in Noah being righteous? What does this story say about a God who created men who are so wicked that he only found one family to spare? Maybe the problem is not the creation but the creator. If it's accepted that God is our heavenly Father, it follows that he is a Father who kills the children he regrets having and spares his one good child. The story of the flood is the antithesis of what Jesus taught in the parable of the prodigal son. The God that Jesus depicts is a Father who celebrates a lost child who returns home. Jesus said suffer the little children to come unto me. God got so pissed that he drowned kids, their parents, and the family dog.

Hurricane Katrina was a terrifying experience for New Orleans. People waited on their roofs until help could arrive. This was a natural disaster that impacted one small segment of our country. Katrina caught the eye of our nation. Yet, the destruction of Katrina is inconsequential compared with Noah's Flood. Think about all those kids crying out to their parents to help them and the parents who themselves are helpless. Think about the people watching their crops being destroyed and livestock drown, but they still have hope that the rain will stop and maybe somehow they can start all over. The point of Noah's Ark is that God gave humankind a second chance when he spared Noah. God spares Noah, and essentially the same type of stuff that got God pissed starts all over again. It seems to me that an all-powerful, all-mighty, all-merciful God should have been able to change the hearts of man to his liking, instead of drowning damn near everybody.

Ken Ham, the president and founder of the creation museum, has embarked upon building a replica of Noah's Ark, called the Ark Encounter. Granted, this project will probably be a successful tourist attraction. However, it does not validate the story of Noah's Ark. If Ham was serious about demonstrating the credibility of Noah's Ark, he would do a documentary building the ark, without the benefit of technology that was obviously not available in the days of Noah, load it with live animals, and live at sea for forty days and forty nights.

I guess he wants a symbol that represents how despicable and sinful God sees man. To be a true fundamental evangelical Christian, it is imperative that you believe a loving God is justified in killing babies and children to make his point.

When Susan Smith drove her car into a lake and let her children drown, she was considered the most despicable mother in America. Killing everybody on earth except for one family is not the best way to prove that you are a loving and just God. This will only appeal to those who believe that all men, including themselves, are so inherently evil that God should kill them all today and take his select few to be in glory with him. The schism between the God of the Old Testament and the New Testament gives credibility that the Bible is myth and that Jesus apparently had a different view from the Old Testament God. The presumption is the Bible is the absolute truth of one God. A God who decides that I will kill dam near everybody and everything because they piss me off. Then he decides that he will be merciful and send everybody to hell except for a select few who commit themselves to ignoring science and common sense to get into heaven.

The Book of Job
The book of Job was also among by favorite Bible stories. My focus was always on the fact that God doubled everything Job had at the end of the story.

In the book of Job, Satan, accompanied by some angels, went up to heaven to have a chat with God. Why God let the devil into heaven is not clear. I thought heaven was for the righteous. In fact, when Satan was kicked out of heaven, I thought it was permanent. God asked Satan, what have you been up to lately? Satan replied, hanging out on earth. Then God boasted about his servant Job. God said:

> And the Lord said unto Satan, Hast thou considered my servant Job, that there is none like him in the earth, a perfect and an upright man, one that feareth God and eschewed evil. (Job 1:8)

Then Satan, in essence, made a bet with God. Satan told God that Job is only faithful because you keep a hedge around him, his household, and everything he has. If you take down your hedge, I will devour him, and Job will curse you. God said you have a bet. You have permission to do what you want with everything he has; however, you can't harm Job.

Let the bet begin. If Satan can get Job to curse God, Satan wins. If Job refuses to curse God, God wins. The only real loser in this bet is Job. A man who fears God and shuns evil is about to go through hell on earth. The only wager at stake is apparently bragging rights.

Satan gets busy, and Job loses his livestock, his crops, most of his servants, house, and children. His wife encourages him to curse God, and he calls her a fool. Job is steadfast in his belief:

And said, Naked came I out of my mother's womb, and naked shall I return thither: the Lord gave, and the Lord hath taken away; blessed be the name of the Lord. (Job 1:21)

As God predicted, Job did not curse him. Job did get to the point that he wished he was never born or had died at birth. Job had nothing to look forward to but the grave, but did he not curse God. He is mocked by his friends, but he held on to his God. Satan wanted to up the ante, and God allowed Job to get sick. Job truly holds on to his faith like no man on earth. Job exemplifies the type of faith God requires. God wins his bet, and all that Job lost is doubled. Job ended up living a long prosperous life.

Everybody loves a story with a happy ending. God replaced Job's children just like he replaced his livestock. According to the book of Job, replacing a child is like replacing a horse. Most parents have a unique bond with their children and consider them irreplaceable. However, since Job lost his children as a result of God placing a bet, his having seven sons and three beautiful daughters at the end of the story justifies the death of his original children. It's like having good car insurance when your car is totaled. A new car is on its way.

There is one point of this story that many Africans Americans get confused. It's this notion that God chooses his best to suffer the most. This concept goes beyond Christianity. I have heard too many comments, from otherwise intelligent Black people, that God chose Black people to suffer because we can handle it. We are like Job. God knows that he will always have Black people praising him. I am amazed at how many Black people are proud of the fact that God chose us to suffer because he knows we are faithful to him. What is more incredulous is the number of Blacks who believe spirituality is some inherent quality of our African ancestry. I have had conversations with Blacks who have left the Christian faith to adopt some perceived African-based religion that is better adapted for the Black man.

I have focused on Christianity and the Black church because this is how I was raised and this is what I know. Unequivocally, I denounce any religion that encourages a dependence on the supernatural. I do not believe that spirituality is an inherent part of our African heritage. Even if it was, it was most likely forced on the tribe by the chief. A religion having an African origin does not exonerate it from the same scrutiny and criticism of Christianity. I realize that religion is incorporated in most cultures. This does not justify the continuance of religious or cultural practices if they impede on the common rights of humanity.

Slave Laws

As an African American, the slave rules in the Bible have given me a better understanding of the American slave trade. My White humanist brothers are more aware of slave laws in the Bible than most of the Black Christians I know. They question why Blacks maintain such a strong allegiance to Christianity, which was used to keep them enslaved.

I am annoyed by Christians who claim that slaves in the Bible were actually indentured servants. I heard one conservative Christian extol the practice of slavery in the Bible because it was an honorable substitute for what we call welfare today. This ignoramus never explained that if there was work for the slave to do, why didn't the slave master just hire the slave for wages? His statement is equivalent to saying that America couldn't get Black people to work for wages, so we had to make them slaves. Many slaves may have worked as household servants, which doesn't mean that there were not slaves who were bought, sold, and treated worse than livestock. The following passage shows that slaves were clearly property to be bought and sold like livestock:

Both thy bondmen, and thy bondmaids, which thou shalt have, [shall be] of the heathen that are round about you; of them shall ye buy bondmen and bondmaids. Moreover of the children of strangers that do sojourn among you, of them shall ye buy, and of their families that [are] with you, which they begat in you land: and thy shall be your possession. And ye shall take them as an inheritance for your children after you, to inherit [them for] a possession; they shall be your bondmen for ever: but over your brethren the children of Israel, ye shall not rule one over another with rigour. (Lev. 25: 44–46)

The following passage describes how the Hebrew slaves are to be treated:

If you buy a Hebrew servant, six years he shall serve: and in the seventh he shall go out free for nothing. If he came in by himself, he shall go out by himself: if he were married then his wife shall go out with him. If his master have given him a wife and she have born him sons or daughters; the wife and her children shall be her master's and he shall go out by himself. And if the servant shall plainly say, I love my master, my wife, and my children; I will not go out free: Then his master shall bring him unto the judges; he shall also bring him to the door, or unto the door post; and is master shall bore his ear through with an aul; and he shall serve him forever. (Exod. 21:2–6)

Now it makes perfect sense why America had no moral issues with slavery. The slave laws in America were using the moral high ground of the Bible as an example of how to practice slavery in a manner that is pleasing to God. Using a man's family to keep him in slavery was a brilliant idea. That is how real gangsters handle their business. I think it's ironic that conservative evangelical Christians, who had no problem breaking up families during slavery, can't understand why Black families are in disarray today.

The following passage describes the practice of sex slavery. How can anyone think it is moral to sell your own daughter as a sex slave?

When a man sells his daughter as a slave, she will not be freed at the end of six years as the men are. If she does not please the man who bought her, he may allow her to be bought back again. But he is not allowed to sell her to foreigners, since he is the one who broke the contract with her. And if the slave girl's owner arranges for her to marry his son, he may no longer treat her as a slave girl, but he must treat her as his daughter. If he himself marries her and then takes another wife, he may not reduce her food or clothing or fail to sleep with her as his wife. If he fails in any of these three ways, she may leave as a free woman without making any payment. (Exod. 21:7–11)

Passages like this make me wonder why the Christian right have an issue with prostitution. I think a woman selling her body for her own benefit is better than a woman being a sex slave. I guess it's cheaper in the long run to just buy a sex slave. Then there is the problem with this fornication issue. I guess screwing a slave does not count as fornication because she's your property. That explains why the Christian right is always talking about bringing back sexual morality. During slavery it is clear by the complexion of the average African American that somebody's been in the gene pool. But since slave masters were screwing their property, it doesn't count as fornication or adultery. Thus, Christian values were being upheld.

What I truly find encouraging about using the Bible as a moral barometer is its rules regarding beating slaves.

And if a man smite his servant, or his maid with a rod, and he die under his hand; he shall be surely punished. Notwithstanding, if he continue a day or two, he shall not be punished: for he [is] his money. (Exod. 21:20–21)

This really shows God's compassion toward humanity. I can envision my ancestor watching a loved one getting a severe beating and asking the master for mercy in the name of Jesus. I can see the master's pious reply: he'll live at least a day or two. If he doesn't, you should feel sorry for me, I paid good money for this nigger.

I submit that these laws seem foolish because they are merely a reflection of what was acceptable at the time they were written. If you take the Bible literally and embrace these laws as being given by God, then I can truly say I do not want to follow God's laws.

The issue that Christians are now under grace and not under the law is irrelevant when evaluating the character of God. If the Old Testament is the true word of God, as proscribed by many, you have to accept that God can be unreasonably cruel by most human standards. I submit that human behavior over time has evolved. What was acceptable behavior six thousand years ago is nauseating by today's standards. To use the Bible as an absolute source of moral guidance today is actually immoral, in many instances illegal and in most cases ridiculous.

"Above all to thy own self be true." I find this Shakespearean quote to be true, but I do not believe that Shakespeare was inspired by God when he wrote it. I believe that much of what is written in the Bible has truth, but it is not inspired by God and therefore a myth.

Bill Moyers hosted a PBS special entitled The *Power of Myth* featuring Joseph Campbell. I recommend this documentary to anyone who is interested in learning more about man's relationship with God, myth, and spirituality. The notion that the Bible is a myth doesn't imply that the Bible has no value. Before science became prevalent, myth explained the world that early man lived in. It explained that which could not be explained otherwise. Myth explains where man came from; what happens after death; why people get sick; why some people kill, love, and hate. Myth was often the foundation for how to manage a tribe, city, or state. Myth provides answers to an array of questions. Myth still has its place. However, myth should be recognized as myth not as divine absolute truth.

If the Bible is a myth, what are these myths based on? Common themes in Christianity are the virgin birth, Jesus rising from the dead in three days, the great flood, and Jesus performing a variety of miracles. The Old Testament declares Jews as God's chosen people and promises them a homeland. The Lord also helped the Jews win several battles. This is a great book to have if you're a nomadic people looking for some respect. Being God's chosen people has to be good for one's image and self-respect.

Fortunately, the Internet makes researching the Bible extremely easy. I have devised what I call a word reality check (WRC). WRC consists of a range of questions designed to help those who live according to the word of God evaluate the Bible beyond what they learn in Sunday school. The Bible, Christianity, and religion have a history. WRC will help you distinguish if your belief in God is a matter of faith or if your belief in God is based on the authority of the Bible. I have not provided any answers to these questions. If you have an interest in the Bible and religion, you will enjoy looking for the answers. If you are a committed Christian, the answers are irrelevant.

Below are the names of five mythological Gods. How many of these Gods are claimed to be by virgin births? How many of these Gods are claimed to have raised from the dead? How many of these Gods are claimed to have given sight to the blind?

a. Horus
b. Attis
c. Krishna
d. Dionysus
e. Mithra

1. Why is Christmas celebrated on December 25th?
2. Why is Easter celebrated on the Sunday following the first full moon of spring?
3. Does Islam teach that Jesus was born of a virgin?
4. What does Islam teach regarding the crucifixion of Christ?
5. In Islam is it believed that the Koran was written entirely by Muhammad?
6. Are all the authors of the Bible known?
7. Why is there a Roman Catholic Church?
8. Who were the Knights Templar? What role did they play in the spread of Christianity?
9. Are there claims that Jesus was buried in India and the location of his alleged gravesite is known?
10. Do poorer, less-educated countries tend to have a higher percentage of people who believe in God?

CHAPTER 13

If You Don't Believe in Jesus, What Do You Believe In?

I AM AMAZED with how much being a believer and being a non-believer overlap. I remember the first time I experienced what I formally considered the work of the Holy Spirit operating in my life, as a humanist. This was an awesome experience. Something I really wanted to happen (something I formally would have prayed to happen) became a reality in a manner beyond what I could have hoped for. What had happened was clearly something that I could not control, predict, or influence. I felt the Lord had delivered exceedingly more than I had asked for. Only I had not asked the Lord for anything. Frankly, after spending most of my life attributing everything positive in my life to the Holy Spirit, I instinctively had the feeling that this must be a blessing from God. Then I reflected on the times when I would pray, fast, and wrestle with the Lord to bless me only to be totally disappointed over what I considered to be a reasonable petition to God. I remembered some of my favorite verses about promises from God: "Delight thyself also in the Lord: and he shall give thee the desires of thine heart. Commit thy way unto the Lord; trust also in him; and he shall bring it to pass" (Ps. 37:4-5). I believed to a fault that my delight was unto the Lord and that he would give me the desires of my heart. I believed that God rewarded those who diligently seek him.

Some Christian theology is grounded in the notion that anyone who walks away from the Christian faith was never a Christian in the first place. This view supports their doctrine that all men are deserving of hell except for the select few who are predestined by God to be saved. Those who are chosen would never walk away from Jesus. I had to address accusations of not being a Christian in the first place on several occasions. My first response was I acknowledged that based on your Christian theology, I understood why you hold this position. I am sympathetic as to why someone who holds your beliefs cannot accept that someone would walk away from the Christian faith. Then I expressed how condescending and arrogant I think such a position is. It implies that all those years I confessed my faith in Christ, I was either incapable of knowing what I believe, a charlatan, or some kind of idiot who thought I believed in Christ but didn't. I believed in Christ irrespective of my intellectual misgivings, often to a fault. It totally ignores that my conversion is the result of my personal growth, my life experiences, my embarking upon intense research of the Bible, the history of Christianity, the inconstancies among various Christian faiths, and the implications of Christianity worldwide, in addition to researching how modern science has disproved many biblical stories and historical claims of the Bible. The thought that as a humanist, I have more peace, a better appreciation of life, an answer to sickness and disease that make sense to me, a God who is much more just than the God of the Bible, and an ineffable appreciation of the universe, is inconceivable to many Christians.

Like most African Americans, a majority of my family members are embedded in the Christian faith. Many of them, especially the older ones, cannot conceive of someone not being a Christian. There is also an indiscernible fear of someone who is not saved. I find it a challenge to be true to myself without being ostracized.

My objective is not to disrupt the faithful but to extend a lifeline to those who are not comfortable in the house of the Lord. To those who are questioning their Christian faith, I challenge them to read the Bible critically, to listen to videos of others who have left the Christian faith, and to research religion in general. But above all to thy own self be true. I can assure you that nonbelievers do not hate God, they hate people who do evil or unjust things in the name of God. They don't hate Muslims, they hate Muslims who blow up planes in the name of Islam.

Most humanist want to insure that government policies are based the Constitution of the United States of America, rather than the religious beliefs of conservative Christians. It is a matter of upholding the principles of separation of church and state. If a humanist supports gay rights, it is because he believes that gay rights is merely rights granted to all Americans and should not be denied to someone solely because some believe a gay lifestyle is sinful. It is insulting that some conservative Christians assert that humanist are for gay rights because they want to prove how much they hate God. These are the same conservatives who assert that humanists who want insurance to cover contraceptives are promoting promiscuity. These are ridiculous arguments that will frustrate any rational person and cause him or her to demonstrate a sense of anger. This anger is not toward God, it is toward trying to have a rational conversation with irrational people.

Since I don't believe I am a sinner saved by grace, I don't believe in heaven or hell, and I don't believe that there is a loving God who intervenes in my life on my behalf, here is what I do believe. I admit that some of my new beliefs are irrational, but like prayer they make me feel good.

1. I believe that the big-bang theory and the creation of God are contemporaneous events. All of life is the result of an event that occurred about fourteen billion years ago. I do not believe there is a God separate from the universe, but I can't prove this belief. Thus, I take the position of Stephen Hawking that there could be a God beyond the universe, but he is not necessary. I do not believe that there is a supernatural being who inspired the Bible, Torah, or the Koran. I believe that all scriptures are man's way of explaining the world based on what they knew at the time. My beliefs are consistent with that of deism and naturalistic theists. I prefer to identify myself as a secular humanist.

2. I believe that life is the result of and a part of the forces and laws of creation. All of life has common elements of survival. This is crucial in understanding sickness and disease. I vehemently reject any notion that a loving God has a higher purpose in sickness and disease. I believe that all life works accordingly to natural laws of the universe; however, these laws are not fully understood. Science explains these laws, and by understanding how these laws work, we can use the laws of the universe to benefit humanity. I believe that cancer research illustrates the relationship between man and nature. Cancer cells, like all other cells and like all forms of life, need a source of energy to survive. A cancer cell is merely trying to survive. However, these cancer cells feed on cells that are needed to maintain good health. Scientists have improved on how to kill cancer cells and how to avoid the development of cancer cells. The point is that cancer, like all diseases, is a result

of nature, not a result of original sin, which in essence is a punishment from God.

3. I believe that it is important to maintain meaningful relationships throughout my life. The quality of my life will be measured by the memories I leave behind. I embrace a simple truth that my life is the aggregate of the memories I have created. I cringe when I hear people proclaim that their best friend is Jesus. You can have a little talk with Jesus and tell him all about your problems, but Jesus will not share a glass of wine with you, break bread with you, or give you a hug. Maybe there is a reason you feel closer to a God you cannot see or touch, rather than a fellow human being you can see and touch.

4. Good and evil is the result of how men choose to respond to the power they have or the lack of power they have. It is an internal choice often based on negative circumstances. I do not believe there is an external force called the devil that is out to deceive us. We deceive ourselves. The primary defense against evil is to be truthful with yourself. The more a person is truthful about his circumstances in life, his abilities, his experience, and his opportunities, the better decisions he can make, which lead to a better quality of life.

5. I don't believe in the Father, Son, and Holy Ghost. I do believe in Truth, Reason, and Logic. I believe that being truthful with yourself is an arduous endeavor. Especially when trying to discover one's weaknesses.

6. I believe that the more people subordinate their religious dogma to the common cause of escalating humanity, the better the experience of life will be for more people worldwide. It seems to me that if God wanted to protect his

reputation, he would prevent the number of wars that are declared in the name of God. I believe that creating heaven on earth is an inherent responsibility of humanity. Not a gift being withheld from our Father who lives in heaven. Humankind has evolved. The world is a better place than it was two thousand years ago. Not because Jesus died on a cross, but because man is continuing to learn that peace, human dignity, and freedom is the best option. Slavery is no longer accepted as a divine right worldwide. Watching men get eaten in a lion's den is no longer considered entertainment. Watching a lynching is not considered the main event of a family picnic (pick a nigger).

7. I believe that people define their own purpose in life. At one time my purpose in life was to find the will of God and do it. I found this to be a very elusive purpose. Then my purpose in life became to fulfill my potential in pursuing the things that interest me. I found that living a good life is a sufficient purpose of life.

8. I accept that life as I know it will end and there is no way to ascertain if there is an afterlife. This makes my life on earth more meaningful and precious. I accept that life is a fleeting moment. Each moment is to be savored.

9. For many people, believing in God and worshipping God gives their life meaning and purpose. I have no qualms with these people whatsoever. However, when people are manipulated to conform to religious behavior at the detriment of their own self-interest, I feel obligated to give them the tools to liberate themselves if they choose. To these people I say use critical-thinking skills as you evaluate your religious beliefs. I also implore that for some walking away from religion is rejuvenating. Howbeit, the

transition from a believer to a nonbeliever can be treacherous. Subconsciously, your former beliefs in the supernatural can influence your decision-making process. The result can be making decisions that are imprudent from every perspective.

10. I find comfort in focusing my thoughts on individuals and circumstances. Some may describe this as prayer and meditation. However, I do not look for supernatural intervention. I am looking to my inner human spirit, which is in everybody as part of being human. I use meditation to clear my mind, to make better decisions, and to cope with difficult situations in my life. I do not purport that this has any external influences on the persons or situations I am focusing on. It is purely for my own gratification, inner peace, and inner strength.

I plan to spend the rest of my life doing what I think is best for me, my family, and close friends (formally known as my church family), without any consideration of their being a God who will either bless me or curse me. I hope that I can be true to my principles and beliefs, which do not include the intervention of the supernatural.

PART 3

*

Life in Holy Roller Land

CHAPTER 14

———— ⚜ ————

Saved, Sanctified, and Queen of the Superfreaks

I WAS FORTUNATE to be raised in a progressive Black church. The type of Black church that I was raised in is now nearly extinct. When I was in high school, the friends I partied with on Saturday nights were the same friends I ushered with on Sunday mornings. In fact, our Youth Usher Board had a reputation of hosting some of the best parties in the city, featuring good food, good music, dancing (fast and slow) women in hot pants, and allegedly spiked punch, all closely supervised by adult members of my church. I dated the women in my church without reservation.

The pastor of my church and the adult leader of the young-adult usher board were very candid about sexual development and never hesitated to talk about contraceptives. Adolescent pregnancy was not a problem in our church. The women who were sexually active used contraceptives. My church did not advocate abstinence only.

When I went to college and was exposed to more conservative views regarding Christian beliefs, I felt the church I was raised in was somewhat substandard. Now I fully appreciate the church I was raised in and realize that common sense mixes well with good religion.

Sunday morning sermons were geared toward "Are you doing something to feed the hungry or visiting the sick or trying to help your neighbor?" Many of the sermons were in the spirit of Martin Luther King regarding a social conscience and love your neighbor. There was an underlying message of how can you best prepare yourself to serve your community. We were also taught how to apply Christian principles and values.

My parents taught me a set of principles and values that helped build my character. I was taught to fight for my principles to the bitter end. Never let anyone disrespect you, your home, or your property. Your name and reputation are valuable assets. Most of all, I was taught that my behavior was a reflection of my parents, and my parents were not going to tolerate their reputations being damaged. I had enough respect toward my parents and fear of my parents that I would never lie to them. On those few instances when my parents received a report on my poor behavior, I was immediately chastised and had to make amends for my bad behavior. This usually resulted in my apologizing in the presence of my parents to the offended.

Today, more and more Blacks, especially women, are attracted to what I affectionately call Holy Roller Land church (Holy Roller Land). These are churches where reason, science, logic, common sense, and personal experiences are strictly prohibited. Holy Roller Land is not exclusive to the Black church. It can be applied to any religious institution where any of the aforementioned attributes predominate. I focus on Black Holy Rollers because it's what I know best. I had Holy Roller roommates, I married a Holy Roller (that was a disaster), and I lived with a Holy Roller (a worst disaster). It appears that in Holy Roller Land, the primary purpose of going to church is to get "your praise on," aka get hit with the

Holy Ghost. In exchange for this, you pay your tithes, which enables the preacher to live large.

People in Holly Roller Land can be very intelligent and successful. But when it comes to church and the power of the Holy Ghost, they adhere only to Holy Ghost logic, which most rational people find to be amusing, irrational, and somewhat humorous.

The following story is based on true events that occurred in Holy Roller Land. The events in this story illustrate the effectiveness of Holy Ghost power, which is usually misunderstood by rational people looking at Holy Roller Land from the outside.

It is indicative of what goes on every day in Holy Roller Land across the country. These events are real! The names have been changed because Holy Rollers are some of the most vicious people around and I don't want to get sued. People in Holy Roller Land insist that every discussion have a biblical reference. To comply with this protocol, I submit the following scriptures:

...I had rather be a doorkeeper in the house of my God, than to dwell in the tents of wickedness. (Ps. 84:10)

For there is nothing hid, which shall not be manifested; neither was any thing kept secret, but that it should come abroad. (Mark 4:22)

Thou shall not bear false witness against thy neighbor. (Exod. 20:16)

Every Holy Roller church I attended has been jam-packed with single mothers, most of whom were in their teens and unwed when they got pregnant. Many of them hold leadership positions in

Holy Roller Land. My criticism is not that they were teen parents, it is their refusal to have any discussion at all with their daughters regarding healthy adolescent sexual development and contraceptives. As a result, many of their daughters have avoidable pregnancies. Their Holy Ghost logic is that any discussion of birth control is conceding to "preplanned sin." These are women who believed that with the power of the Holy Ghost, they could overcome their own sexual desires. Thus, most were not protected during their first sexual encounter. Since they attributed their first sexual encounter to a moment of weakness, they beseech the Holy Ghost for more power to resist the temptation of lust. They didn't realize that the Holy Ghost is not a spermicide and eventually got pregnant. The truly blessed ones had a shotgun wedding.

This is where denial becomes a crucial part of life in Holy Roller Land. These women will never admit that they were overcome by their own sexual desires. They insist it is more honorable to get pregnant by accident than to prevent pregnancy by choice. Irrespective of their own personal experience, they stick to the teachings of the church that the only thing a child needs to know is no sex before marriage.

If there is anyone who should be an expert on teaching abstinence only, it's T. D. Jakes. He makes millions selling the Power of the Holy Ghost. There should be no doubt that what he preaches works in his own home. Just because his daughter gave birth at fourteen, got married at nineteen, and divorced four years later, doesn't mean what Jake is teaching is faulted. It means that Jake is only telling half the story. In biblical times fourteen was a respectful age to get married. Women were not concerned with college and careers. In fact, in those days women had two career choices, being a wife or being a prostitute, and both of them involved screwing. Getting married was simple in biblical times. A guy sees a girl he likes and asks two questions: Can you cook? And do you want to screw? If the answer to these questions were yes, they got married.

The solution to fornication is simple. Holy Rollers should insist their daughters get married as soon as they start getting horny. In biblical times it was common for a female to get married once she reached puberty. For example, if Holy Rollers allowed a four-teen-year-old female to get married instead of waiting until the average age for marriage, which is twenty-six, that's twelve years of either burning in lust or fornication that can be prevented. The best thing is they will be abiding by the Bible and upholding religious customs followed during biblical times.

The Devil in Sheep's Clothing

There are Black pastors and churches that encourage healthy adolescent sexual development. I know three pastors who were fired because they advocated educating teenagers on sexual development and contraceptives. These are pastors who lost their jobs because they believe in physical science, social science, statistics, and common sense.

These pastors are aware that teenage mothers are 89 percent less likely to be married. Their children are more likely to live in poverty, and their chances of completing college in four years is greatly diminished. They understand that the teenage pregnancy rate for Black teens is three times the rate for White teens. They know that pledges of virginity until marriage are ineffective. These pledges only delay sexual activity by about eighteen months. Less than 5 percent of Americans are virgins on their wedding night. This number is inclusive of extremely conservative, reclusive religious groups. This suggests that among urban communities this number is significantly smaller. In urban America the chances of two virgins getting married is close to zero.

Most of all these pastors know that many adolescents who commit to maintaining their virginity until marriage often substitute other sexual behavior to abstain from vaginal intercourse, including oral sex, anal sex, and other high-risk sexual behavior.

A former pastor of mine Reverend Wise shared his experience giving his first report to the Wacko Tabernacle Church Board:

> I have instituted a mentorship program to encourage teens to pursue college or trade school. I established a youth sports program to instill values of sportsmanship, competition, and respect for one's body. Under my leadership the church has instituted youth activities specifically targeted to teenagers, including a day at the mall followed by a movie. I have instituted a Friday night service for our youth that is separate from the adult service. This service includes discussions regarding current hip-hop music (with some sampling), trends on high-school campuses, and of course teenage peer pressure and relationships.
>
> My goal is to minister to all aspects of adolescent development, including sexual development. Of course I teach abstinence. I want every young adult to know the church supports abstinence and they should not feel alone in this pursuit.
>
> I realize that I can preach until I'm blue in the face, and it will not prevent some of our youth from engaging in sexual activity. It is naive to think that because a youth is a member of Wacko Tabernacle, he or she will not face the same temptations or have the same questions as other adolescents.

I strongly believe that it is incumbent upon the church, in concurrence with parents, to give our youth guidance and reliable information regarding sexual development. This should not be misconstrued as an open-door policy of someone asking Reverend Wise, is it OK if I have sex with Jonny, and I give her my blessing. I make every effort to give youth the information they need to make their own decisions.

I warn adolescents about the repercussions they may encounter, emotionally and otherwise, if they engage in sexual activity. I educate them on setting boundaries regarding sexual behavior. I encourage them to demand respect from their sexual partner. I reaffirm to them that their bodies are precious and is not to be shared without serious consideration. I inform them that sex should be a form of intimacy between two responsible parties. I admonish them that if they choose to engage in sex, it should be by their own volition. I let them know that having sex does not make them more of a woman. I ask them if having sex is something they want or are they giving into peer pressure? I plead with them not to engage in sex to maintain a relationship. I emphasize that they should never let anyone coerce them into sexual relationships. I warn them that because a guy says he loves you, it does not mean it is true. What he says has to be backed by his actions. I help them understand that using contraceptives is not a license morally or otherwise to recklessly engage in sexual activity.

I teach them that the use of contraceptives only protects against pregnancy and STDs.

It doesn't mean they will find their sexual encounters spiritually rewarding, morally acceptable, or guarantee a healthy committed sexual relationship. These are issues that they have to deal with on a very personal, intimate level.

If they choose to use contraceptives, I teach them that it is imperative that they have the dignity, self-esteem, and confidence to use the utmost discretion in choosing who they will share their body with, when they will share their body, and where they will share their body.

It was clear to the Board of Wacko Tabernacle that Reverend Wise was not adhering to the word of God and did not understand the power of the Holy Ghost. He was immediately fired! The Board of Wacko rebuked Reverend Wise for exposing his liberal, psychological, man-made propaganda based on years of adolescent sexual-development research to their youth. He was encouraging promiscuity and abandoning their Christian call to be saved, sanctified, and filled with the Holy Ghost.

Teenage Superfreaks are the Solution, Not the Problem

Teenage superfreaks are teenagers who go to parties, get drunk, and then screw for sport and entertainment. Suzie attends a prominent creative arts school in NYC. The superfreaks at her school are extremely creative and talented. They use their creativity to discover new and exciting ways to screw. All imaginable types of screwing is acceptable. One on one, two on one, anal, oral, gay sex, and the use of an assortment of toys and accessories.

Being a member of the superfreak club has a lot of advantages. The main advantage is that screwing at a party is much more comfortable than screwing in the backseat of a car. Another advantage is that guys don't have to worry about buying a woman a Big Mac to get some pussy. They can sign up for the pussy lottery and hope that their name gets called. Karen, you will be screwing Bruce tonight. The best thing about teenage superfreaks is that it ensures the pipeline for teenage porn is alive and well. What I don't understand about teenage superfreaks is, why you would want to screw for the entertainment of others without getting paid?

I'm not sure how teenage superfreak parties started. I surmise a bunch of teenagers were at a party, got drunk, and someone said, "Hey, let's screw," and everybody thought it was a great idea. I also don't know how superfreaks do their recruiting. I suspect they look for others with superfreak tendencies. They also want people who can appreciate superfreak activity and accept it as mainstream adolescent sexual development.

Suzie is the pride of Bedlam Christian Center (BCC) in Brooklyn. She is the lead praise dancer. If there is a youth activity at BCC, she is involved front and center. But most of all, she wrote an article in *The Tabernacle Journal* about resisting the temptation of teenage peer pressure with the power of the Holy Ghost. Suzie truly loves and deserves the adulation that she receives from being a leader at BCC.

BCC like Wacko Tabernacle is a church grounded in the word of God and is guided by the power of the Holy Ghost. Suzie has not been corrupted with any form of sexual education, guidance regarding sexual behavior, or mentoring regarding her sexual desires. Suzie is committed to keeping her virginity until marriage and has been warned that women on birth control are a bunch of whores who will screw anybody, anytime and anywhere.

Armed with this knowledge, Suzie joins the superfreak club. Of course, Suzie is too naive to know that superfreaks are superfreaks. She is convinced that everybody who is not saved behaves like superfreaks. This is a serious insult to adolescents who use contraceptives and engage in sexual activity in private, in the context of an exclusive committed relationship.

At her first superfreak party, Suzie is front and center watching her newfound superfreak friends screw. Suzie is like a kid watching a cartoon. She is elated that watching her friends screw is so much fun. She is amused that women reaching a climax and women who get the Holy Ghost shake the same way. Suzie gets so excited that she starts to anoint herself and speak in tongues.

By the end of the night, Suzie is feeling great. She's thanking Jesus that her new friends are a bunch of superfreaks, who are going straight to hell. They have confirmed what she has been taught in church: women on birth control are a bunch of whores who will screw anybody, anytime and anywhere. Suzie rejoices that with the power of the Holy Ghost, she can resist any teenage peer pressure to actually engage in the screwing. She has discovered a unique opportunity to vicariously satisfy her sexual desires, keep her virginity, and remain saved, sanctified, and filled with the Holy Ghost.

Group Dynamics

Suzie doesn't understand the group dynamics of superfreaks. Her superfreak friends don't see her as saved, sanctified, and filled with the Holy Ghost. They see her as a superfreak with nobody to screw. The guys are hoping to screw Suzie in the next pussy lottery. She also does not understand that by attending these parties, she is giving her implied approval and consent to what is transpiring. She is fully considered one of them, by them. Only in Holy Roller Land is some tenuous distinction made.

If Suzie had been truthful with her superfreak friends (which is rare in Holy Roller Land) and told them "I love watching you immoral whores screw for sport and entertainment. I'm sanctified and would never consider letting guys screw me like they have been screwing you bitches. My body is a temple of God, and nobody gets my stuff until marriage," her sanctified ass would have been dumped immediately. This is why being deceptive in Holy Roller Land becomes an innate skill for survival. It's important to conform to the norms of whatever group one is deceiving at the moment.

Most of all, Suzie is clueless that drunkenness and sexual activity are the prime ingredients to acquaintance or gang rape. A major component of superfreak screwing is the excitement of searching for the next great screw. Once the routine voluntary screwing is over, the search for new involuntary screwing begins. At that point a bunch of drunk and horny superfreaks are not going to be receptive to Suzie's claim of being saved, sanctified, and filled with the Holy Ghost. They will only see Suzie as an untapped pussy. The perpetrator(s) will feel empowered by the group and will equate Suzie's presence as tacit consent. Suzie has no clue that perpetrators of acquaintance rape or gang rape are rarely convicted. Fortunately, Suzie is empowered with the Holy Ghost and has the assurance that she will be delivered from dangers seen and unseen.

A producer of teenage porn will ascertain the ages of the participants and have them sign a legal consent form. This is evidence that all participants are not acting under duress and are competent to make legal decisions regarding their actions. The participants are getting paid and are acting in their own self-interest. This I respect.

In contrast, I find superfreak parties despicable because none of the above assurances are present. First, these parties are notorious for excessive alcohol consumption. Thus, it is reasonable to believe that at least some of those doing the screwing do so because they are drunk and not of sound mind.

Second, there is a tremendous amount of peer pressure to screw. This is akin to screwing under duress. Most superfreaks plan on screwing as soon as they walk through the door. They are eager to get on the top of the screwing list. The question is how many women feel pressured to screw because their boyfriends or "dates" want to show that they can screw better than their comrades? Likewise, how many men are screwing to attract new whores? How many women do the screwing because they can't afford a hotel and confuse a sideshow with true intimacy? How many women start off enjoying the screw but soon realize that the guy screwing them is not concerned with pleasing them but is trying to excite the crowd and win bragging rights for giving the best screw of the night?

Finally, there is no assurance that the women doing the screwing are mature enough to fully comprehend what they are doing. At superfreak parties no one is checking IDs. It is difficult to determine at what age superfreaks start screwing for sport and entertainment. In general, the reason why these women are screwing for the entertainment of others is questionable. Maybe some have self-esteem issues. Others may be screwing out of peer pressure. Maybe some do it to please their boyfriends and keep their relationships. In my opinion superfreak parties have too many unanswered questions.

From Suzie's perspective these questions are totally irrelevant. She has absolutely no compassion regarding why her friends get drunk and screw for sport and entertainment. She contributes their actions to not having the Holy Ghost.

Susie's Next Step

Suzie is so enthralled on superfreak parties that she decides to host one. Suzie does not realize that superfreaks only like to party with other superfreaks. Suzie decides to invite her uptown friends to her superfreak party. Suzie did not realize that her uptown friends are not the superfreak type.

I once dated Suzie's mom, Sister Moore. Sister Moore is extremely active at BCC, being on several boards and part of the pastors' inner circle, which is a privilege second to none. She is proud that Suzie is equally involved at BCC and gave me a full report on Suzie's Christian experience. Based on Sister Moore's report, I agreed to let Suzie host a party, in my Harlem Brownstone, to celebrate her senior year.

I met with Suzie to go over the ground rules. My first question was, how many of her church friends will be attending? The answer was an astounding none! She wanted this to be what she described as "a real party." Here is where I became a victim of Holy Roller Land and kicked all logic to the curb. Here is where my first biblical reference applies:

...I had rather be a doorkeeper in the house of my God, than to dwell in the tents of wickedness. (Ps. 84:10)

Suzie would rather host a party with superfreaks than to host a party with a bunch of Holy Rollers! Suzie did not want any of the friends she worships with every Sunday, the friends she goes to retreats with, the friends who have invited her to numerous sleepovers, and the friends she dances to the glory of the Lord with at her party. She wanted a "real party" with her superfreak friends. I wonder how her "close church friends" would feel if they knew they were passed over for a bunch of teenage superfreaks.

This decision is indicative of Suzie's priorities and appreciation for her church relationships.

I am sure that Suzie would have invited her church friends, but the party was on Saturday night, and she did not want to infringe upon them getting to church on time Sunday morning. She also realized that her church friends may not have enough Holy Ghost power to resist the temptation of getting drunk and participating in the screwing with her superfreak friends. Clearly Suzie has no conflict with being a member of the superfreak club and a youth leader at BCC. She has been doing both for years. The good news is that Suzie is equally deceitful to both her church friends and superfreak friends.

I made it clear that there will be no drugs, no drunkenness, and no smoking inside and joked that nobody leaves pregnant. Suzie assured me that she won't invite anyone if she can't vouch for his or her behavior. She promised to shorten her guest list and invite only her closest friends.

Then Suzie asked if I would stay upstairs during her party. This is where I lost my mind in Holy Roller Land. As an adult, I should have recognized that a request like that is only made when you have something to hide. I let my image of a saved, sanctified praise dancer override my common sense. I asked, what exactly what do you do at these parties? Her response was eat, dance, play games, and do other stuff that's fun to watch. In my wildest imagination, I did not conceive that the other stuff was screwing for entertainment.

Suzie's Party

Suzie lacked the common sense to figure out engaging in clandestine activity is a bad idea when you have loud boisterous friends and someone upstairs who can hear play by play what's going on. This shortcoming is compounded by the fact that once she leaves Holy Roller Land, people know the game much better than she does.

On the night of Suzie's party, the first sign of trouble was when some knucklehead asked if he can get naked. The fact that this knucklehead became irate when the answer was no, is a clue that Suzie has been to parties where nudity was acceptable. It's like back in the day going to a party and asking for some weed. You know when to ask. At this point I suspected that Suzie was a member of the superfreak club, but I was giving her the benefit of a doubt, because of my report from Sister Moore.

Next, I hear bragging about how good the cream pie was (which Suzie neglected to clean off my leather chairs). Now, I am in complete denial. I'm thinking that Suzie has the Holy Ghost and what I think is happening, can't be happening.

It took me a minute to figure out how Suzie combined a party with her uptown friends and her superfreak friends. When the lights go off and the music is pumped up, her uptown friends dance. When the lights go on and the music stops, her superfreak friends screw. Both sides got pissed. Too much screwing for her uptown friends. Not enough screwing for her superfreaks.

I have a sixth sense when it comes to detecting screwing, but this is not evidence. Then I hear some brothers enthusiastically bragging at the top of their lungs about how good "that pussy was pounded." They were in awe with what they saw. This was clear and convincing evidence to me that sex was a major part of the entertainment. Guys don't brag about how good a pussy was pounded unless they saw a pussy get pounded. Their comments were so descriptive that I wasn't sure if I was pissed because of what was going on or, as a friend suggested, pissed because I wasn't invited down to watch. Now, I want to catch them in the act, thinking that was the only way Suzie would make a full confession.

The music comes back, the lights go off, and the last dance is announced. After the last dance, I hear people leave (her uptown friends). I'm thinking the party is over. It was past her curfew, and I gave Suzie a warning call. I had resolved that without a smoking gun, it would be fruitless to disclose that Suzie hosted a superfreak party. I did not realize that Suzie's superfreak friends would insist on ending her party with the last screw of the night. Clearly, they refused to be subordinated to her uptown friends. After all, screwing was the main purpose of the party. Dancing was an intrusion upon their time. It's only fair that a superfreak party end with the last screw of the night.

I went downstairs and caught Suzie front and center watching her superfreak friends screw. It was some poor screwing, but it was screwing. They were on the floor, and Suzie's girlfriend was getting it from behind, reverse cowgirl style. She was riding it hard, working to get her orgasm. Based on her moans and facial expressions, she was about midway through. Suzie and her superfreak friends were cheering them along, like cowboys at a rodeo.

The whore used her dress as a tent. Apparently, this confused Suzie because she described what I saw as inappropriate dancing. She couldn't figure out that underneath the dress her friends were screwing. They were engaging in no music, a dick-in-the-pussy dancing. After a few choice words, I declared her party is over. Suzie walks over and asks if she can have ten more minutes. I guess she felt bad because her friends didn't get a chance to climax.

I don't believe in the power of the Holy Ghost. But something kept me from slapping the Holy Ghost right out of her.

I'm sure her mom would have slapped the Holy Ghost out of her. Here I am standing there watching her superfreak friend put his penis back in his pants, while his whore pulls up her panties, and she asks for ten more minutes. Maybe the Holy Ghost is real. I managed to keep my composure and let her end her party with dignity.

I now have evidence beyond a reasonable doubt that these superfreaks have been screwing all night, as I suspected. With this knowledge, I hereby declare the pride of BCC, saved, sanctified and filled with the Holy Ghost, Suzie Moore, the undisputed queen of the superfreaks. She has introduced superfreak screwing to a whole new audience. Monday morning the whole school will know that if you need a place to screw, contact Suzie.

For there is nothing hid, which shall not be manifested; neither was any thing kept secret, but that it should come abroad. (Mark 4:22)

Most of Suzie's uptown girlfriends found the sex shows degrading to women. One ssister, who was about to whip some superfreak ass, made it quite clear that she came to party, not to watch live porn. Suzie's uptown girlfriends are also very active in church. Like Suzie they love to party, but they never party with their own church members. Some are sexually active, but only with their boyfriends in the privacy of a large closet. They had no clue Suzie was a superfreak. Thus, they got on the Holy Roller Hotline. According to Sister Moore, question's regarding Suzie's party got back to her.

The uptown guys who attended Suzie's party were pleasantly surprised. They took out their videophones and taped the good stuff. They scored each screw accordingly to style, duration, and technique. By a unanimous decision, the golden screw award went to the pounded pussy. Most of all, Suzie went straight to the top of their easy-pussy list. They were absolutely convinced that Suzie had to do some screwing for entertainment at some party, somewhere. Only men in Holy Roller Land understand that while Suzie hosted a superfreak party, she has the Holy Ghost and only watches.

Raymond who had a thing for Suzie had to cut her loose. He just found out that Suzie is a superfreak in front of his boys.

Thou shall not bear false witness against thy neighbor. (Exod. 20:16)

Suzie denies that there was any screwing at her party, which implies that I am lying. I challenged Sister Moore to ask her daughter to explain why I would give her permission to host a party and then make up a bunch of vicious lies about what I witnessed in my own home. Suzie claims to be led by the Holy Ghost, but she is lying. Ask the Holy Ghost to lead you to the truth. This always works in Tyler Perry's movies.

With the power of the Holy Ghost, Suzie makes a big-time confession. "Mommy, my friends are a bunch of whores on birth control who will screw anybody, anytime and anywhere. I'm sure they screwed at my party, but I didn't see it. Mommy, if I had caught my friends screwing, I would have rebuked them in the name of Jesus." It's a shame that Suzie missed all that screwing at her own party. Especially since her party was in an open space.

Here is my assessment of the power of the Holy Ghost. The Holy Ghost lifted Suzie up as a youth leader at Bedlam Christian Center. Then, the Holy Ghost leads her to a bunch of superfreaks so she can satisfy her lust without losing her virginity. Then, the

Holy Ghost blesses her with a party to celebrate her senior year. At her party the Holy Ghost gets pissed because she went overboard with the screwing. So the Holy Ghost exposes that Suzie is a member of the superfreak club. Come Sunday morning, the Holy Ghost is with Suzie as she dances unto the Lord. Suzie, who is saved, sanctified, and Queen of the Superfreaks, makes a deal with the Holy Ghost. I'll keep dancing for the Lord as long as I can lie about being a superfreak. The Holy Ghost is in a dilemma. Sister Moore is praying that Suzie shows her some respect by telling her the truth. Suzie is praying that her mom continues to believe her lies. Every Sunday they both go to church and shout about the power of the Holy Ghost. The Holy Ghost realizes he will never get Suzie to tell the truth, she's in denial and needs Doctor Phil. So the Holy Ghost keeps Suzie as a praise dancer and tells Sister Moore that she's on her own. As a consolation prize, Sister Moore gets to chair a new church committee, and no one at BCC finds out that her daughter is Queen of the Superfreaks.

The Aftermath Is Worse Than the Offense

I have not spoken directly to Suzie about what transpired at her party. Her mom tells me she doesn't understand why I am so piqued about her friends screwing in my home. I'm sure that by her standards, the amount and variety of screwing I witnessed was insignificant. After all, she prohibited complete nudity, and if it wasn't for the dancing, there would have been twice as much screwing.

Sister Moore views this incident as typical teenage poor judgment and something to be put to rest. There is no doubt that teenagers use poor judgment. To me poor judgment was putting the booze bottles in my backyard, not cleaning the cream pie off my leather chairs, and not realizing that I'm upstairs and can hear damn near everything that's going on.

I think it's pathetic that Suzie goes to church every Sunday, is a lead praise dancer, writes an article about teenage peer pressure, has the power of the Holy Ghost, but could not discern that hosting a superfreak party in someone else's home is inappropriate and disrespectful. Maybe BCC should give Sister Moore a rebate on her tithes. Maybe if Sister Moore spent less time in church and more quality time with her daughter, discussing who her friends are and nurturing her, this episode could have been prevented.

I offered to meet with Sister Moore and Suzie several times to discuss what had transpired and make peace. My requests were denied because it interfered with Sister Moore's church obligations. I erroneously assumed that my allegations were serious enough to warrant a day off from church. I know for sure that my mom would have made such a confrontation a top priority. I contend that if Suzie had to confront me face to face, I would have challenged her insidious excuses, and we would have come to a resolution. I strongly suspect that Suzie expected me to tolerate her behavior since I renounced Christianity and don't go to church. Using Holy Roller logic, if I drink, smoke cigars, and am not saved, why should I care about a superfreak party? I resent the perception that humanist have no morals. We do, but our morals are not based on God or the Bible. They are based on reason, logic, and the impact any action has on other human beings, irrespective of their faith or nonbelief. My concern is not that Suzie is a member of the superfreak club. My concern is that she cannot admit that she is a member of the superfreak club and has created a web of lies to hide this. Common sense and healthcare professionals dictate this is not a healthy place to be.

It is easy for me to imagine Suzie hearing a sermon about kids who go to secular parties, not to mention hosting a super-freak party, don't know Jesus, and are going straight to hell. I can empathize with Suzie trying to reconcile her fear of going to hell, the betrayal of her alleged religious beliefs, and her self-esteem with what she knows is the truth regarding her behavior. Religious conflicts are often the foundation of denial. Suzie displays several characteristics of being in denial. She has created falsehoods to redeem her behavior, regardless of the evidence. This is a self-defense mechanism for the immature mind when individuals cannot cope with and accept responsibility for their own actions. Denial diminishes the impact of her behavior to alleviate guilt and impedes her sense of remorse. Most of all, denial is hindering Suzie from having the candid conversations that she needs to fully learn and grow from this experience. Suzie has plenty of people who love her and want her to share with them how she got involved with superfreaks. This is an opportunity for Suzie to experience true intimacy and bonding with those who love her.

If Suzie truly accepts superfreak behavior and wants to continue that activity, she should be mature enough to admit it. Her family and friends will still accept her and love her. However, because of denial these conversations will not happen.

I admonish people in Holy Roller Land and those associated with people in Holy Roller Land to be vigilant. I was completely blinded by the apparent innocence of Suzie. Unfortunately, Suzie is not an anomaly in Holy Roller Land. She is the norm. Holy Roller Land is inundated with adolescents yearning for guidance. I think it's incomprehensible that parents abdicate their responsibility to raise their children to church and the Holy Ghost. I have witnessed the outrage of many women raised in Holy Roller Land.

I have heard their testimonies of how what is taught (or not taught) in Holy Roller Land leads to unplanned pregnancies, promiscuity, prostitution, drug use, and abusive relationships. Several women raised in Holy Roller Land have confided in me how being raised in Holy Roller Land seriously impaired their sex lives, even after they were married. Sex therapists affirm their comments. From this perspective it is easy for me to forgive Suzie's actions, and I do. My forgiveness of Suzie does not preclude me from criticizing the institutions and beliefs that contributed to her unacceptable behavior. It is my sincere desire that Suzie gets the counseling she needs to learn and grow from this unfortunate incident.

I intend to tell more stories about life in Holy Roller Land. I am extremely proud of how Briana, my stepdaughter, recovered from what I consider completely unnecessary hurt and obstacles. Her story proves that being raised in Holy Roller Land can be perilous. Her story also proves that with proper support and a strong desire to move forward, the wounds of being raised in Holy Roller Land can be healed.

I have been adversely impacted by Holy Roller Land, which motivates me to warn others. I have a Holy Roller story for almost every aspect of life.

CHAPTER 15

— ⚜ —

Sister Moore Gets Married

Relationships in Holy Roller Land

RELATIONSHIPS IN HOLY Roller Land are bizarre and the ultimate test of understanding Holy Roller logic. Before I divulge my relationship with Sister Moore, a general background on relationships in Holy Roller Land is warranted. The following are true stories of relationships in Holy Roller Land.

The first dilemma for many women in Holy Roller Land is that they strongly resist dating men in Holy Roller Land. I will use my personal experience to demonstrate this phenomenon. I have dated several Holy Roller women before entering Holy Roller recovery and signing a pledge to refrain from any contact with Holy Roller women.

Women in Holy Roller Land constantly complain that too many Holy Roller men are gay, effeminate, or suspected of being on the down-low. It is common to see these men shake their ass more than women as they do the Holy Ghost two step. I'm sure that gay men find this exciting. Straight women find this to be amusing. However, they don't look at these men as someone who can give it to them hard.

The truth is that most women in Holy Roller Land prefer to screw bad boys. They become prime targets for worldly men looking for good sex. These men know women in church are emotionally on the edge and sexually frustrated. Some straight men are willing to play the Holy Roller game if they think the pussy is worth it. I know one brother who viewed Sunday service as a stage performance. Every now and then, he would pretend to catch the Holy Ghost just for the fun of it. After service he would take his woman home, give her some weed, and get busy.

When I see a woman get the Holy Ghost, I observe how well she shakes her ass and the flow of her titties. If she is having an orgasm with the Holy Ghost, I know her pussy is burning up. If she is shouting in church, I know she will shout once she gets some good dick. The problem is her pulpit pimp wants to control all the pussy in his church. Pulpit pimps don't want outsiders screwing their women. They only want the Holy Ghost screwing their women. Occasionally, they screw their women for quality-control purposes. Don't take my word for it. Check out this sample reading list:

> *Warning to Ministers, Their Wives, and Mistresses. Avoid the Road to Destruction*—This book was written by Betty Price, the wife of Apostle Fredrick K. Price. It is admirable that Dr. Price wrote this book. The fact that she took the time and energy to write a book to address ministers who screw members in their church speaks for itself.

> *Pimps in the Pulpit*—Written by Shannon Bellamy, this is another book that warns women about the prowess of pulpit pimps. She was being counseled by her married pastor and ended up being his lover.

Jamel Bryant presents the pimp's view on how cheating on his wife and getting a divorce is the work of the Holy Ghost. In his interview with Roland Martin, he explains how breaking every principle he once taught regarding fidelity made him a better preacher.

I listened to one of his lectures on relationships where he warned that women should wait for the man God sends them so that they can avoid infidelity. I would think that his ex-wife believed he was the man that God sent her. After all he is a preacher.

Reverend Bryant adroitly presented the standard Holy Roller bullshit defense to redeem himself. When the preacher gets an outside piece, it's the work of God preparing him for greater things. When someone else gets an outside piece, it's because he or she doesn't know Jesus and have the Holy Ghost. Any reasonable person should be able to come to the conclusion that some people cheat and some don't. Being called reverend, bishop, apostle, or any other Holy Roller title has nothing to do with someone being righteous. The assertion that these men are anointed by God with the power of the Holy Ghost is absurd, approaching insanity. There is no proof whatsoever that Holy Ghost power exists. There is plenty of proof that these men are delusional. There is an abundance of proof that these men are a bunch of charlatans who can convince thousands of people they are anointed. To those who claim that their pastor has never been caught in a sexual scandal and is truly anointed by God, I say that there are good people who have never stepped foot in a church and who are faithful. There is no correlation between being faithful and being a Christian. People are people. I have never seen any evidence that Christians who have the Holy Ghost can escape the flaws of humanity. Maybe if an apostle goes to a strip club and sits through a lap dance without getting an erection, I will believe it's the power of the Holy Ghost. Then again, he might be on the down-low.

Steve Harvey outraged a lot of humanists when he proclaimed a woman in church should run from a nonbeliever. He argued a man who does not believe in God is not capable of being a leader in the home. I listened to an interview of Steve Harvey's ex-wife. She did not sound like a woman who was getting good counsel from her Christian husband.

I agree with Steve Harvey's conclusion that men who do not believe in the Holy Ghost should stay away from Holy Roller women but for totally different reasons given by Steve Harvey. The first problem an intelligent man is going to have with a Holy Roller woman is she will rarely receive advice offered from any man who does not have the title of bishop, apostle, or elder. Holy Roller women refuse to accept advice that is based on sociology, psychology, common sense, or logic. They rely on advice from their anointed pimp. Men who are anointed by the Holy Ghost and refuse to bring worldly knowledge to the situation.

Not all Holy Roller women are equally damaged. I have been exposed to a broad spectrum of Holy Roller women. One thing they have in common is their ability to be deceptive. Holy Roller Land cultivates deception. Every Holy Roller woman I have talked with confessed they say amen to things they don't believe on Sunday morning. While I don't expect people to agree with everything they hear from the pulpit, I would expect them to believe in the basic teachings of their church regarding their lifestyle. From my experience, most people who attend Holy Roller churches do not believe in the premises of "living a righteous life." There are a very few who find this lifestyle acceptable, and the rest simply live a double life. I have yet to receive a cogent argument on why people choose to live this way, but I am still searching.

To partake in what reasonable people consider a good life, is clandestine activity in Holy Roller Land. Having married a Holy Roller, I have firsthand experience with how Holy Rollers live double lives. First, my ex-wife would not dance because it went against her spiritual life. Yet she would go to a club with me and watch. She would wear dresses with a cut in the back two inches from her crack and a split up the middle inches from showing the panties. She would never wear this dress around her church folk. The women I partied with would never wear such a provocative dress.

I took my then wife to dinner at an exquisite restaurant, and we had a glass of wine together. She relaxed, and we had a great time. When we got home, she felt guilty. She was so conditioned that enjoying worldly pleasure was a sin, that what I thought was a great night became a spiritual conflict with the teachings of her church. I took her to a Patti Labelle concert, and she was almost excommunicated from church. Needless to say my marriage was a terrible experience and didn't last long.

Every Holy Roller church I know has an underground social network. This network is a select group that lives life just like everybody else but pretend that they are living a righteous life come Sunday morning. These are people who enjoy sex out of marriage, go to Atlantic City, party at clubs, and enjoy a glass of wine at dinner. They have no conflict about going to church and getting their praise on and living a good life, in spite of the crap they hear coming from the pulpit. These are the fortunate ones since they somehow are immune from the nonsense they hear on Sunday morning.

After my divorce I vowed to never attend a Holy Roller church again. I have basically kept this promise. When I met Sister Moore, I knew that she was a Holy Roller, but she seemed to have a minimal amount of Holy Roller brain damage. She liked to dance, was sexually active, enjoyed a glass of wine with dinner, and went to clubs. I made it clear that I don't attend church, and this was not a deal breaker for her. She had never dated a man in church and admitted that she has always been attracted to bad boys.

We had what I considered a good relationship for about four years. Our relationship was grounded on the Chris Rock principle, we loved to eat together and we loved to screw each other. In between we went to museums, concerts, family events, school events, nice restaurants and hosted a number of family holiday dinners. Occasionally we would indulge in a weekend getaway. I guess the downfall was that I would not attend any of her church functions, which were frequent.

After dating Sister Moore for about two and a half years, she moved into a vacant apartment I had available. She was in a bind, so I let her and her daughter move upstairs. For all practical purposes, Sister Moore slept with me, and her daughter used the upstairs apartment as her bedroom. We had meals together as a family. In my mind, we were a family. I do not make a distinction between living together and being married other than the legal ramifications. Since we lived under the same roof, we were a family. This is where I made a fatal flaw. A family in substance is still living in sin.

I took seriously trying to be a positive male role model for Suzie. I have a former stepdaughter and was somewhat experienced in the role of being a male presence in someone else's child. I only use the term "former stepdaughter" because I divorced her mom. We still retain a stepdaughter-stepfather type of relationship. I would have typical adolescent-type conversations with Suzie. Suzie had stated that her mom had never had a discussion with her regarding sexual development. My response was that's impossible. I later talked to Sister Moore and had to apologize to Suzie. Since I was not a blood relative, I could not have any meaningful conversation with Suzie regarding her sexual development. Thus, I arranged a special dinner with her mom to discuss issues I urgently felt she needs to address with her daughter. I wrote them down and explained why I thought it was important they talk about these issues, based on my past experience and research I did on the Internet. Sister Moore agreed to discuss these issues with Suzie.

I submit that if I was a prophet at a Holy Roller service and proclaimed that the Holy Ghost told me "You need to talk to Suzie about her sexual development," Sister Moore would have urgently spoken with Suzie regarding the issues we discussed. But, since I have no religious title and in fact don't go to church, my advice was of no significance. My advice was based on conversations I had with Suzie, my knowledge of adolescent psychology, and what I learned from being a stepdad. This is where Steve Harvey's stupid comments apply. You don't need the Holy Ghost to give sound advice. Sister Moore had time for all of her church commitments but never found time to speak with Suzie until after her party.

Sister Moore is on the Usher Board, Trustee Board, Retreat Committee, and Special Event Committee at Bedlam Christian Center (BCC) in Brooklyn. When she was asked to join the Deaconess Board, she was required to give a full report to her pastor regarding where she lives and who she's screwing. Thus, I was immediately cut off, no questions asked, no discussion needed.

I will admit that I never anticipated being dumped for the Deaconess Board. Sister Moore actually complimented me for my emotional support, for my financial support, and on how she appreciated the new things that I exposed her to. An acquaintance of mine, who once lived in Holy Roller Land, advised me that Sister Moore's perceived spiritual needs outweighed everything I brought to our relationship that I deemed as important. This is why she is dominated by her pastor and her church. I entered this information into my Holy Ghost Logic database for further research. Maybe if I had a girlfriend while Sister Moore was spending so much time in church, I would have responded better to her dumping me for the Deaconess Board.

My first inclination was to not disclose what had transpired at Suzie's party. I soon realized that would be irresponsible and her mom had the right to know what had happened. I expected Suzie would fully confess to her transgressions and we could all move forward from this experience. My first approach was to ask Sister Moore to have her daughter explain what they were doing when the music was off. I told Sister Moore sex was a part of the entertainment. Suzie denied everything regarding sexual activity at her party. At this point, I asked Sister Moore and Suzie to move in as soon as possible. At that moment my concern was Suzie would make up false accusations against me, especially if I pursued with my accusations. I no longer saw Suzie as an innocent praise dancer and unofficial stepdaughter. I now saw her as a horny, confused teenager who will do anything to protect her image of righteousness. To protect myself I made a full disclosure to a family member and investigated taking a polygraph examination. I also secured legal counsel to determine what legal ramifications regarding the sexual activity could be held against me.

I had four years invested in a relationship with Sister Moore. I decided that it was worth fighting to keep our relationship together if possible or civil under any circumstances. I called Sister Moore six times on a Saturday night and asked her to skip church so that we can spend a day together and try to work things out. I was convinced that her daughter only looked at superfreak parties as fun and games and was oblivious to the inherent dangers of such activity. I was devastated when my request for her to miss one day of church was denied. I had truly underestimated the influence a pulpit pimp has over his members. The contrast is also true. I overestimated the importance I thought I had in Sister Moore's life. This was the beginning of a journey that would change my views of life forever.

I was relieved when Sister Moore moved out. I resented that she did not see her daughter apologizing to me as a priority. Sister Moore's moving out put us both in somewhat of a dilemma. Sister Moore wanted to remain lovers, at least for a season. Given her position in church, I was a safe way to satisfy her sexual desires. I was so hurt and angry that I refused her offer. After my anger subsided, I reconsidered, primarily because she never kept her last promise to me. We had a ritual that we termed Margarita night. Margarita nights were not about sex, they were about romance. They always included a romantic candlelight dinner, private dancing, lingerie, Margaritas, provocative conversation, and making love all night, in all positions. Before she moved out, she promised me one last Margarita night so that we can end our relationship on a positive note. This was important to me. I wanted to share with her what I had learned from our four years together. I had questions that I wanted answered. I wanted her to speak her mind about what was good and what was bad. In my mind, my last Margarita night was to be a night to celebrate what I considered to be a good four-year relationship. If there was any chance of a reconciliation, it would have surfaced then. I could not entertain reconciliation while I was angry.

I approached Sister Moore about us having our last Margarita night. She claimed to be on board. In reality, I think she enjoyed the attention of my sexual desires but had little intention of fulfilling them. Sister Moore moved out in early April. At the end of May, I asked if she was still interested in having our last Margarita night. She assured me she was and asked that I be patient. In June, I invited her over, and she refused because of a foot injury, of which she sent me a picture to confirm. In July she brought me a box of cigars for my birthday and was surprised when I did not ask for my last Margarita night. I was thinking our last Margarita night is imminent. Then none of my e-mails were being answered, and none of my phone calls were being returned. I decided to call and e-mail for a week straight until I got a response as to why I was cut off cold. I received the following e-mail response from her daughter who had hacked her mom's e-mail:

From: Deacon Henry
To: Sister Moore
Sent: Thursday, August 15, 2013 9:47 PM
Subject: Good Morning

I am disappointed but not surprised

- that you decided to cut me off cold;
- my questions were not answered;
- that I never received my promise of our last Margarita night; and
- that I am being treated like an abusive ex-lover.

When life goes sour, your best recourse is to make lemonade. I have learned a lot about my weaknesses and Holy Roller Land. I have addressed both. If you should choose to address any of the above, feel free.

Deacon, you shouldn't be disappointed nor surprised anymore, because my mom is already happily married to the man of her dreams a couple of months ago and she has moved on with her life, and I suggest you should do the same and stop abusing her. You deserve to be cut off cold a very long time by my mom for the things you accuse me, Suzie, of. What you say about me and our pastor, Apostle Bandit, is not true. I am innocent to your accusations, and now I am going to let Apostle Bandit know that you are accusing him of being a pimp. If you're man enough about what you're accusing me of, my mom, her husband, and I attend church every Sunday—and I know you're well aware of the church address: 666 Satan Avenue, Brooklyn (BCC)—from 10:30 a.m. to 2:30 p.m., and I am willing to testify in front of my apostle against you (liar). I know my mom is going to be upset, but I don't care because I know she already told you she's married. She told me what you said about me, and I am mad.

I must admit that e-mails like this make me think that maybe there is a Holy Ghost. Receiving an e-mail like this is the answer to an unselected prayer. I could not have asked for a better reason to confront the almighty Apostle Bandit. I was piqued that a seventeen-year-old superfreak would talk to me like I'm her bitch. Moreover, this e-mail confirms how much Suzie is in denial and needs professional help. I feel blessed that she did not speak this way to me in person. I would have been locked up for whipping her ass. I did not take Suzie's claim of her mom being married seriously. Before she cut me off, I had every indication that my last Margarita night was on its way. I responded to Suzie's treat by showing up at church with a package for her pastor. Again, maybe it's the work of the Holy Ghost, but Suzie and her Mom were not there. Here is the body of the letter I left with the almighty Apostle Bandit:

Dear Apostle Bandit:

First, let me commend you for your ability to dominate the members of your church. I can personally attest to the commitment and dedication of one of your members, Sister Moore. Ms. Moore and I dated for about four years.

At Ms. Moore's request, I rented an apartment to her and her daughter for about a year and a half. For all practical purposes, her daughter had her own room upstairs, and Ms. Moore slept downstairs with me.

I have witnessed Ms. Moore wake up at 2:00 a.m. to make sure that your reports were completed on time. Often, Ms. Moore would come home from church exhausted, and I had to wake her up so that she can keep her commitment to call you. Regardless of her school commitments, health, lack of rest, or personal commitments, I have never witnessed Ms. Moore missing a day of church, without prior clearance from you or some other church official. However, I have witnessed Ms. Moore alter personal plans to accommodate her church obligations. Sometimes at a moment's notice.

Our relationship ended abruptly when Ms. Moore decided to pursue a deaconess position at Bedlam Christian Center (BCC). You can be proud that Ms. Moore immediately stopped sleeping with me and became exclusively a tenant. Prior to our breaking up, I promised her daughter a party to celebrate her senior year of high school. Unlike Ms. Moore, keeping promises are important to me, and I kept my promise to her daughter. Enclosed is a satirical essay based on what transpired at this party. It is to be part of a book I'm writing. I am also trying to sell it as a magazine article for exposure. I owe Ms. Moore, her daughter, and BCC for providing me with a story that I could have never made up.

I know how important it is for you to monitor the personal lives of your congregants. This is understandable for the pastor of a church that proclaims "Continuing the Legacy of Righteousness."

I considered my allegations serious enough to merit missing one day from church so that Ms. Moore, her daughter, and I could discuss what transpired. This was the only time in four years that I asked Ms. Moore to miss a day from church. Of course this request was denied. Again, this is a testament to Ms. Moore's commitment to you and BCC. Nobody can control a woman better than preachers and pimps.

I know that reason and logic are not a part of the Holy Roller mindset, but maybe if you use a little of the above and call upon the power of the Holy Ghost, which to date has been useless, you will see that my allegations are true. Based on the attached e-mail, I am sure that as their revered and esteemed apostle, they will be truthful with you. You can take pride that Ms. Moore moved out in a timely manner upon my request.

Since I don't live in Holy Roller Land, I can unabashedly say that since neither Ms. Moore nor her daughter felt that a personal apology to me was a priority at best or warranted at worst (mainly since her daughter feels that her behavior was no big deal and that I am lying) and I feel that Ms. Moore has completely disrespected me as the "other man" with you clearly being her first priority, exposing the truth provides me with a sense of justice, vindictiveness, and closure. Moreover, my actions are a result of my principles (another concept foreign to Holy Roller Land). My parents taught me to never allow anyone to disrespect you or your home. To have someone disrespect my home and then imply I am lying about what transpired in my home, after I granted her permission to use my home, is appalling. In addition, to endure several broken promises and be denied of any closure exacerbates the situation. These actions have no statute of limitations.

I am not sure how you, as a pulpit pimp, will handle a situation like this. I surmise that your first priority is not to lose a tithing member. Maybe Ms. Moore will have to sit in the back of the church for a month. Maybe you will engage in some Holy Roller chicanery and use the "I see a spirit of deceit or lust" routine, anoint her with oil, and then speak in tongues. I have seen this performed before, and it is very dramatic when executed properly. Maybe you will ignore this, which seems to be a standard practice in Holy Roller Land. I have not had any meaningful conversations with Ms. Moore for several months. Maybe Ms. Moore already gave Jimmy Swaggart's "Lord I have sinned" speech.

I would hope that you convey to your congregants that if they had the decency to talk with me and if Ms. Moore had kept her last promise, this letter would not have been written, and they could have maintained their facade of righteousness, without any interference. You may want to advise them that men who don't live in Holy Roller Land get a real attitude when you call them liars, disrespect them, and don't keep what they consider reasonable promises. Moreover, to accuse me of not being man enough to speak with you directly (see e-mail) is truly an insult coming from a seventeen-year-old who hacks her mom's e-mail. I received a hacked e-mail earlier, which contained language I don't use, and I don't have the Holy Ghost.

I will concede that part of their deception may be an issue of culture as well as living in Holy Roller Land. I am an African American, and once we get busted, we make a full truthful confession, often with boldness and attitude. To be blunt, telling incredulous lies once you get busted is typical White boy bullshit, which is the crowd that caused the problem in the first place. I feel that the anger is vented at me since I am the one who made the bust and disclosed the truth.

Finally, I know that in Holy Roller Land, all things work for good for those who love the Lord and are called according to his purpose. I'm sure, based on the example of Bishop Eddie Long, that after a couple of testimonies and sermons on repentance and redemption, Ms. Moore will be exalted as a Christian who was attacked by the devil (me) but delivered by the power of the Holy Ghost, which to me, to borrow your phase, is merely a "Spiritual Orgasm." I am sure that Ms. Moore and her daughter will continue to be a part of "Continuing the Legacy of Righteousness" at BCC.

I trust you have the integrity to read the enclosed article carefully and pay close attention to the end. I concede it is very sarcastic and uses blunt language; however, it contains some serious points, which I researched and footnoted. For the record, I have offered to take a lie-detector examination to confirm that I am telling the truth, if I get reimbursed should I pass. The cost is about $600. I also consulted an attorney regarding any legal ramifications that could be charged against me.

Exposing the truth is very cathartic.

Christopher Henry II, CPA

I was not sure what the reaction to my correspondence would be. I found out later that one of Sister Moore's friends who came by while we were living together recognized me and informed her that I visited her apostle. Remember that deception is an integral part of Holy Roller life. I had given Apostle Bandit my contact information, but he never responded. My charges regarding Suzie's party are in my view serious. I expected Apostle Bandit to take some action, including taking action against me for defamation of character if he believed I was lying.

Eventually, Sister Moore called. She did not mention anything about being married or that Apostle Bandit had talked to her. In the past when Sister Moore would call, I would ask for my last Margarita night. But not this time. The conversation was curt. This reinforced my belief that Suzie's claim of her mom getting married was a bluff. This belief was substantiated when I received an e-mail from her mom stating that it was refreshing to hear my voice and she questioned why I did not acknowledge her birthday. I took this opportunity to congratulate her on getting married and that I did not think it was proper for me to call a married woman on her birthday. I was being sarcastic. Likewise, I thought she was being sarcastic when she thanked me for congratulating her on her new marriage and explaining why I did not acknowledge her birthday. Once again I found myself in Holy Roller denial. To me it was inconceivable that Sister Moore, a dedicated church woman, would get married and continue to talk to me about having our last Margarita night. I was not convinced that Sister Moore got married. Finally, I had my last conversation with Sister Moore. She asked me about what was in the package I gave to her apostle. I told her that I responded to an e-mail that Suzie sent me. Suzie claimed you got married and assumed you told me. I asked Sister Moore point-blank, are you married? She confessed that she got married a couple of months ago. I asked her why she did not tell me. Her response was she wanted to tell me in person, but I never gave her a chance because I was too busy degrading her. I told her that I never want to hear her voice again. Now that you have a new husband, there is no reason for you to hear my voice. I have not spoken to Sister Moore since. I did send her several e-mails to collect the $5,000 she owed me.

Sister Moore showed no concern with how her actions impacted me. She was extremely concerned regarding what I gave her apostle. In Holy Roller Land, pissing off your apostle is second only to blasphemy of the Holy Spirit. Thus, the only recourse I had against Sister Moore for playing me like a cheap secondhand bitch was to bring darkness into the light. So I sent her beloved apostle two more letters:

Dear Apostle Bandit:

I hope your daughter and son delivered the package I prepared for you as they promised. I want to apologize for reacting on information that I did not know was true.

First, I hope that you did indeed read my letter and my article. I stand by my claim that the events and issues are true. Ms. Moore's daughter did hold a party in my home. I stand by my claim that oral sex and sex in general was a planned part of the entertainment and that I caught her daughter watching her friends having sex as part of the entertainment. There was a degree of drunkenness that was totally unacceptable, and this is coming from someone who has a drinking lifestyle.

As a writer, I have the audacity to ask you for your comments regarding the structure of my article. I just found out today that you did not discuss what I sent to you with Ms. Moore. I think not responding to such serious allegations demonstrates your lack of integrity, leadership, and is somewhat irresponsible. I also found out today that indeed Ms. Moore did get married. Knowing this I owe you and her daughter a big apology. As a humanist, I try to be truthful and acknowledge my faults.

Ms. Moore's daughter was justified for making the accusations she made against me. She only made one misjudgment. Ms. Moore never mentioned that she had gotten married until today. This confession only came after some aggressive questioning on my part. I am truly sorry that I reached out to you based on what I considered a bluff and a challenge to my manhood.

I am thankful that Ms. Moore's daughter told me the truth. I am sure that as a pastor, you are sick of hearing this, but if I had known Ms. Moore was married, I would have moved on with my life as her daughter suggested. I will confess that I sent Ms. Moore e-mails that were totally inappropriate to send to a married woman. When I confronted Ms. Moore about her relationship status, her response was always that she was not ready to move on yet. She never said, "Deacon, I am involved with someone and I am committed to my new relationship." This, in my opinion, is a situation where the truth would have prevented a lot of unnecessary anger and hurt. I consider myself to be very intelligent and am trained in professional scrutiny. I am embarrassed that I was this deceived and can only say again I apologize for reaching out to you. To be truthful, I am perturbed that I was played like a cheap secondhand bitch.

Finally, I really hope that you read my entire article. I really think it covers some serious issues that the Black church needs to address. I use satire to take the edge off serious issues. I am willing to discuss the issues in my article any place, anytime, and anywhere.

September 27, 2013

Christopher Henry II, CPA

Dear Apostle Bandit:

Acknowledgment of receiving and reading my correspondence delivered on September 1, 2013, along with my correspondence delivered on September 23, 2013, would be greatly appreciated. I consider this to be a reasonable courtesy, considering it was a member of your congregation who requested that I grant her an opportunity for her to call me a liar in your presence. I have presented my side of the story and would appreciate confirmation that you have at least read my arguments, as presented in my article. I trust that you will be objective as you judge who is being truthful. I would like to respond to any parts of my story that you deem are unreasonable or raise doubts (not including the obvious satire) about my story being truthful. The article I submitted contains reasonable and easy-to-confirm questions, which I am sure will help guide you to the truth. For example, what is Ms. Moore's daughter's explanation on why she invited a bunch of White superfreaks to her party rather than her church friends? You can ask for a credible explanation of how she did not see any of her friends screwing yet concedes they screwed. Most of all, people don't just show up at a party and start screwing. Not even superfreaks. Her party was part of a protocol where screwing is part of the entertainment. She had to know this prior to inviting them.

Based on circumstantial evidence, I surmise that Ms. Moore married a brother in your church. This assumption is based on comments made by her daughter that "a brother in the church told her that he wants to marry her mom." This comment was made close to a year ago. I guess this is the same guy who Ms. Moore admitted she likes to flirt with upon being confronted by me.

It also explains why her marriage took place in such a timely manner. I am certain that avoiding fornication was a primary reason she got married so quick. I hope that marrying a brother in the church will enhance Ms. Moore's coveted goal of becoming a deaconess.

I am distraught as to why Ms. Moore never even alluded that she is seeing someone, not to mention that she got engaged and married. I never doubted that Ms. Moore would move on. She is a woman with great attributes. Thus, I made continuing inquiries about her relationship status. Some of my inquiries were very blunt.

Maybe it's because I'm not a Christian and I don't have the Holy Ghost, but I feel it was disrespectful not to share this information with me. Especially when you consider the nature of the conversations I was having with her. I can only assume that she enjoyed the fact that I was expressing my sexual desires toward her. But, to her credit, she never succumbed to my offers. In June she refused one of my offers because she had a foot injury. She e-mailed me a photo to prove that this was the only reason she was not coming over. If she got married in July, I would think that she was at least engaged or considering engagement in June.

I know that Holy Rollers love to give testimonies. I can imagine the amount of praises and testimonies that transpired at Ms. Moore's wedding. Yet, Ms. Moore never testified to me that the Holy Ghost had delivered her from my evil ass and revealed to her the man of her dreams. If you review the e-mail Ms. Moore's daughter hacked, you will notice a sense of pride that her mom was happily married to the man of her dreams and moved on. It seems to me that Ms. Moore should have been eager to tell me she has found the man of her dreams and that I should leave her the hell alone. I would have obliged. I have been told this in the past by other ex-lovers. Instead, all I heard was a bunch of bullshit that I can't stomach to repeat and that she is a long way from moving on. She missed an opportunity to share how the power of the Holy Ghost intervened and changed her heart. I suspect that Ms. Moore got married in July. This is ironic since she sent me a box of cigars for my birthday in the same month. She called to confirm that I received my gift without any mention of being engaged or married. In fact, after we talked, I was thinking my chances of my last Margarita night are getting better.

I appreciate Ms. Moore's daughter for helping me discover the truth, even though it was inadvert and without her mother's consent or knowledge. I find it quite amusing that her trying to piss me off was actually to my benefit. Without her e-mail I would not have questioned her mother when she called to say "I just want to hear your voice" about a week ago. I was even more bamboozled when she asked why I didn't acknowledge her birthday. I think it is poetic justice that Ms. Moore had no clue that her daughter had sent me an e-mail, telling me the truth. That's why it's important that deceitful people coordinate. The best thing that happened is her daughter opening the door for me to expose the truth to you. Her e-mail was truly a blessing to me.

If it was not for Ms. Moore's daughter's intervention, I would still be wondering what I did that caused her mother to cut me off cold, and I would still be trying to get my last Margarita night (review e-mail I sent to Sister Moore on August 15, 2013). It is refreshing to realize that I was merely a victim of deceitfulness. That being said, I still asked Ms. Moore to explain to me what I did that caused her to treat me like an abusive ex-lover. I never received a response. Henceforth, I deserve to be treated like an ex-lover who retaliates when he is disrespected and deceived. You should be pleased that I am firmly committed to never speaking to Ms. Moore again.

During our four-year relationship, I had several conversations with Ms. Moore regarding how to manage a sidepiece. Rule number one, never disrespect a sidepiece. Clearly, Ms. Moore had to know that not telling me she got married was disrespectful. Otherwise, I would presume she got married to save face with her church and was considering me as a potential sidepiece. It's like trading the sin of fornication for the sin of adultery. Of course this is preposterous, since I would never play second fiddle to a Holy Roller. Plus, *Adultery 101* dictates that such an arrangement would have to be discussed and preapproved prior to marriage. Only a complete moron would contemplate getting married without telling her ex-lover and then approach him for a sidepiece.

Al Sharpton often uses the phrase "Confession comes before repentance."

I am happy that Ms. Moore married a good Christian brother who has the Holy Ghost and is involved in church.

Since he is a good Christian brother, I am confident he will not be susceptible to the lies, deception, and disrespect I had to endure as a heathen.

I am sure Ms. Moore's new marriage is built on a foundation of truth and honesty and is ordained by the power of the Holy Ghost. I am confident that she has confided to her new husband that she deliberately did not tell the man whom she lived with, up to April 6 of this year, that she got married. As a marriage sanctioned by the Holy Ghost, I am sure these things are irrelevant. The germane issue is they are married and not living in sin.

I congratulate Ms. Moore's new husband for being blessed with the bride he has been praying for. Truly, this is a testament of how the power of the Holy Ghost answers prayer. Without the power of the Holy Ghost, I can attest that Ms. Moore would not have changed so many of her views so quickly. Somewhere between phone calls, she went from I'm not ready to move on, to I'm open, to I got married two months ago. I find this amazing. For people who do not recognize the power of the Holy Ghost, they attribute this type of change to frustration and peer pressure from her church.

I am hoping that Ms. Moore's daughter finds the maturity to confess to you the truth about what transpired at her party. However, this is very unlikely unless she gets professional guidance.

The good news is that I have my next episode of life in Holy Roller Land. This time featuring Sister Moore. As I mentioned, I have written an article based on this experience. Some find it hard to read, but fortunately others find it to be entertaining, humorous, and a truth that needs to be told. I could never make these types of stories up.

Again, as a professional clergyman, I would appreciate an acknowledgment that you have reviewed my material. In corporate America this is considered professional courtesy. As a pastor of a church that promotes "Continuing a Legacy of Righteous," I hope you appreciate that I am exposing the truth about two prominent leaders at BCC.

I trust that you will e-mail me at HenryII@xyz.com to acknowledge receipt and review of my material. All I expect is a quick line. Of course any comments or questions that you may have will be addressed.

Thank you for your time and consideration.

Christopher Henry II, CPA

I found sending these e-mails to Sister Moore's pulpit pimp to be very gratifying. Then I started to analyze the various lies that Sister Moore was telling me. Too many of her lies started to contradict each other. I had to dig a little deeper to get to the truth. To my dismay, I was again in Holy Roller denial. I could not accept that Sister Moore did not want to keep her promise and grant me my one last Margarita night. In my letter to her apostle, I presumed that Sister Moore would not screw a leader in the church without the benefit of marriage. I consulted with Briana, my primary Holy Roller expert. She confirmed that even by Holy Roller standards, her marriage was extremely quick. Then I realized that outside of Holy Roller Land, the first assumption that is made when someone gets married so quickly is pregnancy. I had put Sister Moore on a pedestal thinking that she got married to save face in church. The harsh reality was I did not want to face the fact that she had started to screw a brother in the church while she was still promising to screw me. When I pieced together all the evidence and the timeline, I came up with the following scenario.

Sister Moore screwed a brother from the church, but evidently it was not hard enough. Thus, she sent me some cigars for my birthday and offered a Margarita night not knowing she was pregnant. Once she found out she was pregnant, she got married as soon as possible so she would be married before she started to show. There is nothing worse than two leaders in a Holy Roller church screwing before marriage. This makes sense considering she described her getting married as, "It wasn't planned, it just happened." This explains why she never mentioned that she was engaged or dating. She was only screwing and got pregnant. I wonder if her daughter and apostle were smart enough to figure this out, or did they assume she got pregnant on her first night of marriage. When e-mailing Sister Moore about paying off my loan, I asked her if she was pregnant when she got married. She refused to answer, which is her way of saying, yes, but I will never admit this to you. If the answer was no, she would have proudly said so. By chance my theory was confirmed. A pregnant belly is hard to hide. A friend of mine who knew Sister Moore from when she lived with me had moved to Brooklyn. He saw her in Brooklyn from a distance and noticed she was pregnant. He called me and asked if I was the father. With great pleasure I told him I was not the father. Sister Moore did not see him, but he was sure it was her. I guess the Holy Ghost is obsessed with bringing darkness into the light.

I find some comfort in knowing the truth. It is important to note that knowing the truth is not the same as understanding the truth. When I reflect upon some of our conversations regarding her past and her relationship with church, she seems to find living a double life somewhat exciting. It's akin to living the life of a secret agent. It is hard for me to understand why anyone would choose to partake in an institution that promotes values that go against his or her own nature. I am convinced that Holy Roller

Land cultivates behavior that simply cannot be mentally healthy. I also wonder, who is the real Sister Moore? Who is the real Suzie? Maybe both of them are enamored with the adulation that comes with being a church leader. I am sure that they have a belief in God, but they clearly do not believe in God as preached at BCC. It is beyond me why they don't attend a church that is closer to their personal convictions. From what I do know about Sister Moore, it is hard to imagine her living a Holy Roller lifestyle on a fulltime basis. I hope that her husband is as deceptive as she is or that her apostle has delivered her from the worldly lifestyle I know she enjoys. Either way I don't begrudge her getting married to a brother in church. It makes sense considering the amount of time, money, and energy she commits to BCC.

My anger against Sister Moore is not that she got married. My anger is that she did not bury me properly before she got married. I was hoping that our four-year relationship would end with respect, dignity, and memories of a final Margarita night. I have been able to maintain friendships with love gone bad in the past and expected the same with Sister Moore. Instead everything that was good about our relationship has been eradicated by how our relationship ended.

I have finally learned to not let anyone's religious affiliation influence me regarding his or her potential behavior. I now concur with my friend who asserts that if you are involved with someone in Holy Roller Land, it is critical to immediately establish that you will not be subordinated to his or her pulpit pimp. My experience is that many women in Holy Roller churches have a strong need to be dominated. They will be dominated by either the man in their lives or their pulpit pimp. I have heard this from too many women who have broken away from Holy Roller Land for this claim not to have some merit. It is an arduous task to break the domination of a pulpit pimp.

When dating, I always hated getting stuck on friends. With Sister Moore I got stuck between giving her the freedom to adhere to her religious beliefs and not letting her beliefs infringe upon our relationship. I signed a pledge to never date a religious woman again. I am looking forward to being in a relationship where we can have breakfast on Sunday mornings and our schedules are not dictated by her church obligations. I want a relationship where I am respected as a man. I may not be an apostle, but I am responsible, educated, and experienced in life. Most of all, I look forward to a relationship where I won't have to compete with a pulpit pimp.

My experience with Sister Moore and Suzie have brought to my life a new meaning to the phrase "Anything in life can happen."

CHAPTER 16

—⚜—

Gay's in Holy Roller Land

BEFORE I ENGAGE in a discussion regarding gays in Holy Roller Land, I want to make some disclosures and general comments about gays in the Black community. First, I am not gay. I do not consider myself a gay activist by any standard. I have a few gay acquaintances and no openly gay friends. I support gay rights because I see gay rights as a constitutional issue. I believe that any biblical references to being gay as being sinful are totally irrelevant. I believe those who claim that they were born gay. Just from observations growing up, it's hard to believe some of my gay classmates chose to be gay. I also believe the testimonies I heard from gay men who say if it was a choice, they would have chosen to be straight. Especially, older gay men who had to live during the time when staying in the closet was the norm. I tend to believe that bisexuality is likely to be by choice, with the exception of gay men trying to maintain the facade of being straight. I think claims that gays choose to be gay because they hate God are beyond absurd. I have heard testimonies from gay Christians that the Lord made them gay. I have also heard testimonies that God is sovereign and that babies born with birth defects are part of God's plan. It seems to me that God would be better off making healthy gay babies, rather than straight babies who are born with severe birth defects.

I have a sensitivity toward gays because my mom thought I was gay. Frankly, I have been presumed gay on numerous occasions. This once angered me, primarily for the reasons given by those who eventually admitted to me that they thought I was gay. I soon found out that many of my colleagues were also presumed to be gay for the same reasons.

In the Black community, being gay is not necessarily an indictment to your sexual preference. It is an indictment as to characteristics you lack, regarding what is perceived as being "A Real Black Man." To put in very blunt terms, sometimes if you don't come across as a "real nigger," you are presumed to be gay. Whites who complimented me by saying "You are not like most Blacks" are expressing the same sentiment. They are essentially saying I don't come across as a "real nigger." However, they don't assume that because I am not a "real nigger," I am gay. To be candid many White women find intelligent, well-spoken Black men to be very appealing. But that's a different story.

Two primary reasons that my colleagues and I were presumed gay is that we talk too proper and dress too neat. I had conversations on this topic that bring a new meaning to the term "nigger logic." The Black community has two challenges. First, to remove the stigma that somehow being smart is being gay. The next is removing the derogatory connotations of being gay.

You don't have to be a gay advocate to realize that gay rights and the acceptance of the gay lifestyle is a major issue in the Black church, especially Holy Roller churches.

The reelection of George W. Bush is a prime example of Black Holy Rollers being successfully manipulated over the gay rights issue. The Bush campaign convinced enough Black churches that as Christians, they could not support a gay rights candidate, in this instance John Kerry. Consequently, Bush doubled his percentage of the Black vote, and this was the decisive demographic that gave him the victory. My guess is that too many Black Christians felt that if they didn't vote for Bush, their sons will become gay.

In my view, Black churches that use Christianity to suppress other groups are ignorant. Black Christians who put suppressing gays in the military over economic growth, civil rights, and unnecessary military action voted against what is in the best interest of Black America. The economic progress of Black America was severely damaged by the Bush recession. Yet, those who voted for Bush can say with pride that the repeal of don't ask, don't tell did not happen under the Bush administration. Black preachers held Bush up as a "man of God who is led by the Holy Spirit." For a reasonable person, this is proof that leadership, in government or anywhere else, has nothing to do with the Holy Spirit or any biblical agenda. Bush led this country into the worst recession since the Great Depression. The millions of people who lost their jobs and homes due to Bush policies can rejoice in the fact that gay soldiers who died while Bush was commander-in-chief were denied the honor and dignity of dying for their country as openly gay soldiers. I am willing to change my view if a Holy Roller can greet a cargo plane filled with caskets of soldiers killed in action, and pick out the ones who are gay. If they get it wrong, they should immediately be put in harm's way. Log cabin republicans should be ashamed of themselves. I am not a gay advocate. I am a Black secular humanist with enough intelligence to know that any man or woman, regardless of race or sexual orientation, deserves as a human being, to be buried with dignity if they died serving my county. I have no inclination to associate with any party, religion, or bigots who feel otherwise.

During the reelection of Barack Obama, there was a backlash from Black churches over Obama's policies for gay rights. It is amazing that Holy Rollers use the same Bible that justified slavery to deny the rights of gays.

T. D. Jakes said he would never hire someone who is openly gay. A Black man against equal opportunity can only happen in Holy Roller Land. Jakes says that homosexuality is brokenness, which implies to me implies that a powerful Christian minister who has the full force and power of the Holy Ghost should be able to fix this brokenness. News flash! T. D. Jake's gay son Jermaine Jakes gets busted masturbating during a gay-sex sting in a public park.

I have two questions for Bishop Jakes.

1. You became rich and famous preaching about the power of the Holy Ghost. How come you couldn't pray the gay away from your own son?
2. Don't you think your son would be better off in a healthy gay relationship, like maybe marriage, instead of jerking off in a public park?

Since you believe in living by the word, according to Scripture Leviticus 20:13, "If a man also lie with mankind, as he lieth with a women, both of them have committed an abomination: they shall surely be put to death; their blood shall be upon them." As a preacher committed to upholding the word of God, are you willing to pull the trigger on your own son? Do you have the same faith as Abraham?

Bishop Eddie Long called homosexuality "spiritual abortion." He then gets charged by four teenage males for sexual coercion. They claim Long wined them and dined them and then had inappropriate contact with them for spiritual healing. Bishop Long vowed to fight these allegations. He's a man of God. He has the truth and the power of the Holy Ghost on his side. He will win this battle like David defeated Goliath. He then settled out of court for an alleged $15 million so he can focus on his ministry. But first, he took some time off while his wife filed for a divorce.

To make his grand entrance back to the pulpit, Bishop Long staged an elaborate show where he gets crowned King Long by a rabbi. He got wrapped in a Hebrew scroll signifying that he is now wrapped in the word of God. This was truly an entertaining scene to watch. If you don't believe me, google "King Eddie Long." What I find totally disgusting about this charade is that the only people who objected were from the Jewish community for the misrepresentation of Judaism. I applaud the Jewish community for doing this. I did not find one prominent Black clergy say that Bishop Long is a disgrace and needs to stay out of the pulpit. T. D. Jakes and Creflo Dollar, who both head mega churches, only commented that Bishop Long is covered by the blood of Jesus. Neither of them, to my knowledge, called for Bishop Long to resign. Creflo Dollar encouraged members who left Long's church to attend his church to go back to Long. I call this behavior the pulpit-pimp brotherhood. It's based on the principle that a pimp should not take another pimp's whores.

This is an indication of how hard it is for God to get good help these days. Bob Guccione, who was the founder of *Penthouse*, spent a fortune in legal fees defending his name. He published the Vanessa Williams pictures, with the intent of suing the pageant if they took away her title. Obviously, things did not work out as he had hoped. This does not negate that Bob Guccione was a man who believed in fighting for his principles. I would think that a man anointed by God would have the same tenacity to legally clear his name as a publisher of pornography. It is extremely difficult to believe that an innocent man would agree to pay at least a $15 million settlement rather than pay legal fees to exonerate himself and fortify his reputation. It is very easy to believe that a man who wanted to avoid possible criminal charges and go to jail would pay over $15 million to settle out of court. Pulpit pimps convince thousands of naive but sincere believers that they are anointed by God and forsaking them is equivalent to forsaking God. As a Black man, I am embarrassed that someone like Bishop Long can survive in the pulpit.

To my knowledge, Bishop Long has never publically admitted any wrongdoing. He has never apologized to those who brought forth the charges and has never admitted to being bisexual. I have gay acquaintances who claim that within the gay Christian community, Bishop Long, among other preachers, are indeed gay. But that is hearsay. I suggest that you look at the picture he texted to the young men he was mentoring and make your own judgment.

What pulpit pimps don't seem to realize is YouTube is a readily accessible source of what they claim to believe. I listened to a sermon by Bishop Long about how someone can be delivered from homosexuality. Maybe Bishop Long is like Jesus on the cross. He can deliver others, but he cannot deliver himself.

The most absurd thing about gays in Holy Roller Land is the homosexual-deliverance services. CCN broadcasted a clip of one of these services that looked like a skit from *Saturday Night Live*. The head pimp commands the homosexual spirit to leave as he anoints the young man with oil. He is surrounded by a bunch of women praising God as they watch such foolishness. When I watched this tape, I once again felt a sense of shame and embarrassment. This tape reminded me of how Africans were depicted in Tarzan movies, only this was real.

As a straight man, there is something about gay men in Holy Roller churches I can't comprehend. I talked to some gay acquaintances of mine who left Holy Roller Land and now attend common-sense churches. They were as perplexed as I am. The only insight they gave me was many gays are attracted to the music and dancing. In Holy Roller Land, the pastor knows that half his choir is gay. He brags about how blessed the church is to have a choir anointed by the Holy Ghost. Then he starts preaching that homosexuality is a sin from the pits of hell and the whole choir shouts amen. To me this behavior is like Blacks attending a KKK rally. It makes no sense.

I once attended a Holy Roller church that aggressively denounced homosexuality. One of its key leaders was Mitch. He led the praise service, directed one of the choirs, and was a deputy pimp to the head pimp. When he danced unto the Lord, he could shake his booty better than most of the women. I have yet to meet anyone who does not consider Mitch gay. This includes many of his fellow church members. This might explain why Black Holy Roller churches supported don't ask, don't tell. It works for them. Mitch dated my ex-wife for over two years, and they never kissed or had any sexual contact. My ex's explanation was Mitch understands her spiritual needs and realizes if they start something, she will want to finish it. She was firmly committed to no sex before marriage. For her no physical contact was a blessing from God. They were two church leaders dedicated to avoiding fornication. To those around her, it was a red herring. Mitch never proposed, and they broke up. No official reason on why they broke up. The unofficial reason was Mitch did not want to marry on the down-low.

I have been advised from several reliable sources that Holy Roller churches are full of gay men who marry on the down-low.

For many Holy Roller women, understanding their spiritual life is of the utmost importance. Straight men going to Holy Roller churches are rare. Women will accept a down-low husband who will attend church with them and accompany them to a profusion of church events. Of course the golden rule of don't ask, don't tell must not be violated.

My experience with women in Holy Roller Land corroborates this assertion. I have dated several women in Holy Land who had a strong aversion to dating men in Holy Roller Land. One of the main reasons given was too many of them are gay. The next reason given was they wanted it hard on Saturday night. The third reason was they wanted to live a lifestyle that most men in church would not approve of. This included everything from the way they dress, going to clubs occasionally, having a glass of wine with dinner in a romantic restaurant, attending secular concerts, and doing other things that they profess as sin on Sunday morning.

Being gay and attending a Holy Roller church is symptomatic of the denial that is rampant in these churches. Very few find what is preached in these churches as a preferable lifestyle. Yet, for reasons I don't understand, these churches have a strong hold on their members. What I do understand is these members love getting hit by the Holy Ghost and they love participating in church functions. Everything in between seems to have no merit.

CHAPTER 17

———— ✣ ————

Prosperity Preachers

I FOUND THE movie *The Butler* to be a great story, with a main plot and several subplots, which mixes well with the history of the civil rights movement. Early in the film, I started to wonder what role "Black Prosperity Preachers" played in the civil rights movement. As far as I can tell, the answer is none.

Historically, Black churches played a major role in the civil rights movement. However, the theology of the traditional Black church during the civil rights movement was in stark contrast to the Black prosperity Gospel that is prominent today.

The traditional Black church had been a catalyst for social change and human rights. These churches aligned themselves with the National Association for the Advancement of Colored People, Southern Christian leadership Conference, progressive Whites, and others, to bring justice and equality to America. Black Theology is a discipline addressed by Dr. James Cone and others. Suffice it to say the traditional Black church abandoned scriptures that kept Black people subjugated and embraced scriptures that asserted we are all God's children who should be treated equally according to the Constitution of the United States.

Holy Roller churches during the civil rights movement, which are comparable to the mega prosperity churches of today, provided its parishioners with a weekly dose of the Holy Ghost, promises of heaven, and then passed the collection plate. Likewise, evangelical

Christians held on to their scriptural justification for the status quo. Their concern was that Black people accept Jesus as their Savior. Everything else was a political or legal issue, which they shunned. If a Black man accepted Jesus at a revival, he was part of an evangelical preacher's headcount. The living condition of the Black man who got saved was Jesus's problem. Both the Holy Rollers and the evangelicals offered prayers that the Lord will touch the hearts of America.

The Butler illustrates that civil rights and social change was the result of people of all races and all faiths, working together to bring forth a better America. It was the result of peaceful protest, civil obedience, protesters being jailed, strategic alliances, marches, buses being burned, churches being bombed, televised beatings, innocent people being hosed, and dogs attacking students. Black leaders and White leaders were killed for standing up for justice in America before most of America was ready to accept it. It was not the work of the Holy Ghost.

Now, let's scrutinize some of the assertions of Black prosperity preachers and review them within the context of the civil rights movement.

First, God wants you to prosper financially. I guess for years Blacks were paid less than Whites because they did not claim equal pay "in the name of Jesus." I guess this is the same reason that qualified Blacks were denied jobs in the first place. They did not claim their jobs in the name of Jesus. Racism could not have been an issue, because Jesus is the same yesterday, today, and tomorrow. Presumably, if Blacks knew that God wanted us to prosper, the fight for civil rights could have been avoided.

Second, join a ministry that properly teaches the power of God's word. The word of God supersedes any of man's laws or circumstances. Imagine if Rosa Parks (who was a Christian) had told the bus driver, according to the word of God, I should be able to sit here, and the Holy Ghost intervened. The whole Montgomery boycott could have been avoided.

The Reverend Dr. Martin Luther King and a host of other Black clergy, too many to mention, just did not understand the power of God's word. If they had, the marches, boycotts, and protests would have been unnecessary. All Blacks had to do was pray for equal rights according to the word, and God would have handled it.

Today's prosperity preachers clearly have a superior understanding of scriptures when compared with preachers from the civil rights era. Resolving civil rights so that Black people could fully partake of the American dream was merely a matter of recognizing the power of the word.

Finally, God will bless you with prosperity if you tithe and become a financial partner with an anointed ministry. This must be the root of the problem. I guess the Sixteenth Avenue Baptist Church was not anointed. I am sure if it was anointed by God in the manner of today's prosperity mega churches, God would have covered those four innocent girls attending Sunday school with the blood of Jesus, and their lives would have been spared.

I am not against the pursuit of prosperity. However, I contend that any correlation between tithing, being a financial partner with a particular ministry and achieving prosperity is not supported by evidence, critical thinking, and logic, with one major exception; preachers who successfully sell the power of the blood of Jesus and are on the receiving end of the tithes and financial gifts always prosper. There is a strong correlation between race, education, occupations, and prosperity. If you don't believe me, go to any upscale neighborhood and count the number of Black people who live there. Then ask the residents what they do for a living. Finally, ask them what church they tithe to. I predict that overwhelmingly you will find the residents are White, have high-paying jobs or profitable business, and don't tithe to any church.

I often wonder if Black prosperity preachers have ever read a US history book. Slavery is an integral part of American history. Slaves were Christians. Granted slaves could not read. The implication of prosperity preachers is that if slaves had the ability to read the word and understand that God wants Christians to prosper, slaves would have prospered as much as the slaveholders. The only advantage the slaveholders had over slaves was that they could read, not that they were White. I also wonder if Black prosperity preachers ever read the scriptures pertaining to slavery. Clearly the Bible endorses slavery. Jesus never condemned slavery. So when did God's word and the power of the Holy Ghost become the key to financial success? It seems to me that if God wanted all Christians to prosper, he would not have provided the rules for how to manage slaves. The history of slavery in America does support the argument that God wants White Christians to prosper and niggers to remain slaves.

In defense of Black prosperity preachers, I will concede that prosperity is relative. House niggers would have been prosperous when compared with field niggers. Free niggers were prosperous when compared with house niggers. The problem is all of the above were still niggers. The premise that the key to prosperity is the word of God, the power of the Holy Ghost, or Christianity in general is outrageous in the context of African American history. When did God change his mind and decide that niggers should prosper also? Where was God during the middle passage? Where was God during four hundred years of slavery? Where was God during Jim Crow and the KKK lynching's? It seems to me that God didn't want Black people to prosper until the '70s, sometime after the Watts riot, affirmative action, the civil rights bill, the assassination of Martin Luther King, and a host of other civil rights victories and tragedies. I also find it amusing that prosperity churches are often found in more affluent Black communities. These communities just happen to be occupied with Blacks who have benefited from the civil rights movement. I have never seen a Black prosperity church start in a poor Black community and, by preaching the Gospel of prosperity, converted it into a prosperous Black community.

CHAPTER 18

— ⚜ —

Let's Talk

I THINK THAT before individuals can call themselves a bishop or apostle, they need to demonstrate how much Holy Ghost power they possess. They should turn water into wine or feed the whole church with two fish and three loaves of bread. Instead, they have a fancy service, and before you know it, they are transformed into an apostle or bishop. They are now deemed by some to be anointed by God, which means absolutely nothing to most reasonable people. However, they surround themselves with faithful sycophants who don't have the courage to challenge them. In essence they become Pulpit Pimps. Women pay them 10 percent of everything they earn. Some pay tithes before they pay rent. They will take time from their family to make sure that all of their pimp's wishes are fulfilled.

I noticed preachers know everything about God during Holy Roller hours but are never willing to defend their beliefs in a debate. I want to offer any Holy Roller pulpit pimp an opportunity to debate me and prove to their congregation they have evidence to support their claims. This will be a formal, timed debate, not a Holy Roller sideshow. This is an opportunity for pulpit pimps to demonstrate their prowess in defending the faith. I will invite some of my humanist colleagues.

Here are my proposed guidelines:

1. There will be a referee we can both agree will be fair. The referee will have the power to interrupt if someone goes over time and question each of us for clarification. I recommend a professional journalist.
2. The format will be as follows:
   a. Opening statement fifteen minutes each
   b. Rebuttal to opening statements ten minutes each
   c. Questions from the audience ten minutes
3. To address issues that are rarely discussed in the Black church, each debater must address the following issues in their opening statement:
   a. The role that Christianity played in the American slave trade
   b. The authority and origin of the Bible
   c. Evidence (not testimony) of the Holy Ghost
   d. Evidence (not testimony) of healing

There was a debate between Bill Nye and Ken Ham regarding evolution verses creationism. I see this debate as having the same merit. Presumably apostles or bishops anointed by God and filled with Holy Ghost power would welcome an opportunity to prove to their congregation and colleagues that they are preaching the truth.

I surmise that no genuine pulpit pimp will accept my offer. They are not concerned with dealing with the truth, their only concern is making sure that their church members dance on Sunday and pay their tithes.

This offer is expended to Holy Roller pulpit pimps only. Progressive preachers who bring reason and common sense to the

Gospel need not apply. Sorry, Al Sharpton, you do not qualify for this offer. I watched your debate with Christopher Hitchens. Your ability to reason on relevant issues clearly disqualifies you. For example, your position on gay rights makes too much sense for an authentic Holy Roller pulpit pimp.

PART 4

Life without a Heavenly Father

CHAPTER 19

❧

Deacon Henry's Postmortem

AFTER SPENDING MOST of my life developing a relationship with a God who does not exist, I had to painstakingly examine how depending on divine intervention impacted my decision-making process. I had to learn how to live without Jesus. I was appalled when I realized how much my trust in Jesus was betrayed. But, like most Christians, I always proclaimed that Jesus had something better planned or that God had a reason for my misfortune. I decided that my only alternative was to bury Deacon Henry. I soon discovered how much religion hindered my life. I will probably never fully recover from life with Deacon Henry. Fortunately, my experience with religion is not typical. There are plenty of people who practice religion in a superficial manner. They are able to adhere to a religious tradition without any significant dependence on the supernatural.

I wonder how many people needlessly died from disease because they were expecting the Lord to heal them and did not get medical treatment in a timely manner. I think about those who spend their life serving the Lord and end up getting strokes and heart attacks just like everyone else. Deacon Henry accepted human suffering as part of a divine plan of a loving God. I now believe the concept of human suffering as part of a loving God's divine plan is absurd.

I grew up believing in divine justice. I had more confidence in God than I did in myself. I believed the Lord would make a way out of no way. To this day I wish my former beliefs are true, but there is overwhelming evidence that these beliefs are false. The Bible is a myth. God does not heal. Prayer does not change things.

I find it ironic that George Zimmerman claimed that his killing Travon Martin was God's will. On the day his verdict was announced, Travon's mom was in prayer up to the moment the verdict was read. George Zimmerman was exonerated, which supports his claim. I am sure that to many Black Christians, this makes no sense. At virtually every crisis that impacts the Black community, you can expect to find Black clergy calling for justice in the name of Jesus. I challenge Black Christians who have doubts about their Christian faith or religion in general to read the entire Bible critically. African Americans should scrutinize the history of Christianity and slavery and then apply common sense to their Christian experience. They should ask themselves, is it reasonable that the same God who allowed us to suffer in slavery had a change of heart and now wants us to prosper?

On June 17, 2015, a twenty-one-year-old White male attended a prayer meeting at Emanuel African Methodist Episcopal Church in Charleston, South Carolina. He murdered nine church parishioners in cold blood. This shooting echoed the bombing of four young girls at Sixteenth Avenue Baptist Church in Birmingham, Alabama.

The killing in South Carolina is a hodgepodge of racism, gun violence, and a walk down memory lane for those who fought for civil rights. I can only speculate that the killer was ignorant of the struggles Black Americans still face. The notion that "Blacks are taking over our country" is so absurd that no comments are needed. The assertion by some that this attack was violence against

Christians because it took place in a church is diabolically absurd. The killer spared one of the parishioners so she can tell his story. He told her he wanted to kill Black people. They are taking over our country and raping our women. He considered other venues to kill Black people but decided on a church, probably because their only defense is prayer. I found the response of the church members to be troublesome and indicative of what I consider a major flaw in Christian theology.

Immediately after the shooting, a group of Black men held hands in a circle and prayed. They pleaded for the Lord to protect them. I feel this image depicts weakness, not strength. Obviously, the Lord failed to protect the nine people who were just murdered. For whatever reason the loving, sovereign God they were praying to allowed this to transpire. It was by default "God's sovereign will" that these innocent Christians get murdered during prayer meeting. If God did not protect them, why should you expect him to protect you after the fact? I suspect that outside of the Christian right and Holy Rollers, most Americans saw these men as pathetic. This image definitely does not invoke the fortitude of Malcolm X.

When the killer was having his hearing, the judge granted church members an opportunity to address the accused killer. All of their comments made me cringe. They told the defendant that they forgive him. The defendant offered no apology. They have not had time to grieve. The defendant admitted that he wanted to start a race war. He confessed he was treated well by the people he killed but had to kill them for a greater cause. The urgency to tell this man he is forgiven is close to insanity in the name of Jesus. I am not suggesting that the survivors harbor hate. Some forgiveness is probably warranted at some point to move on. I am suggesting that these attitudes are a reflection of the notion "they are sinners saved by grace." I surmise that as "Christians" they feel obligated to forgive, since Jesus forgave them. Their concept of forgiveness is misconstrued. They should not correlate Jesus forgiving them with their obligation to forgive the defendant, unless they killed nine innocent people.

The problem with Jesus dying for the remission of sin is clearly illustrated here. Jesus dying for the sins of the world is merely a biblical concept. People are born into sin and by default worthy of eternal damnation. Jesus replaces individual responsibility for how someone lives his or her life with faith in him. Believers call this mercy. I call this an injustice to all who live a good life and do not accept Jesus as their personal Lord and Savior. The defendant still has a chance to repent and go to heaven. In heaven he can attend a praise service with the people he murdered. The people he murdered are happy to see him since a new soul has entered into heaven. The parishioners who admonished the defendant to get saved exemplify a Christian slave mentality. It's equivalent to "Master done got mad and killed some of his niggers. We better pray for Master." This mentality is the last vestige of the mental chains of slavery. It's time that we break this last shackle of slavery.

But the natural man receiveth not the things of the Spirit of God: for they are foolishness unto him: neither can he know them, because they are spiritually discerned. (1 Cor. 2:14)

The above scripture is true. As a natural man, I see asking the defendant to repent as pure foolishness. What concerns me as an African American is our propensity to depend on the Lord and see ourselves as impotent. I have no inclination to forgive the defendant. It sends the wrong message. A message that Black Christians are docile targets, depending on their sky daddy for mercy, forgiveness, and protection. It sends a message that we will forgive anyone regardless of what they do to us. It sends a message that we don't have the self-respect to condemn those who attack us. I suggest that Black Christians watch some old John Wayne movies to learn how White folks view themselves in these situations. They will learn that the solution to conflict often entails defeating your enemies before you forgive them. After the assassin is convicted and the families have had time to grieve, maybe forgiveness is in order.

CHAPTER 20

Life without Deacon Henry

JUST LIKE GRIEVING the physical death of a loved one, I grieved the death of Deacon Henry. I had to learn how to live life without God, similar to a man learning to live after his lifelong spouse has died. This sounds simple, but in reality it is a very arduous task. I never realized how many bad decisions I made because of my dependence on Jesus. I felt like a junkie learning to live life without drugs. The foundation of my decision-making process was predicated on my religious experiences and beliefs, which in essence were little more than emotions centered on what I believed was the will of God. Fortunately, for most of my life, the bad decisions I made using this paradigm were innocuous. Unfortunately, at a critical point in my life, my belief in God and my belief in my own personal judgment collided and changed the course of my life forever. I will always regret that I allowed my Christian faith to lead me into the abyss. I was in the midst of a universal conundrum for people of faith. How much of life is the result of hard work, good choices, opportunity, and luck in contrast to your life being a part of God's divine plan? I believed that God ordered my steps in the world for most of my life. I attributed all of my success to God's grace. I firmly believed that God was about to take me to the next level. I had been faithful to God, and God had been faithful to me. Subconsciously, I developed a view of my future that was entrenched in my belief that God will take care of me. Regrettably, I discovered too late how much this erroneous, infantile belief system was impeding my decision-making process. In spite of my professional training and experience in making sound decisions, in my personal life, I was submerged in a completely irrational belief system. Consciously, I was in control of my life and making sound decisions that were being sabotaged by my subconscious. I was at the pinnacle of my career when the faith of Deacon Henry and the reason of Christopher Henry II. intertwined. It became evident to Christopher Henry that the God he once worshipped was an illusion. I (Christopher Henry II) could no longer justify what was happening in my life was "part of God's divine plan." I became convinced there is no God who knows the desires of my heart. If there was, my life would be different. I would no longer trust in God and then make excuses to explain why my trust was betrayed.

For sure some will argue that my problem was not Christianity but a lack of proper Christian teaching. Others will argue that I lacked the faithfulness that Jesus requires. I am sure that most would argue that I have been chastised by God for being disobedient to his word and speaking against the Holy Spirit.

My rebuttal is that once I left Christianity, I was fully able to appreciate how much of the Bible in substance and fact is not true.

Deacon Henry lived so deep in my subconscious that he maintained a profound influence on my actions and decisions. Deacon Henry asserted that if I had held on to my faith, God would have delivered me. Deacon Henry still believed that Christopher Henry was a sinner not worthy of success beyond God's grace. Deacon Henry held on to his faith to the point where it was self-destructive. While at times I mourn the death of Deacon Henry, I know his death was necessary. When Deacon Henry died an ineffable part of me died. This I regret. I have an answer to the story about the man who was in a flood praying for God to save him.

He refused to get into a rescue truck because he was waiting for the Lord to save him. He refused to get in a rescue boat because he was waiting for the Lord to save him, and he refused to get in a rescue helicopter because he was waiting for the Lord to save him. He eventually drowned and then asked God why he didn't rescue him. God told him that he sent a truck, boat, and helicopter to save him, what else did he expect? I submit the man drowned because he became mentally paralyzed trying to figure out why God allowed him to get stuck in a flood. Once he was mentally incapacitated, his cognitive mechanisms became distorted. Consequently, he was expecting his rescue to come from some undefined supernatural intervention, not some mundane intervention from man. He refused to accept that man had the solution to his dilemma. If man was going to deliver him, why was he praying to God? The Lord has never performed open-heart surgery, hired a single person, or taken a beating in the name of civil rights. But he gets the praises for all the above and more.

CHAPTER 21

— ⚜ —

Religious Rehabilitation

FOR OVER FIFTY years, my life was centered upon my Christian faith. Now that I denounced the Christian faith, especially the work of the Holy Spirit, I experienced an unexpected phenomenon. I have the same experiences that I once attributed to "the work of the Holy Spirit." This happens repeatedly. Soon I realized other experiences that I thought were uniquely the work of the Holy Spirit were still very much a part of my life. To this day, I am amazed how well the Holy Spirit works in the life of an unbeliever. Consequently, I developed a keen interest in the connection between religion and psychology, how the brain works, sociology, and the mystery of the mind.

As an African American, I am particularly interested in the impact that Christianity has had on the Black community. I discovered an online series entitled "Slave Sermons" produced by Jeremiah Camera. Mr. Camera does a superb job of exploring the history of Christianity, the Bible, and the role of the Black church in our community. His work is concise and in my opinion is an accurate picture of how the Black church and Christianity has contributed to the stagnation of the Black community. I would strongly recommend that any African American who is struggling with his or her Christian faith, religion in general, the history of Christianity, the role of Christianity in slavery, and the pitfalls of the Black church visit his website at www.jeremiahcamara.com.

Dr. J. Anderson Thomson, MD, has done extensive research on why people believe in God from a psychological perspective. He foresees the psychology of religion becoming a standard part of professional psychological training. I recommend his book *Why We Believe in God(s): A Concise Guide to the Science of Faith.*

I began to watch several documentaries regarding the existence of God. Many of them featured former evangelical Christian leaders, who repudiated their Christian faith.

I would listen to debates and lectures that featured the four horsemen: Christopher Hitchens, Daniel Dennett, Sam Harris, and Richard Dawkins. Between these four, virtually every aspect of religion and God is explored.

I found the most amusing source of information regarding God and religion to come from illusionists. I find their presentation of religion to be both entertaining and informative. For several decades the James Randi Educational Foundation offered a million dollars to any psychic who can prove his or her psychic ability under controlled circumstances. No one has never collected the million dollars. Randi would use his skills as a magician to expose how some "physic" tricks are performed. Likewise, Derren Brown has duplicated alleged supernatural gifts, using his skills as an illusionist, hypnotist, and skills in mind control. I encourage believers and nonbelievers to view his show *How to Covert an Atheist.* Penn and Teller use magic tricks to expose many of the flaws in Bible stories.

I wish *The Ebony Exodus Project: Why Some Black Women Are Walking Out On Religion and Others Should Too* by Candace R. M. Gorham, LPC, was mandatory reading for Black church women. The following book description from Amazon.com speaks for itself:

Black women are the single most religious demographic in the United States, yet they are among the poorest, least educated, and least healthy groups in the nation. Drawing on the author's own past experience as an evangelical minister and her present work as a secular counselor and researcher, *The Ebony Exodus Project* makes a direct connection between the church and the plight of black women. Through interviews with African American women who have left the church, the author reveals the shame and suffering often caused by the church—and the resulting happiness, freedom, and sense of purpose these women have felt upon walking away from it. This book calls on other black women to honestly reflect on their relationship with religion and challenges them to consider that perhaps the answers to their problems rest not inside a church, but in themselves.

The more I learned about human nature, the more I realized what I once attributed to the Holy Spirit was simply life happening. I exchanged my pursuit of knowing God to knowing the truth. I found that truth has a power comparable to what I once called the power of the Holy Ghost. When my perception of truth is affirmed, I get the same feeling as being in the will of God. Truthfully, defining an issue is half of the solution. I don't know what happens after death. I do know that life as I know it will end. Everything else is speculation, not a statement of fact. I don't believe that God has a plan for my life. If he does it makes no sense to me. I know I enjoyed most of my life. I made some bad decisions based on my belief in God. Based on how my life unfolded, my steadfast beliefs that I was living according to the will of God were egregiously wrong.

CHAPTER 22

— ⚜ —

Wide Is the Road to Destruction

WHEN I ABANDONED Christianity, I inadvertently drifted out of my lane. I made choices that were not consistent with my personal preferences or character. I rebelled against some of my Christian strongholds and went to places I was never attracted to anyway. I eventually ended up dating a woman whose life experience was everything mine wasn't. She was a model who once lived and worked in Europe. She was well educated and spoke three languages. She had some success running a boutique modeling agency. Her personal background was dark and complicated. I was absolutely overwhelmed with how much she had accomplished, given her past trials and tribulations. She was able to restore a vision that I haven't had since college. A vision of finding love and building a life together. I achieved most of my success as a single man. I had never really experienced starting from scratch with someone and moving forward. This is where our lives merged. We both were at a crossroad in life. We both had attained a good measure of success, which was decimated by the Bush economic crisis. We both were looking to rejuvenate our lives individually and collectively. We both had several doses of love gone badly. We both were hoping that this would be the relationship that would lead us to the promised land.

Stacy had lived across the street from me for over ten years. She was always pleasant and had a great smile and a walk I could recognize from down the street. I always wondered why she was apparently single. At times, I thought she was a lesbian. I am sure at times, she thought I was gay.

I never asked Stacy out until she moved off the block. There was a rumor that she was evicted because her landlord became aggravated with her weed consumption and occasional selling of weed. Her story was that her landlord significantly raised her rent. As a landlord, who experienced two evictions, I knew this was not true. New York City is extremely pro-tenant. Her apartment was rent stabilized. Drug use is one of the few grounds to expedite an eviction. She was staying at Quaheem's apartment, which belonged to a friend who was singing in Japan. Quaheem, who everyone called "Q," had a gangster-rap style, and from what I could see, he was very talented.

On our first date, I took Stacy to the Post, which is where old soldiers go to party. We agreed that it was somewhat of a duty date for both of us. There was no real interest, but at least we could say that after ten years of waving at each other, we went out at least once. She was looking for a place to stay before Q returned from Japan. She had found a place on Craigslist but was hesitant about having a male roommate. In the interim, I invited her over for dinner. I was mesmerized by our conversation. We also enjoyed good food, good wine, and a little dancing. She smoked cigarettes, which was a nuisance to me but far from a deal breaker. I smoke cigars and dated a smoker for several years without any problems at all. She mentioned she smokes weed daily. I was taken a little back by this. Not because she smoked weed. I have friends and relatives who smoke weed. I occasionally put weed in spaghetti sauce. Ninety percent of the people I know have at least tried weed during college. Initially, I felt that it was usual for someone in her age bracket to smoke weed daily. In retrospect it was more of a generational issue. Generally, my generation would smoke weed during college but give it up within a few years after graduation. I was so fascinated with Stacy that I did not give her use of weed much consideration.

Maybe it was my rebellion from Deacon Henry, maybe I was lonely after not living with someone for over two years, maybe I was looking for love in all the wrong places, maybe I was looking for something new and exciting. Probably it was all of the above. I asked Stacy to move in with me after two dates. I felt it was a win-win situation. I planned on relocating from New York City soon, so why not. She was looking to relocate to Chicago by year-end.

I learned some harsh lessons soon after Stacy moved in. First, I learned I was a bitch. I had to admit I was a bitch before I could address the problem. Second, I learned that sometimes the truth is in front of me, and I lacked the fortitude to admit it and take action. Third, I learned that since I abandoned Christianity, it was imperative that I establish who I am and what I stand for. I had to accept that I have beliefs that overlap with my former Christian beliefs, and I must continue to embrace them.

When Stacy first moved in, we faced the normal challenges that any couple would upon knowing each other for such a short period of time. We spent most of our time talking and getting to know each other better. Stacy was in her mid-forties and was at a stage in her life where she was seeking marriage. She had never been married, and while she had several long-term relationships, this was her first encounter living with someone. The distinction being she did not have her own place. I had been married and was not interested in marriage at this stage in my life. Eventually, I became open to marriage. I also gave serious consideration to moving to Chicago. I smoke cigars a couple of times a week, and always outside. She is a heavy smoker and is accustomed to smoking inside. Plus, she smoked much more weed than I ever imagined. As a result, I found myself living under conditions that were inconceivable before living with Stacy. I dread the smell of weed, but I invited her to stay here and tried to be accommodating. I soon went from being accommodating to being a doormat.

We came up with a routine that I found to be a good compromise. We would go into the backyard, and I would smoke a cigar while she smoked weed and cigarettes. I considered this to be our sanctuary. She would constantly convey how important Q was to her. This was my first stage of entering bitch land. She also made it a point to mention that most of her friends are male and this has been a problem in her past relationships. I took this information in stride. I generally cook large meals on Sunday and often invite friends over for dinner. Stacy asked if Q could come over for dinner so I could meet him. I had no objection and conceded to her request. The next thing I knew was Q is coming over every Sunday and a couple of times during the week. Whenever Q came over, he would have quality high time with Stacy in my backyard. At one dinner Q made it clear that he was upset about not being able to contact Stacy on Friday night. Fridays was our date night and apparently the only night she was Q free. When Q complained that his girlfriend would go over Stacy's when he wasn't home, even a bitch like me started to ask questions. I asked Stacy why she wasn't screwing Q. Her response was "I am not his type, we are just friends. We like getting high together." This was my first lesson in pothead protocol. This was a lifestyle I knew nothing about, but I was learning real fast. Not being a pothead, it's hard to believe that a man and a woman can get high on weed and alcohol virtually every day and not screw. I personally have engaged in unexpected sex upon reaching the proper alcohol level in a conducive environment. I find the chances of screwing to exponentially increase when the woman involved openly admits that weed makes her horny. More on that later.

Now, I was beginning to seriously question my judgment to get involved with Stacy. Her constantly getting high with Q was bizarre. I was out of my lane, yet I developed an emotional attachment to her. She was a good person. I enjoyed how she treated me in our relationship. My hope was I could cope with her use of weed as long as it doesn't impact me. This hope was short-lived. I planned a special weekend for the sole purpose of us bonding and moving forward. Friday was our date night. I brought her flowers and cooked a special dinner. That night was on the money. Saturday we had some sunrise sex followed by brunch at her favorite restaurant in New York City. The restaurant was elegant and pricey. We then went to the Hayden Planetarium. We had planned to go several times earlier, but this time I made it happen. Instead of going out for dinner, we decided to go grocery shopping. She cooked enough Saturday night so that we could relax on Sunday and the kitchen would be closed. Grocery shopping was a simple way of reinforcing that we are a couple doing couple things. We had a nice Sunday breakfast, and all was well. A friend of mine came over who I would normally ask to stay for dinner, but not tonight. I wanted this weekend to be about me and Stacy. I wanted to end this weekend with some quality time with my girlfriend. I was looking forward to an intimate meal, listening to Luther Vandross, and making love all night long. I wanted this to be a memorable weekend and a turning point in our relationship. On both counts it was.

Stacy was upstairs when I heard someone knocking on the door. It was Q. Stacy had invited him over for dinner earlier that day. Now the bitch in me saw the light. Sundays was about Stacy having quality high time with Q, and I was the host. I was stunned. All my efforts to make Stacy feel special and take our relationship to the next level was rewarded by her having quality high time with Q. All of my friends advised me that I should have asked Q to leave on the spot and to take Stacy with him. But I was still living in bitch land. Stacy made sure that Q was comfortable, and I became invisible. After dinner Stacy advised Q that she was ready for him. She then escorted him to the backyard. There I was watching my live-in girlfriend, sitting in my backyard, in my chairs, in our sanctuary, having quality high time with her pothead pimp. Only a bitch would tolerate this behavior. A real man would have shut this down immediately. Like a little bitch, I left and went to a club. This is when I realized just how strong the pothead brotherhood is. Stacy and Q shared a mutual love for weed, which created an emotional bond I would never be able to penetrate. This is when I knew I was not with a woman who smokes weed but with a woman emotionally attached to weed. Stacy was so enthralled with getting high that she never considered that her actions were totally disrespectful toward me. To her it was as simple as "I love to get high with Q." When I returned home, we had a heated argument regarding what had transpired. Her strongest argument was that when she lived across the street, she would regularly cook for Q and her friends. Then they all get high together. Next she argued Q needed her emotional support while he was trying to get back with his girlfriend. She kept the conversation as short as possible so she could get back to me. My response was, if you still lived across the street, your cooking for Q and getting high with him would not be a problem. It's only a problem because you live with me and claim you want a serious relationship with me. Then, I told her that putting me on hold so you can cater to Q is the ultimate form of disrespect. If you are so concerned about Q's love life, you should be screwing him. Next, she argued that when she invited Q over, she didn't know I wanted to spend quality time with her. This is when I learned another lesson in pothead protocol. It never occurred to me that I needed to get clearance from Stacy to confirm she hadn't made plans with her pothead pimp. I presumed that if we are a couple, and she is living in my house, and we had spent the weekend together, and we never had any conversations about inviting a guest over for dinner, I was by default entitled to have dinner with my girlfriend without Q. Then she bitch-slapped me, and I had to give her some credit. She argued that Q had been coming over every Sunday since he was introduced, so she presumed it was not a problem to invite him over. Stacy was correct. I became her bitch, and she presumed that I accepted Q as part of a package deal. My job was to provide the backyard, and his job was to provide quality high time. Her final argument was the most ridiculous. Q is her friend, and she wanted to make sure he had a good meal. She declared she has no need to get high with Q because she keeps plenty of weed on hand and most of the time gets high by herself! I had a simple comeback. Q is a grown ass man who can afford Popeye's.

I again told Stacy that she should be screwing Q, not me. She assured me that she has never screwed Q. I believed her, but not because of the bitch in me. I contend that Q is a closeted gay man. This is based on substantial corroborating evidence. Q would get high with Stacy damn near every night in her apartment. Stacy is sexually appealing, and weed gets her horny. Every straight man I know would want to screw her at least once, on general principle. However, if Q is on the down-low, their pothead bond makes perfect sense. Stacy is a voluptuous woman. She wants a masculine, sexually dominating man. She finds the thought of screwing a feminine man who's on the down-low repulsive. Thus, she can get high with Q all day and all night without giving up the pussy. When Stacy wants to get laid, she goes elsewhere. Likewise, Q is turned on by scrumptious men. No matter how high he gets, he finds the thought of trying to sexually please a vixen like Stacy repugnant. To protect his rapper-game face, Q dates a sweet little church girl who doesn't get high or know the streets. She conveniently lives out of state and is too naive to detect that Q is on the down-low. As part of Stacy's pothead bond with Q, she is committed to protecting Q's clandestine relationships with men. Her friendship with Q's girlfriend is a convenient facade for both of them. From the moment I saw Q greet Stacy, I presumed he was gay. All my friends presumed Q was gay. When Stacy invited Q and some of his friends over, I became convinced he's on the down-low. I never viewed Q as a sexual threat. My accusations of such were purely out of frustration and partially for entertainment. I knew that Stacy wanted to tell me she has no desire to screw Q because he's on the down-low, but she was bound to the pothead protocol. This frustrated the hell out of Stacy. For me, it was the better side of being a bitch. Telling Stacy to go screw Q was really telling Stacy to make a lifestyle choice. Since you prefer quality high time with Q rather than Luther time with me, the fact that you don't screw Q becomes irrelevant. I immediately shut down my emotions for Stacy and asked her to move out as soon as possible.

Stacy found a place and wanted to talk before she moved out. She apologized for not telling me she had invited Q over for dinner and stated it was an oversight. I told her inviting Q over was not an oversight, it was a reflection of what is important to you. Your priority was quality high time with Q. I have been in enough relationships to know when a woman is connected with me. If you were connected with me, you would not have been thinking about Q. You would have been thinking about what lingerie to wear and how good you're going to give it to me.

At this point, deep within I knew that if Stacy did not see a problem with inviting her pothead pimp over for quality high time, she was living in a world centered on getting high, and things would only get worse. This was when I knew Stacy and I were not suitable for a serious relationship. I became bewildered as to why Stacy wanted to be with me, when so much of her behavior demonstrated how prevalent weed is in her life. Stacy accused me of being the problem. She's been smoking weed for over twenty-five years virtually every day, and I am the only person to complain. None of her previous boyfriends smoked weed. They all accepted that she likes to get high, and it never affected their relationship. This made me wonder how many of her previous boyfriends cared about her personal growth. Maybe it's the bitch in me, but I find it incredulous that a man who knew her history would not be concerned about her abuse of weed, alcohol, and cigarettes. Maybe that's why her last boyfriend kept women on the side rather than deal with what's going on emotionally with her. Since Stacy never lived with her previous boyfriends, my presumption is she adroitly concealed how much she really gets high. However, this is an extremely pious attitude. I know firsthand that Stacy is a very loving, caring, ambitious woman. It was my own disposition that could not reconcile her passion for weed with my pursuit of tranquility. All of the positive attributes I loved and appreciated about Stacy were being overshadowed by her propensity to be controlled by weed. This control indirectly controlled me. It limited my ability to bond with someone I love. I instinctively rebelled against being controlled by any substance, directly or indirectly.

After our conversation, I decided to stay with Stacy. The bitch in me could not man up to the truth. I can't explain why I went against my own reasoning and logic to stay with Stacy. Sometimes, I was haunted for not yielding to my instinct to immediately end this relationship. Stacy stopped inviting Q over, but she would stop by his place and get high before she came home. I felt like I was dating Q's leftover whore. They might not be screwing, but Q had complete control over her mind. Q did not care that Stacy was in a relationship with me. When he wanted some quality high time with his whore, she made herself available. When his whore wanted some quality weed, Q delivered. It was a relationship made in pothead heaven.

Stacy is not into foreplay. I was a little dismayed about this since I consider foreplay one of my fortes. I have always been able to get a woman in the mood with foreplay and a good licking all over. I am proud of the fact that I received several accolades from past lovers for giving them the proper attention in this area. They appreciated the emotional and physical bonding of foreplay. Stacy was very candid about weed made her horny. Before we would make love, she would take a ten-minute weed break and come back ready to screw. I found this extremely intrusive and frustrating. Too often I would lose my erection and desire by the time she came back smelling like weed. Too many nights she would return to bed high and horny, while I went to sleep irritated and horny. Stacy's passion for weed hindered us from developing an intimate sexual relationship. I exchanged sexual intimacy for sexual endurance. I abandoned the ecstasy of foreplay and would ride it as long as I could when she was high. Needless to say, I started to look for sexual intimacy elsewhere. Maybe it's my male ego, but I found having to wait for Stacy to get high before we screw to be degrading. I was deprived of the satisfaction that comes from getting my woman in the mood. While I cared for Stacy outside of the bedroom, in the bedroom I felt like she was my hooker. Me getting screwed was more about her being high than me turning her on.

One evening I told her I was going out but decided to sit on my steps and smoke a cigar instead. I was appalled when a man pulled up in front of my house looking for someone. Stacy came out, greeted him, and supplied him with some weed. She was invited to hit some with him, but by that time she noticed I was watching and declined. She explained that he was a friend visiting from out of state. He was looking for some good weed for his visit. With great pride, she declared that her friends contact her when they are in town because they know she has the best weed around. It must be true since the same guy showed up the next day. Stacy sold him some more weed but insisted that she is not a dealer. She often bragged about the quality of her weed to my friends, often with a demonstration of her weed paraphernalia. I had clear and convincing evidence that the rumors of her weed parties and the occasional weed sale were true. She was evicted due to her abuse of weed, not because of a rent increase.

I started to do research on marijuana addiction. I was able to witness at least nine of the twelve symptoms of addiction to marijuana (according to data published by Marijuana -Anonymous. org). The other three I never asked her about. The most important thing I learned about marijuana addiction is that it develops gradually, and this is why most potheads don't realize they have a problem. In addition, most potheads are functional addicts. They can hold a job and be responsible. Marijuana is part of their lifestyle, and in my opinion, they have no incentive or reason to stop smoking. I must admit I was completely at fault for dating someone who is addicted to weed and then complaining about her addiction. I think the main issue regarding Stacy and I is not my assertion that she is addicted to weed, rather we are not equally yoked when it comes to weed. She has a lifestyle that is conducive to having a mate with the same lifestyle. Stacy needs a man she can share a joint with when she comes home from work and share a pipe with before they screw. Her weed habit inevitably affected me and us as a couple. Even a bitch like me can figure out that her actions were not consistent with her claims that she's happy in our relationship. Her happiness with me is contingent upon me remaining a bitch and in essence remaining subservient to her passion for weed.   I found living with someone whose lifestyle is focused on her next high to be a pain in my ass. At first it was amusing. Soon it became very intrusive. I learned that marijuana is a psychological addiction. Potheads get addicted to the mental state of being high. There are several factors that contribute to addiction, including genetic predisposition, PTSD, depression, anxiety, mental illness, and schizophrenia. Prolonged use of marijuana can inhibit the brain's natural process to produce dopamine, a chemical that produces a sense of well-being. Consequently, a dependence on weed develops a sense of well-being. From my personal experience, potheads are clueless of the impact their addiction has on others who don't have the same passion to get high. Maybe that's why they prefer to be with other potheads. It is easier and a lot more fun to get high with your fellow potheads than it is to seek professional help to address the underlying problems.

My research on the addiction of weed caused me to reflect on my former dependence on religion. I discovered a correlation between substance addiction and religion addiction. Potheads cannot imagine life without weed. I could not imagine a world without God, in spite of the number of people who live happy, productive lives without any belief in God. Potheads are often advised by friends that their use of weed is excessive. I had a girlfriend in college who warned me that I had too much dependence on God. Pot can have a negative influence on relationships. I have been in relationships where religion had a negative influence. I accepted that I was among a small percentage of religious people who took my faith in God (which is a good thing for most) and abused it.

I was not only a critic of Holy Roller Land but also a victim. I discovered that some of my behavior was just as distorted as Holy Rollers. My judgment was impaired by religion, just like pot impairs the judgment of a pothead. I realized that religion has the potential to become just as destructive as drugs. I started to understand why so many ex-drug abusers end up giving testimonies on Sunday morning. They simply went from being hooked on drugs to being hooked on Jesus. Surrendering to Jesus is much easier then addressing the underlying issues that contribute to your addiction. I wonder how much the Black community would flourish if we were not sedated by drugs and religion. I started to examine my circle of friends, both Blacks and Whites, and assess how many had strong religious beliefs and how many had little or no religious beliefs. Overwhelmingly, the least religious were more prosperous, contrary to claims of prosperity preachers. There were a few extraordinary exceptions. But overall, my non-religious friends have more self-confidence, a positive perspective about life, a better appreciation of life, and are more fun to be around. They are more informed, and our conversations are far beyond the wrath of God.

At this point, I find it difficult to accept that the Black community would be inundated with churches if it was emotionally, financially, and psychologically on par with Whites. I am convinced that Christianity is the drug of choice for many African Americans. We go to church, get our praise on, and go home. We wait on the Lord to solve our problems, while at church we embrace the praise and prestige of being on the Deacon Board, Head of the Pastors Appreciation Committee, or being the head usher. Being hooked on Jesus may not be cheaper than drugs, but at least it's legal. You simply do not find the same obsession with church in affluent White neighbors. My guess is that affluent Whites view having a job as a reasonable expectation and not a miracle from Jesus. They have financial investments and are not interested in tiding to receive a financial blessing. They hold positions at work that give them a sense of prestige and power. They have absolutely no incentive to send up praises to God to receive their blessings. Mainly because they are clearly already blessed, partially due to the advantages of being White. If they want to dance, they can afford to go to a club. Black people spend hours in church asking God to give them the life that most White people take for granted.

Process addiction is someone who develops a dependence on an activity rather than a substance. I have been involved with women who in an attempt to grow spiritually committed more and more time to church at the sacrifice of family relationships. I know Christians who would pay their tithes before they would pay rent. I've heard plenty of testimonies from believers who just can't get enough prayer. I listen to jazz, classical, and R&B. I know numerous people who only listen to Gospel and exclusively watch nothing but the word channel. These believers refuse to face the harsh reality that life is hard. They focus on the word and Jesus to isolate themselves from world events. They believe that the world is in God's hands, but they refuse to be informed about what's happening in "God's world," because it's too daunting. They prefer to stay focused on Jesus and the afterlife. I contend that they are afraid to learn too much about what's going on in the world around them, because they might be tempted to think and ask questions. They use Jesus, the way a pothead uses weed, to filter out those aspects of life they don't want to cope with.

When I think about the men and women who filled the church I grew up with, I am sure that they had a true desire to worship God. I am equally sure that most of them had no place else to go. They had been scared by racism, a lack of education, Jim Crow, and having the unique privilege and honor of being second-class citizens. Church became their extended family, a place where they were always welcomed, a place where they could walk through the front door, a place where they were not considered niggers, a place that offered them dignity and respect. The truth is that for too long the Black church has been the only place Black people can be somebody! The Black church was fertile ground for growing leaders and organizing for positive change. As a child, church dinners was the closest I got to experiencing a family restaurant. I will always have a love and respect for the Black church legacy. However, I cannot accept the Black community holding on to Jesus. I believe a true sign of maturity is confronting your addictions and accepting the inherent pain of personal growth. This applies to addiction to Jesus as well as addiction to weed. Black clergy are quick to march for more jobs, better education, and justice for the Black community. They constantly look for opportunities to curb drug abuse, especially among our youth. The Black community is still the most religious segment in America and still on the bottom of everything. Religion is on the decline in White America. We are again far behind. I submit that the White community has recognized that Christianity (religion in general) is fundamentally flawed and has moved on.

I adamantly believe that Christianity is the last shackle of slavery. It will be the hardest to break because the Black church has become a sacred cow, controlled by Black people. I contend that the Black church is holding on to a Christian tradition that was imposed upon us. Black people have refined Christianity to accommodate our unique condition as former slaves. More Blacks need to accept that Christianity is fundamentally flawed and move on. For those who are accustomed to attending church service on a regular basis, I recommend attending a church that emphasizes humanist values and does not adhere to traditional Christian doctrine. Progressive Black churches need to abdicate their affiliation with their established Christian denominations. In essence a church without Jesus is an idea whose time has come.

Stacy abused weed, which is enjoyed by most without any negative repercussions. I do not want to infer that being a pothead equates to a lack of success in life. Some potheads use their personal success as proof that they are not addicted to weed. I contend someone's addiction to weed and personal success are two non-related issues. I made some horrible decisions based on my belief in God. I wish I could blame them on drug abuse. But I can't. I was just stupid.

As a man recovering from religious addiction, I can sympathize with Stacy's struggle with weed addiction. I have tremendous empathy with Stacy. I can understand how after twenty-five years of embracing a lifestyle that uses weed, alcohol, and cigarettes to alleviate some of her emotional wounds, the idea of confronting her abuse of these substances is terrifying. My primary impetus to scrutinize my Christian faith was how inequitable life is. The very first night I invited Stacy over for dinner and she told me her story, I fell in love with a fantastic woman who, through no fault of her own, experienced some of the atrocious elements of life. She not only survived, but she also thrived. Her addiction to weed does not diminish what she has accomplished in her life. It is not an indictment against her personal fortitude. It has no moral overtones. It is merely an emotional bandage she uses to heal some of her battle wounds in the war of life. If she chooses, I earnestly believe Stacy can demolish her addictions and let her underlying wounds fully heal. To thy own self be true. I vigorously confronted my favorite quote. My first major decision after the demise of Deacon Henry was not going too well. Indeed, at this point, I wish I had a nice church girl. Life with Jesus did not work, and thus far, life without Jesus was not too promising. I came to the conclusion that I would seek professional counseling. I wanted to get an objective, independent, professional evaluation on my ability to assess my problems and address them. I definitely wanted to get rid of my inner bitch. I was totally disappointed in myself for not telling Q to leave and take Stacy with him. All of my colleagues firmly believe that a woman inviting her pothead pimp over unannounced was an immediate deal breaker, no discussion necessary. I was learning that life without Jesus is not easy. In part because my skills to live without Jesus were still under construction.

Before the Q fiasco, both of us were optimistic that our relationship would lead to marriage. Consequently, Stacy invited me to Chicago to spend Thanksgiving dinner with her family. I was reluctant to spend Thanksgiving in Chicago with Stacy post Q's invited intrusion into our relationship. However, I had paid for the plane tickets and wanted to visit Chicago before I relocate. Stacy is very close to her family, and I was again hoping this would be a positive changing point in our relationship. Stacy was eager for me to meet her family, but her first phone call upon landing was to Lindsey, her Chicago pothead pimp. She wanted to get high with him and pick up a supply of weed for her visit. Her plan was to get high with Lindsey, while I wait in the hotel. Stacy's passion for quality high time is innate. Again, I was kicked to the side while she pursued her first priority. Again, she did not see her actions as being disrespectful to me. I bought plane tickets so we can have time together, and the first thing on her agenda was to get high with Lindsey. She justified getting high with Lindsey because she is a friend of his wife, who doesn't smoke weed. My response was that if he was fully committed to his wife, he wouldn't be getting high with you. You are a potential sidepiece to him and all your other pothead pimps who get high with you and then go home to their wives, who don't smoke weed. If a man is getting high with you, why wouldn't he want some pussy on the side?

Again, I was schooled on the pothead protocol. Lindsey won't cheat on his wife with Stacy because they get high together. Apparently, Stacy is held in such high esteem that her pothead pimps don't want to marry her or screw her. She is exclusively for quality high time. Thus, if Lindsey was horny and looking for a sidepiece, he would never screw Stacy, regardless of how high and horny she was.

Stacy was disappointed that Lindsey had family obligations and quality high time with her was not his top priority. Again, I found myself being angry at Stacy for being Stacy. Again, I blame myself for getting involved with someone who's not in my lane. Her behavior was appropriate for those who are a part of her element. When I invited Stacy to my family reunion in Las Vegas, her first response was she has a pothead pimp in Vegas to supply her with weed. I'm sure she expected me to wait in the hotel while she got high with him also. Stacy's insatiable desire for quality high time was not a personal condemnation against me. It was simply part of her pothead protocol. From Stacy's perspective she was treating me how her pothead pimps treat their wives. Unfortunately, relationships still have double standards. Ultimately, a man does not want to be treated like a bitch. Fortunately, her cousin provided her with enough weed for the weekend. I was glad I made this trip after all. I somewhat enjoyed watching her go weed crazy around her family. She smoked weed behind the family tent by herself after Thanksgiving dinner. It never occurred to her that this alone makes her appear to be a pothead, especially to the adults who knew she's behind the tent smoking weed. I was thinking that if she was with Q, she wouldn't have to be getting high by herself on a holiday. She smoked weed before breakfast the next day. I enjoyed watching her cousins experience the same annoyance I experience daily. All the adults knew she was high. Their facial expressions conveyed the message "damn bitch, can't you give it a break." Then they looked at me as to say "Damn Brother, can't you handle your woman?" One of her cousins expressed his observations to me and let it be known that her behavior was tolerated, but not appreciated. The subtext was, I hope you can put Stacy in check. Meanwhile Stacy was enjoying her solo high, totally unaware that she was embarrassing herself, embarrassing me, and putting her family in an awkward position. She wore her reputation as the family pothead as a badge of honor. To the younger adults, it was. To the older adults, it was a badge that needs to be retired.

Everything I researched about weed addiction had been confirmed. At this point I was starting to reach out to my family and close friends for counsel. I was beginning to believe that this was God's retribution toward me for talking about church women. In the past, I would have considered myself to be a backslider and my experience with Stacy was God calling to repent. But now, I had enough experience and done enough research to know that I was enduring the consequences of a bad decision. In many ways, I was approaching my final test of faith or lack thereof.

Stacy's use of weed was now clearly a point of contention in our relationship. I insisted that she was addicted to weed and her weed habit was affecting me and our relationship. She admitted she likes getting high every day, but insisted that she was not addicted and wasn't going to stop getting high.

I use writing to journalize my emotions, good and bad, at any point in time. It is my way of confronting my daily struggles in life. If I did not have writing as my refuge, I too might succumb to substance abuse. I use great caution choosing who I write to. I want people with different points of view and life experiences. The people I correspond with have never betrayed my trust and confidence. They all know I only confide with them on serious issues that are dear to my heart. It is a given that I would not bother them with my personal issues unless it was someone I deeply cared about. The positive things I saw in Stacy were firmly established. I was seeking guidance on the obstacles we faced. To be more candid, they all knew, without any reservations, if I didn't love Stacy, I would have left her by now. I would not waste my time and their time unless I thought she was worth fighting for. My track record in other relationships prove this. I wrote to my sister who is a Christian marriage counselor. I wrote to my cousin Jessie who is my mentor and knows the intimate details of my past relationships. I wrote to Linda, a lifelong female friend. I wanted her perspective as a woman who once had a passion for weed. Her view was similar to mine, been there, done that, and moved on before she reached thirty. I wrote to my friend Rafael. We have shared our relationship experiences, good and bad, for over thirty years. I shared with each of them some aspect of what I was experiencing with Stacy. They all agreed that the issues I raised had merit, especially when contemplating marriage. I needed to be assured that our schism over her use of weed was firmly resolved before

I make a full emotional commitment. I did not see a resolution but was still looking. I concede that anyone who read my e-mails out of context could get a distorted view of my intentions. I was writing to my most trusted confidants about my genuine concerns regarding someone I love. Most of the time, I was writing to divert my immediate anger and frustration away from Stacy until I had time to think things out and approach her in a more meaningful manner. Everything I wrote was supplemented with personal conversations, which put everything in its proper perspective.

Stacy had stopped smoking weed to prepare for a job fair to be held in Chicago. I immensely enjoyed her being sober. Spending time with her without her high breaks was refreshing. I always had a lingering suspicion that she was still getting high but was getting better at concealing it.

Stacy had a dialogue with her aunt and uncle. They somehow convinced her that inviting her pothead pimp over for dinner was not a good decision. They also convinced her that most men would have a problem with their woman having quality high time with other men. Stacy apparently saw the light. She proposed to stop getting high with her pothead pimps. She will keep in contact to get her weed but will only get high with me. I found this amusing but gave her claim little credibility. She said she would only get high with me when I smoke my cigars. The problem was that we tried this, but she invaded our sanctuary with Q. Now, I had no inclination of smoking anything with her. Second, this would entail a tremendous reduction in her consumption of weed. Most of her friends smoke weed. I would be naive to think she would now restrict herself to getting high with me. I definitely could not envision Stacy not getting high with Q. Third, at this point I was utterly frustrated with her pothead protocol. I was confounded as to why Stacy could not recognize she's addicted to weed. I encouraged her to get professional counseling, and she did attend one session. Subsequently, she briefly acknowledged that she was addicted to alcohol, cigarettes, and weed. However, she never expressed a genuine interest to address any of these addictions. She hinted that she might cut back on smoking and drinking but weed was off the table. Eventually, she continued to deny any addictions. I yearned for her to acknowledge her addictions and to continue getting professional help. It was my desire to support her wholeheartedly with her recovery. However, unless Stacy admitted she has a problem with weed and decided to give it up for herself, my only recourse was to accept her addiction or move on. I had no reason to believe that Stacy could deliver on her proposal. Yet, her proposal sparked in me another glimpse of hope. When she returned from the job fair, I prepared a special meal for her. My cousin Jessie challenged me on this. Based on our conversations and my actions, he came to the conclusion that I was already too emotionally connected to Stacy. He accused me of not treating her like a woman I was ready to let go of. He predicted that we will be together for years to come. Stacy questioned why I went out of my way to welcome her back. This caused me to think my cousin was correct. I had too much of myself invested in Stacy. Maybe it was the dregs of the bitch in me. Maybe I had some distorted messiah complex and wanted to be the one who supports Stacy as she defeats her weed addiction. Maybe this was my first betrayal of my newfound mandate to let reason and logic dictate my decisions. Maybe I was in love with Stacy more than I wanted to admit and more than she realized. I was hoping that Stacy and I would maintain an amicable relationship and over time we would bond, resolve our issues, and ultimately get married. This was the consensus of all my confidants. Each, in his or her own way, recommended I give Stacy more time to fully embrace professional counseling.

Hopefully, she will realize that addressing her substance abuse is something she wants for herself. If this occurs, we will have a solid foundation for a satisfying relationship. Otherwise, I should do what's best for me and leave.

I noticed that many of the phrases I used in my e-mails were being quoted by Stacy. Twice I asked her if she was reading my e-mails. Both times she denied it. Then it became obvious that she was reading my e-mails. I aggressively accused Stacy of hacking my e-mails, and she confessed to getting my e-mails on her cell phone. She then vehemently accused me of throwing her under the bus, based on the e-mails she had read. I was trialed and convicted based on purloined confidential e-mails. She refused to show me how she hacked my e-mails. I wanted to know how to protect myself from future intrusions. She claimed that she had a legal application to do this. My speculation is that anyone who can get illegal medical marijuana would have no problem getting an illegal application to steal e-mails. I was able to determine she surreptitiously set up my user ID to remember my password. When I pleaded with her to sit down with me and discuss what I wrote that was not true, she refused. She had plenty of time to talk with Q about how to save his relationship but no time to talk with me about saving our relationship. I asked her if she had read my last e-mail. She said no. I pleaded that we read it together. I warned her that she doesn't have the complete picture. She refused. She read the names of the people whose e-mails she hacked and adamantly proclaimed she had all the evidence she needed to prove I threw her under the bus. At this point, if I still believed in Jesus, I would say this is the work of the Lord. My last e-mail was to my cousin Jessie. I told him he was correct; I love Stacy more than I realized, irrespective of her weed addiction. I was convinced that if I can recover from the Q incident, and she moderates her weed consumption, we have a future together or at least a fighting chance. The problem was that my e-mail was in response to a phone conversation and a game we play called Christopher jeopardy. Without this information, the e-mail didn't make much sense. I tried to explain this to Stacy. I told her to call my cousin to confirm I was telling the truth. I told her the people I sent e-mails to saw me as showing true concern for someone I love. Stacy's solution to our conflict was to get high and leave on the spot, in her pajamas. I considered this to be conclusive evidence that she was a pothead. She never considered that I was a man who loved her and was deeply concerned with how dependent she was on weed, alcohol, and cigarettes. She convinced me that I was not the man she wanted or needed in her life. I was not the type of man who was going to sit around and watch someone I love engulf herself in substance abuse. She can do that by herself or find a man of like mind.

Eventually, I was delighted that she got high and left. I really don't want to be with a woman who does not understand my true character. It makes no point to be with a woman who cannot distinguish between someone who cares about her and someone "throwing her under the bus." From my point of view, the latter is part of the marijuana-induced paranoia I researched. She was so preoccupied defending her use of weed and alcohol as fun that a serious conversation with me was not warranted. I was expecting a heartfelt conversation that would ultimately help us break some barriers and move forward. I abruptly learned another lesson in pothead protocol. The best way to prove you don't have a problem with weed is to get high and leave, while the man you claim to love is trying his best to defend his love for you. My conjecture is that she made up her mind to leave a while ago. When she read my e-mails, she convinced herself that I was going to ask her to leave. This precluded her from seeing that my actions were saying I love you and still want to work things out. Maybe she became so accustomed of me being her bitch that she was outraged when I had the audacity to challenge her. I surmise that Stacy's leaving me was her way of making a statement against me. I became such an unbearable person that she had to leave me on the spot. I'm sure she became disillusioned, living with someone who was not in her lane.

Stacy completely eschewed the issue of breaking into my e-mail as a serious betrayal of trust. She had access to my personal and professional information. She invaded my right to have confidential conversations with my family and friends. Most of my e-mails had absolutely nothing to do with her. My family and friends feel she invaded their privacy also. They are rightfully concerned Stacy might hack their e-mails. They are reluctant to e-mail me anymore.

Stacy suspected that I was writing about her use of weed and without remorse boasted that what she read justified her breaking into my e-mail. She was correct. I was writing about her weed use. She contended I made her sound like a pothead. I was telling the truth about her behavior and a pothead is what she saw.

The most perplexing issue regarding her breaking into my e-mail was her betrayal of trust. Trust is the foundation of any relationship. How did she expect to keep my trust by breaking into my e-mail? I ponder how much of her poor judgment was the result of her habitual use of weed. Maybe that's a good question for Dr. Drew. My instincts about Q and the pothead protocol were correct. Once I had evidence that I was dealing with a pothead, I should have known that things would only get worse.

I have not spoken to Stacy since she moved out. The last time I saw her she was leaving Q's place high, smelling like a weed factory. We politely ignored each other. I can now explain why I didn't stick with my first intuition and insist Stacy leave immediately after the Q incident. She convinced me of her vision that at this stage in life, two people can find love and start a new life together. I wanted this vision to happen with us. It took me a while to accept that I was out of my lane. I refused to continually invest my love and emotions with someone who instinctively made weed her first priority and consequently completely disrespected me as a man. I believe that Stacy loved me but not as much as her first love, which is weed. I still have some compassion for Stacy. She is a woman who sees weed as the solution to her problems, not the problem. She believes that those who encourage her to get professional help are rejecting her and do not accept her for who she is. Her concept of unconditional love is to let her do whatever she wants, regardless of how much it harms her or those around her. A good friend of mine who has been addiction free for over twenty-five years, assures me that my assessment is correct. He says I should be thankful she left. It is a relief not having an illegal substance in my house. My tenant appreciates that the lobby no longer smells like weed, my reputation of possessing a weed-free zone has been restored, and my house smells much better. My biggest relief is Stacy's addiction to weed is no longer a concern of mine. I no longer worry about her getting busted. I no longer worry about her conducting a weed sale in front of my house. I no longer play second fiddle to Q and all her other pothead pimps. Since I am no longer considering Stacy as my potential wife, her addiction to weed and her pothead lifestyle are totally irrelevant to me. I fully embrace her choice to depend on weed to bury her past and impede her personal growth.

I once hoped that Stacy and I would remain friends and maybe friends with benefits. Our friendship is over. My friends would never break into my e-mail. My friends always give me a chance to explain my side of any story. My friends communicate with me, and they don't get high and walk out on me because they don't like the topic of discussion.

I still have a vision that I can find love and start a new life. I could conveniently conclude that how my relationship with Stacy ended was by divine intervention. I had finally come to accept that Stacy was addicted to weed, but I loved her anyway and was willing to hold on. She had concluded, based on my hacked e-mails, I did not love her and I was throwing her under the bus. I feel much better now that she is back in her own element and I am back in my own lane. I truly have a feeling that God was looking over me and protecting me from myself. I feel blessed. This begs the question, what is being blessed? Is it God's intervention, Karma, good luck, or the intersection between preparation, hard work, logic, reason, and good fortune?

I could easily repent and say, "Lord, I have sinned." There are many who would welcome me back into the flock. The feeling of God looking over me does not change the facts about the Bible, the history of religion, Christianity, or my personal experiences of feeling totally abandoned by God at a critical time in my life. It means that in this instance I am pleased with how things worked out. I have grown as a person. I finally defeated the bitch in me and watched Stacy walk out of my life with no concern about where she was going. I learned to accept that our relationship was over based on her actions. I relinquished my original desire to maintain a friendship with her. This is a milestone for a man who was the epitome of being Stacy's bitch.

I will continue to learn how to live without God. I will strive to be the best person I can be in all respects. I have no religion other than seeking the truth. I no longer have a friend in Jesus. However, I cherish my family and friends now more than ever. I remember as a child learning the Bible verse "God is Love." This verse remains a quagmire for me. I don't believe in God, yet I certainly love my family, my friends, and humanity. I believe it is infinitely more important to love your brother who you can see, rather than love God who you cannot see. I have not met any rational person who does not believe in love. I have met many rational people who believe in love but do not believe in God. The proposition that one cannot love without believing in God is unequivocally false.

I have redeemed myself from a world of faith, sin, mercy, and trusting in that which I cannot see. I hope Briana and Suzie find redemption from being raised in a world that defies human compassion, common sense, logic, and reason. For reasons unknown, too many people are born into dire circumstances. Yet, most of them find a way to have fulfilling, meaningful lives. To me this is a tribute to the human spirit. It is a type of redemption that too many people born into more fortunate circumstances fail to see. Redemption in this life is more important than redemption from sin in some afterlife. Jesus Christ is no longer my Lord and Savior. My life as a Christian is over, and I have moved on. I still have scares from my past transgressions. It is still difficult for me to accept the consequences of walking by faith and not by sight. I wish I had embraced the truth earlier. My first challenge as Lord of my life is to accept my past, learn from it, and build a better future starting today. When I was a child I had an invisible friend named Skip. I not sure when I decided I no longer needed Skip as my friend. Maybe, I traded my invisible friend named Skip for my invisible friend named Jesus.

Obviously, what I view as personal growth will be perceived as losing my faith and forfeiting heaven by my family and friends who remain faithful. I assure them that I earnestly pursued the truth, believing the truth would lead me back to Jesus. It did not. I found no credence in the scripture: "For God so loved the world that he gave his only begotten Son that whosoever believeth in him shall not parish. But have everlasting life" (John 3:16). While the pursuit of my own truth was daunting, frustrating, and aggravating, it ultimately made me a better person. Most of all I assure them that my love for them has not changed, only my belief in the supernatural. While I understand their concern, to myself I must be true.

Bibliography

Atheist Community of Austin. Cable, Louis W. *Slavery and the Bible.* http://www.atheist-community.org/library/articles/read. php?id=676 (May 11, 2016)

CNN: Belief Blog. *Bishop Eddie Long Settles with Accusers.* John Blake. May 26, 2011. http://religion.blogs.cnn.com/2011/05/26/bishop-eddie-long-settles-with-accusers/ (May 11, 2016)

CNN: Keeping Them Honest. *Analyzing The Bishop Eddie Long Sex Scandal.* Hosted by Anderson Cooper. September 29, 2010. https://www.youtube.com/watch?v=dimPfYD5xrs (May 11, 2016)

Daily News. *Stephen Hawking in 'The Grand Design': God did not create the universe.* Michael Sheridan, September 2, 2010. http://www.nydailynews.com/news/world/stephen-hawking-grand-design-god-not-create-universe-article-1.145933 (May 11, 2016)

Dallas Voice. *Son of Dallas' Pastor TD. Jakes Arrested for Indecent Exposure.* John Wright. February 13, 2009. http://m.dallasvoice.com/son-of-dallas-pastor-t-d-jakes-arrested-for-indecent-exposure-1018795.html?mobile-redirector-transfer=true (May 11, 2016)

Dr. Phil Show, The. *Sarah Jakes, Daughter of T. D. Jakes, Shares Her Personal struggle.* April 1, 2014. https://www.youtube.com/watch?v=jZsecbqO1v4 (May 11, 2016)

Elements Behavioral Health. *Can Religion be an Addiction?* November 19, 2013.
https://www.elementsbehavioralhealth.com/behavioral-process-addictions/can-religion-be-an-addiction/ (May 11, 2016)

Essence.com. *Making it work: Bishop T.D. Jakes' Daughter Sarah Henson On Motherhood*, Ministry, and *Marriage*, Charli Penn, May 3,2012
http://www.essence.com/2012/05/03/making-it-work-sarah-henson-on-motherhood-ministry-and-marriage (May 11, 2016)

Essence.com. *Sound-off: Bishop Long, innocence doesn't cost 15M.* Demetria L. Lucas, May 27, 2011
http://www.essence.com/2011/05/27/bishop-eddie-long-15-million-settlement-sexual-abuse-accusers (May 11, 2016)

Fox 4 News KDFW. "Steve Harvey's ex-wife speaks out from behind bars following arrest." Dionne Anglin Sarah Crandall. December 20, 2013.
http://www.fox4news.com/news/1631335-story (May 11, 2016)

Guttmacher Institute. *Facts on American Teens' Sexual and Reproductive Health.* June 2013

Healthline News. *Marijuana Addiction is Rare but Very Real.* Rachel Barclay. July 20, 2015.
http://www.healthline.com/health-news/marijuana-addiction-rare-but-real-072014 (May 11, 016)

Larry King Live interview with Joy Behar. Guest: Steve Harvey, May 30, 2009.
https://www.youtube.com/watch?v=9hTnmZkHnTE   (May 11, 2016)

Mayo Clinic. *Denial: When it helps, when it hurts.* Mayo Clinic Staff. May 20, 2014.
http://www.mayoclinic.org/healthy-lifestyle/adult-health/in-depth/denial/art-20047926 (May 11, 2016)

New York Times, The. *Charismatic Church Leader, Dogged by Scandal, To Stop Preaching for Now.* Kim Severson and Robbie Brown. December 4, 2011.
http://www.nytimes.com/2011/12/05/us/eddie-long-beleaguered-church-leader-to-stop-preaching.html (May 11, 2016)

Psychology Today.com. *Is Marijuana Addictive?* J. Wesley Boyd MD, PhD. November 3, 2013.
https://www.psychologytoday.com/blog/almost-addicted/201311/is-marijuana-addictive (May 11, 2016)

Psychology Today.com. *Marijuana Addiction Today.* Lynn E. O'Conner PhD. May 2, 2012.
https://www.psychologytoday.com/blog/our-empathic-nature/201205/marijuana-addiction-today May 11, 2016)

RolandMartinreports.com. *Drama in the church: Temptation ended his marriage, nearly destroyed the ministry of Pastor Bryant.*
https://www.youtube.com/watch?v=dimPfYD5xrs (May 11, 2016)

Strange Fire Conference. "Grace to You." October 16, 17, 18, 20, 2009.

WashingtonPost.com. *How Stephen Hawking, diagnosed with ALS decades ago, is still alive.* Terrence McCoy. February 24, 2015. https://www.washingtonpost.com/news/morning-mix/ wp/2015/02/24/how-stephen-hawking-survived-longer-than-possibly-any-other-als-patient/ (May 11, 2016)

World Union of Deists. Johnson, Robert L. *The Bible's Ungodly Origins'* https://www.deism.com/bibleorigins.htm (May 11, 2016)

About the Author

CURTIS O. SANDERS Jr. was raised in Santa Monica, California. He is a graduate of California State University, Long Beach.

He studied filmmaking at New York University, School of Continuing Education. He wrote and produced *Sons of a Dark Voyage*, which won him a Tally Award.

The Secret Life of Deacon Henry is his first novel. He was impelled to write a novel upon the reelection of George W. Bush. He was appalled by how many Black Christians voted for Bush because he was a "born-again Christian" who was against the repeal of don't ask, don't tell. They believed since Bush was born-again, he would be led by the Holy Spirit and lead the country into prosperity.

The Bush recession was devastating to the economic progress made in the Black community. Mr. Sanders believes this should be a warning for the Black community to challenge the Black church and especially current trends within the Black Christian community. Consequently, he challenged his own Christian experience. He discovered that he was psychologically and emotionally damaged by his Christian experience and transitioned to humanism. He is committed to exposing, educating, and healing those who have had a negative experience in the Black church.

Mr. Sanders lives in Harlem. He invites you to visit his website at curtissandersjr.com. You will find information regarding speaking engagements, his film, poetry, essays, information on his next project, plus general information and commentary.